Bhartiya Vaastu Shastra

An Ancient Science of Architecture

Author

Jyotish Bhushan
Lakshmi Narayan Sharma
M.A.(Geography), B.Ed., S.R.H.

Bharti Publications

Bharti Publications, Khandsa Road, Gurugram –122001(Haryana)
©Copyright : Author
Author : Lakshmi Narayan Sharma
First Edition: 2024

// Shri Ganeshaya Namah //

**Gajananam Bhutganadi Sevitam, Kapittha Jambuphal Charu Bhakshanam /
Uma Sutam Shokvinashkarkam Namami Vighneshwar Padpankjam //**

**Vakratund Mahakaye Suryakoti Samprabha /
Nirvighanam Kuru Me Deva Sarva Karyeshu Sarvda //**

// Dedication //

Dedicated to my Parents
Late Pt. Chhaju Ram and Smt. Ram Devi
whose blessings and memories are my inspiration and strength.

FOREWORD

Past few decades have witnessed great upsurge in the field of Vaastu knowledge. Intelligentsia have become receptive to Vaastu theoretical principles and their application aspects leading to tangible benefits to the followers. Our veteran author Shri Lakshmi Narayan Sharma has brought into full play his research experience and analytical acumen for shaping the contents of this new book titled " Bhartiya Vaastu Shastra ". This book is an important and useful addition to the existing literature on the subject.

Besides giving historical background of Vaastu Shastra, this book puts forth useful and comprehensive Vaastu guidelines for construction and remedial measures for all types of buildings such as residential houses, farms, flats, commercial buildings, government offices, factories, malls, clubs, religious places etc.

This is the sixth book to the author's credit. Huge body of Vaastu knowledge has been segmented into Sections A to F which includes 31 chapters in this detailed book. Specific criteria have been laid out for selection of plot, positioning of house within the plot and location and details of components of inside area, such as drawing room pooja room, kitchen, bedroom, garage, etc. This book seems to contain answers to all Vaastu queries.

I warmly congratulate my long-time friend Shri Lakshmi Narayan Sharma for his valuable contribution in the form of the present book "Bhartiya Vaastu Shastra" and highly and unhesitatingly recommend this useful treatise to all Vaastu enthusiasts as well as general readers.

R.V.Venkatachalam
MA (Economics)
Sr. Central Govt. Officer (Retd.)

26th Jan. 2024 Gantantra Divas

PREFACE

When humans started to settle down at one place from their nomadic life, they applied their understanding about natural, cultural, religious beliefs and sensory comfort to make their dwelling more congenial.

Hindu sages and seers have known the secrets of balancing the 'Panch bhootas' the five elements in the human body. The universe and all its inhabitants are governed by the influences of magnetism and gravitation. This book captures Vaastu in its entirety from its historical documentation to its understanding as a science and, more importantly, its application in the building design and construction.

I intend this book as a 'handbook to implement Vaastu tips' with complete understanding of the Vaastu Shastra's guidelines related to geo-patterning, directional implications, locational criteria, inner structural and design recommendations for a balanced and Vaastu aligned building. The book also describes the auspicious moments or Muhurats for deriving ideal benefits of starting construction work and occupying the Residential, Commercial and Office buildings, Educational and Medical Institutions, Religious places etc.

There are increasing proofs that Vaastu compliance heavily contributes to the enhancement of prosperity, peace, happiness, and health for the inhabitants.

Author hopes that Vaastu enthusiasts and general readers will get the benefit of all Vaastu related requirements. Formative suggestions from them will be highly appreciated.

Lakshmi Narayan Sharma
House No. 77, Sector-10 A,
Gurugram-122001(HR.)
Mob. 9911287445
Email : lakshmi77parwati@gmail.com

Contents

Sec. F – Remedial Measures through Vaastu & Feng Shui

i) Chanting of Mantra for releasing the mind from hindrances and impediments.
ii) Application of Yantras for helping in rectification of aura problems.
iii) Precious Gems for polarizing energy and mental peace.
iv) Color Schemes for peace and prosperity.
v) Herbal Bath for cleanliness, health and happiness.
vi) Ganesh puja, Navgrah puja, hawan/yagya for happiness, peace and prosperity.
(b) Remedial measures Through Feng-Shui
i) Wind Chime for diffusing negativity
ii) Buddha Statue for diffusing negativity and having Prosperity.
iii) Lion for confidence and power
iv) Camel for growth of career.
v) Pyramid and Pakua Mirror for maximum source of energy
vi) Doves, Dolphins, Tortoise for happiness, harmony and stability.

Chapter
1
What is Vaastu Shastra?

<u>**Vaastu Shastra Definitions in Nutshell**</u>

1. **Vaastu Shastra** is an ancient and vast science of healthy, wealthy and prosperous living.

2. The word **Vaastu** is derived from the Sanskrit root word **ol~** means **oluk (Dwelling)** and Hindi root word **okl (Vaas)** means **vkokl (Aavas)** or **fuokl (Nivas)** Dwelling Place.

3. **Vaastu Shastra** is the **Textual part of Vaastu Vidya or Shilp Vigyan.** The knowledge is a collection of ideas and concepts, with or without the support of layout diagrams.

4. **Vaastu Shastra** is one of the ancient teachings from the Indian civilization developed by Hindu sages and seers for designing and building.

5. **Vaastu Shastra** is a **Traditional Hindu system of Architecture,** which literally translates to "An Ancient Science of Architecture".

6. **Vaastu Shastra** is the science of directions that combine all the five elements of nature and balance them with man and materials.

7. **Bhartiya Vaastu Shastra** is based on Ancient Science of house building that indicates good or bad direction out of total eight directions. An individual can select a good direction as per his birth Sun sign of zodiac as described below.

Vaastu Shastra is an ancient and vast science of better living, where one can enjoy happy, healthy, wealthy, comfortable and peaceful life. The great author **Vrahamihir** in Brahat Samhita used Vaastu for a limited area i.e. only for residential houses, while guidelines for construction of houses, buildings, palaces, temples, cities etc. differ from each one, however all appear in the purview of Vaastu. Jaipur city is an example totally constructed as per Vaastu guidelines and worth to be seen. It is the main reason that Vaastu Shastra is also called **Sthapatya Veda** a part of **Atharva Veda.**

Vaastu Shastra is the **Textual part of Vaastu Vidya.** Vaastu Vidya knowledge is a collection of ideas and concepts, with or without the support of layout diagrams that are not rigid. Rather, these ideas and concepts are models for the organization of space and form within a building or collection of buildings, based on their functions in relation to each other, their usage and to the overall fabric of the Vaastu. It helps to get natural benefits of five basic elements of universe, which are Earth, Air, Water, Fire and Space. These elements influence our deeds, fate and behavior. They guide and change the living styles of all living creatures including human beings. Vaastu Shastra is based on various natural energies like Earth Energy, Space Energy, Solar Energy, Lunar Energy, Electric Energy, Magnetic Energy, Thermal Energy, Wind Energy, Light Energy and Cosmic Energy etc.

Vaastu Shastra is one of the ancient teachings from the Indian civilization. It is an ancient Mystic science developed by Hindu sages and seers for designing and building. It deals with the science of the architecture and tells how a building should be planned to channelize the positive energy in our lives. The proper implementation of Vaastu techniques has brought peace and prosperity to many households for centuries. Though Vaastu first started out with the construction rules for Hindu temples such as **Balaji Temple (Tirupati), Meenakshi Mandir (Madurai), Surya Mandir (Konark), Rangnath Swami Temple (Mysore), Vivekanand Temple at mainland of Vavathurai-Kanyakumari) etc.** It soon spread out in its application to residential houses, office buildings, place for vehicles, sculpture, paintings, furniture etc. The science of Vaastu is mostly based on directions and the building materials used, along with many other minor factors. The Indian civilization is the oldest in the world and has a rich heritage of developing different branches of science. Vaastu Shastra is one such discipline that developed over the years based on the traditional knowledge gained from studying the nature. The age-old Indian philosophers knew a lot about the five elements that made the universe.

Vaastu Shastra is a **Traditional Hindu system of Architecture**, which literally translates to "An ancient science of architecture". These are texts found on the Indian subcontinent that describe guidelines of design, layout, measurements, ground preparation, space arrangement and spatial geometry. **Vaastu Shastra** incorporates traditional Hindu beliefs. The designs are intended to integrate architecture with nature, the relative functions of various parts of the structure, and ancient beliefs utilizing geometric patterns/**yantras**, symmetry and **directional** alignments. We can be prosperous and live in harmony by eliminating negative energies and enhancing positive energies around us.

<h1 align="center">Vaastu for Better Living</h1>

Figure-1

Indeed, **Vaastu Shastra** is the science of directions, which combines all the five elements of nature and balances them with man and materials. It is all about the impact of various forms of effect on a living person. It aims to create a subtle conducive atmosphere in a structure in which we can bring out the best in ourselves, thereby paving the way for enhanced health, wealth, peace prosperity and happiness in an enlightened environment. Like any other science, Vaastu is universal, reasonable, viable and useful. Thus, it is a science.

Bhartiya Vaastu Shastra is based on Ancient Science of house building that indicates good or bad direction out of total eight directions. The importance of orientation of a building is not only for saving energy, but also to have a better healthy house design, which not only gives comfortable living, but also gives good health, prosperity and wealth to the house owner/occupier and his family. There lies a co-relation between the rotational scenario of the planets and the house design and their different directions with respect to North. The building of any type and its construction fulfils the purpose, if proper orientation has been given using suitable local building material. It increases not only its life span but also improves the condition of occupant/resident.

We can proudly conclude that our ancient sages and sears invented Vaastu Shastra for the wellbeing of humans. It mainly deals with such an art/science of constructing or building a house, where one can enjoy all comforts in life. The Interior Decoration of the house must be attractive and solid as per Vaastu Guidelines. A house must be technically feasible and realistic for the resident or the inhabitant. Main gate may be in any direction, but resident or inhabitant might feel happy, healthy, comfortable and peaceful in the house. Therefore, an individual should select such a beneficial plot/house, which may give an idea as to which direction house

11

should face depending on house owner's Sun sign of zodiac. Individual's Sun signs of zodiac are given below.

Aries (Mesha) People

This is the first sign of Zodiac. This represents the **East** direction. The favorable ruling planet is Sun (Surya). For the people of Sun sign Aries, East facing house is more beneficial. East is the most powerful direction. East facing house gets more Sunlight, which helps in keeping the house free from bacteria and other germs. You can draw a favorable symbol of Swastik or other in bronze color or place a Swastik sticker of bronze color at the main gate of the House. Swastik and other symbols are given below.

| Swastik | Ya Allah | Ek Onkar | Almighty |

Figure-2

Taurus (Vrishabha) People

This is the second sign of Zodiac. The favorable direction for the people of Sun sign Taurus is **North-East** (Eshaan) corner and its ruling planet is Jupiter (Guru). North-East is the most sacred direction. Buying or building a house facing the North-East direction proves lucky and favorable for a Taurus person. The house facing this direction brings in wealth, health, power, prestige and prosperity along with all other forms of happiness in life. Light yellow color is lucky for Sun sign Taurus people.

Gemini (Mithuna) People

This is the third sign of Zodiac. **North-East** is the favorable direction for the people of Sun sign Gemini. The ruling planet for Gemini is Jupiter (Guru). It is most beneficial planet. Buying or building a house in the North-East facing will be lucky and favorable to the house owner. Use yellow color shades for getting maximum benefits. For house positivity place a favorable symbol/sticker at the main gate of the house.

Cancer (Karka) People

This is the fourth sign of Zodiac. North is the favorable direction for the people of Sun sign Cancer. Its ruling planet is Mercury (Budh). This direction is associated with the God of wealth "Kuber". Cancerians should build their house facing **North direction.** Use light green color for North facing walls. For house positivity place a favorable Swastik symbol or other made of silver or green colored Ganesh Idol at the main gate of the house.

Leo (Simha) People

This is the fifth sign of Zodiac. **North-West** (Vayavya) is the favorable direction for the people of Sun sign Leo. Moon is the ruling planet. Such people should build their houses facing the North-West (Vayavya) direction as per Vaastu guidelines, otherwise they will lose their health. For better health place a Swastik symbol or other of bronze color or sticker of the shining Moon made of silver on the North-West wall and at the Main gate of the house. Use cream color for happiness.

Virgo (Kanya) People

This is the sixth sign of Zodiac. **North-West** is the favorable direction for the people of Sun sign Virgo. Moon is the ruling planet. They can build their house facing the North-West (Vayavya) direction as per Vaastu guidelines, otherwise they will have to face health related problems. Cream color on the wall and main gate is favorable and beneficial to the people of Sun sign Virgo. Place red color Hauman symbol/sticker or other at the main gate of the house.

Libra (Tula) People

This is the seventh sign of Zodiac. **West** is the favorable direction for the people of Sun sign Libra. Saturn is the ruling planet. West facing direction is auspicious for houses of Librans. They will never face any economic crisis. Librans should avoid North-West direction always to feel free from fear of enemies. The house owner should place a Tulsi (Basil) plant outside the house or offer Prayers to the almighty God Vishnu or other every week.

Scorpio (Vrischika) People

This is the eighth sign of Zodiac. **South** is the favorable direction for the people of Sun sign Scorpio. Mars is the ruling planet. Though South facing house as per Vaastu guidelines is generally considered to be inauspicious for other signs, yet for Scorpions South facing direction is auspicious with a condition that ruling planet Mars is placed in an auspicious house/sign. It will prove to be very lucky bringing happiness, peace and prosperity in their life. Use red/pink/grey color on the South wall and at the Main gate of house.

Sagittarius (Dhanu) People
This is the ninth sign of Zodiac. **West** facing house is considered auspicious and more beneficial for the people of Sun sign Sagittarius. Saturn is the ruling planet. The people living in this house will not face any social problem. Build the house away from facing the main road otherwise the owner will have to face enemies. So, avoid construction of Main gate facing North-West (Vayavya) direction. Place a Tulsi (Basil) plant outside the house or offer Prayers to lord Krishna or other favorable daily.

Capricorn (Makara) People
This is the tenth sign of Zodiac. **South** is the favorable direction for the people of Sun sign Capricorn. Mars is the ruling planet. Though the South facing houses are generally not considered to be auspicious to all as per guidelines of Vaastu, yet this direction is auspicious for the people of Sun sign Capricorn with a condition that the ruling planet Mars is placed in the auspicious house/sign. It will bring wealth, happiness and prosperity in their life. Such residents should keep the South floor of the house higher than East.

Aquarius (Kumbha) People
This is the eleventh sign of Zodiac. **South-East** (Aagneya) will be favorable direction for the people of Sun sign Aquarius and Venus is the ruling planet. South-East corner is the corner of fire element. Though South-East facing plot is not recommended for residential purpose in general, yet it is favorable for the people of Sun sign Aquarius. If Pomegranate plant (Anar) is planted in the house garden, it may bring happiness, peace and prosperity in the South-East (Aagneya) facing houses. Swastik symbol or other favorable of bronze color may be fixed at the Main entrance.

Pisces (Meena) People
This is the twelfth sign of Zodiac. **South-East** is the favorable direction for the people of Sun sign Pisces. Venus is the ruling planet. As per the guidelines of Vaastu South-East direction is the Aagneya corner in the house with the fire element. Generally South-East facing house is not recommended for residential purpose, yet for the people of Sun sign Pisces, it brings happiness, peace and prosperity to the resident and his family. Plant a Pomegranate tree in the house garden for good health or fix a bronze color Swastik symbol or another favorable symbol at the Main gate.

Note for our Readers :

Please see below table for the Best Direction of the building for an Individual as per his Sun Sign of Zodiac.

Best Direction for an Individual as per his Sun Sign of Zodiac

Sr. No.	Individual's Sun Sign of Zodiac	Best Direction
1	Aries (Mesha)	East
2	Taurus (Vrishabha), Gemini (Mithuna)	Northeast
3	Cancer (Karka)	North
4	Leo (Simha) Virgo (Kanya)	Northwest
5	Libra (Tula) Sagittarius (Dhanu)	West
6	Scorpio (Vrishchika) Capricorn (Makra)	South
7	Aquarius (Kumbha) Pisces (Meena)	Southeast

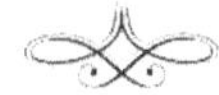

Chapter
2
The History of Vaastu Shastra

The History of Vaastu Shastra in Nutshell

1. On the basis of deep studies made by the great historians **James Fergusson, Alexander Cunningham and Dr. Havell,** we find that Vaastu Shastra was developed between 6000 BCE and 3000 BCE. Excavations in the archaeological sites of Harappa and Mohenjo-daro indicate it.

2. Indian Vedic literature Samhitas, Brahmans, Aaranyaks, Upanishads, Vedangs etc. are very famous. **Rigved is first Samhita**, in which two Suktas regarding construction are famous and available. One Sukta **Vastoshpati** Sukta is called the God or lord of house/building construction. Vastoshpati is remembered, worshipped and prayed at the time of construction of house for resident and family always to be healthy and prosperous. Sukta or shloka from Rigveda 7/54/1-3 and 7/55/1 below:

वास्तोष्पते प्रति जानीह्यस्मान् त्स्वावेशो अनमीवे भवा नः।

यत् त्वेमहे प्रति तन्नो जुषस्व शं नो भव द्विपदे शं चतुष्पदे।।

वास्तोष्पते प्रतरणो न एधि गयस्फानो गोभिरश्वेभिरिन्दो।

अजरासस्ते सख्ये स्याम पितेव पुत्रान् प्रति नो जुषस्व।।

वास्तोष्पते शग्मया संसदा ते सक्षीमहि रण्वया गातुमत्या।

पाहि क्षेम उत योगे वरं नो यूयं पात स्वस्तिभिः सदा नः।।

अमीवहा वास्तोष्पते विश्वा रुपाण्याविशन्।

सखा सुशेव एधि नः।।

Vastoshpate Prati Jani Hayasmaan Tatwavesho Anmi Bhawa na |
Yat Tawemahe Prati Tanno Jusasva San No Bhaw Dwipade San Chatushpade | |
Vastoshpate Pratarno Na Aiedhi Gayasphano Gobhishvebhirindo |
Ajrasaste Sakhye Siam Pitev Putran Prati No Jusasva | |
Vastoshpate Sagmaya Sansda Te Sakshimahi Ranvya Gatumatya |
Pahi Kshem Uat Yoge Varam No Yuyam Paat Swastibhi Sada Na | |
Amivaha Vastoshpate Vishwa Rupanya Vishan |
Sakha Susheva Aiedhi Na | |

3. In Sutra literature **Shankhyayan** and **Ashvlayan** there are three chapters regarding guidelines of house/building construction. In

Matasya Puran there are eight chapters. In **Garud Puran** there are four chapters, which describe construction of houses, army stations, temples etc. In **Agni Puran** also there are 16 chapters about Vaastu.

4. The art of Vaastu originates in the **Sthapatya Veda,** a part of the **Atharvana Veda.** It subsequently used to be a purely technical subject and was only confined to architects (Sthapatis) who handed over to their heirs.

5. In **Mahabharta, Ramayan and Buddisth** literature references are that big buildings and individual buildings were constructed on the basis of Vaastu guidelines.

6. Man came on the scene perhaps in **Tretayug** and the origin of Vaastu Shastra was traced to this period only.

7. The study of **Vaastu Shastra** starts with the knowledge of the basic five elements of creation Earth, Air, Water, Fire and Space.

Excavations pertaing to ancient cultures of Harappa and Mohenjo-Daro Civilization indicate the time-period of **development of Vaastu between 6000 BCE and 3000 BCE.** Indeed, the Vedic social system and all its elements were based on logical reasons essentially required for bringing about the overall welfare of individual. This whole structure of Vaastu Science was aimed at defining a proper system that creates synergy between cosmic energies and human shelter. In Vedic times, the scholars were well-versed with advanced scientific applications known as Shubh-Vaastu. After proper permutation and combination of various elements involved in building construction, suitable directions for everything related to building can be effectively drawn. Each guideline described in Vaastu Shastra is strongly backed by the scientific causes and vivid impacts of natural powers. The network of causes and effects are clearly explained in Vaastu Sukta.

In Indian Vedic literature Samhitas, Brahmans, Aaranyaks, Upanishads, Vedangs etc. are very famous. They are full of Sanskrit Shlokas or Suktas. **Rigveda** is **first Veda (Samhita),** in which two **Shlokas/Suktas** regarding construction are available. One sukta **Vastospati** is called the God or lord of house/building construction. At the time of Grah-Pravesh Vastopati is worshipped for the safe and healthy, wealthy and prosperous living of the house owner and his family. In **Yajurveda,** the **second Veda (Samhita),** the Sukta description of crematoria is called primary design of Vaastu Vidhya. In the same way **Shala Nirman Sukta in Atharva Veda,** the **fourth Veda** is also famous. The words such as **Vansha** (Beam) and

Sthupa (Pillar) are used. In Brahmin literature **Yup, Vedi, Shamshan** etc. words talk about Shilp Vigyan. In chapter **Agnividhya of Kathopnisad** there is a famous Shloka that points out Shilp Vidhya –

'लोकादिमग्निं तमुवाच तस्मै या इष्टिका यावतीर्वायथा वा
स चापि तत्प्रत्यवदद्यथोक्तम् अथास्य मृत्युः पुनराह तुष्टः।"

**Lokadimagnim Tamuwach Tasmai Ya Istika Yavteervayatha Va |
Sa Chapi Tatpratayavadththoktam Athasya Mritue Punrah Tusth ||**

In Sutra literature **Shankhyayan** and **Ashvlayan** there are three chapters regarding guidelines of house/building construction. In **Shulba Shastra** there is a paragraph how to arrange Bricks to construct **Vedi for Hawan**? In certain Puranas many chapters deal with Vaastu Vidhya. In **Matasya Puran** there are eight chapters about Vaastu Vidhya and three chapters about establishing a Statue. In chapter 252 the names of 18 Vaastuvids are given. In **Garud Puran** there are four chapters which describe construction of houses, army stations, temples etc. In **Agni Puran** there are 16 chapters about Vaastu. Out of these chapters two chapters enunciate for guidelines of house construction, thirteen chapters about fort and temple construction and one chapter for city planning. Besides these **Kautilaya ArthShastra, Mayamatam, Mansar, Samrangan Sutradhar, Muhurat Chintamani etc.** also quote about forts, palaces and their right time of construction. Ancient Vaastu Shastra guidelines include those for the design of Mandirs or **Hindu temples**, and the guidelines for the design and layout of houses, towns, cities, gardens, roads, water works, shops and other public areas.

Learned Todarmal in his book **"Vaastu Saukhyam"** wrote that Brahma ji is the first knowledgeable Deva of Vaastu Shastra. Following Shloka indicates the same.

वास्तुज्ञानं प्रवक्ष्यामि यदुक्तं ब्रह्मणा पुरा।
ग्राम सद्मपुरादीनां निर्माणं सूक्ष्मतोऽधुना।।

**Vaastu Gyanam Pravakshmi Brahmna Pura |
Gram Sadampuradinam Nirmanam Sukshmatoadhuna ||**

Vaastu Shastra is an ancient Indian science of Vedic origin that deals with proper construction of a house. It is a part of astrology. There are eight branches of Vaastu. The names are (1) Yagiya Vaastu (2) Grah Vaastu (3) Nagar Vaastu (4) Praasad Vaastu (5) Udhyan Vaastu (6) Jalashya Vaastu (7) Vimaan Vidhya and (8) Yantra Vaastu. An age-old technique, Vaastu defines building of homes in sync with the natural forces. A Vaastu perfect

18

home not only attains complete harmony with natural forces, but also brings in prosperity, good thought and sound health to its residents. There are certain basic guidelines that are considered Vaastu-logically correct for the making and designing of the house. Following these guidelines, while constructing a house or even choosing one would be highly beneficial and advantageous. Read more in the paragraphs about the fundamental guidelines of Vaastu-Shastra.

Those days the system was absolutely different. Nowadays the entire construction has been totally changed from mud to cement and concrete with steel structures. The guidelines of the Science laid down during those days were based purely on the effect of Sun-Rays during different times of the day. The observations and corrections made were noted and concluded. Vaastu is a part of Vedas, which are believed to be four to five thousand years old. Through penance and meditation, yogis of that period posed their questions and acquired appropriate answers believed to have descend from the cosmic mind itself. Hence Vedas abound with divine knowledge. The art of Vaastu originates in the **Sthapatya Veda**, a part of the **Atharvana Veda.**

It used to be a purely technical subject and it was only confined to architects (Sthapatis) who subsequently handed over to their heirs. The guidelines of construction, architecture, sculpture etc., as enunciated in the epics and treatise on temple architecture, have been incorporated in the science of Vaastu. Its description is there in texts like Matsya Purana, Skanda Purana, Agni Purana, Garuda Purana, and Vishnu Purana. There are some other ancient Shastras that pass on the knowledge of Vaastu Shastra to next generation, like **Vishvakarma Prakash, Samraangan Sutradhar, Kashyap ShilpShastra, Brahat Samhita, and Praman Manjare.** Vishwkarmprakash written by Vaastu Expert Vishvakarma and Maymatam written by Mayasura are very popular ancient books of Vaastu Shastra. It is said that Vishvakarma was a Vaastu Consultant for Suras (Devtas), and Mayasura was a Vaastu Consultant for Asuras (Devils).

Ancient Buildings as per Vaastu

1. In **Mahabharata** it is said that a number of houses were built for the kings who were invited to the **city Indraprastha** for the Rajasuya Yagna of King Yuddhistira. According to **Sage Vyasa** these houses were as high as the peaks of Kailash Mountains, perhaps meaning to say that they stood tall and majestic. The houses were free from all obstructions. They had compounded with high walls and their gates were of uniform height and covered with numerous metal ornaments. Even the "**Maya Sabha**" building in **Mahabharta** was built by **Mayan** civilization on the ancient

guidelines of Vaastu. On this **Auspicious Moment (Muhurata)** the king Yudhister obeyed all the rules while worshipping for Better Future. The relevant Shloka is given below.

तस्मै युधिष्ठिरः पूजां यथार्हमकरोत् तदा।
स तु तां प्रतिजग्राह मयः सत्कृत्य भारत।।

Tashme Yudhistharah PujamYatharhumkarot Tada |
Sa Tu Tam Pratijagrah Mayah Satkritaya Bharta | |

2. It is said that the **site plan of Ayodhya,** the city of Lord Rama was similar to the plan found in the great architectural text **Manasara.** Even the **"Ramsetu"** a bridge to **Srilanka** in Ramayan was based on the guidelines of Vaastu. In Balmikk Ramayan the following Shlokas indicate about Vaastu-

आयता दश द्वे व योजनानि महापुरी।
श्रीमती त्रीणि विस्तीर्णा सुविभक्तमहापथा।।
राजमार्गेण महता सुविभक्तेन शोभिता। मुक्तपुष्पावकीर्णन जलसिक्तेन नित्यशः।।
ता तू राजादशरथो महाराष्ट्रविवर्ध्नः। पुरीमावासयामास दिवि देवपतिर्यथा।।
कपाटतोरणवतीं सुविभक्तान्तराणाम्। सर्वयन्त्राायुध्वतीमुषितां सर्वशिल्पभिः।।

Aayta Dash Dwe Va Yojnani Mahapuri |
Srimati Trini Visteerna Suvibhakatmahapatha | |
Rajmargen Mahta Suvibhakaten Shobhita |
Muktpushpavakirnen Jalshikten Nityash | |
Ta Tu Raja Dashratho Maharashtravivardhanam |
Purimavasyamas Divi Devpatiryatha | |
Kapat-toranvatim Suvibhakatantaranam |
Sarvyantrayudhvatimushitam Sarvshilpbhi | |

3. In **Buddhist literature** references are that the big buildings and individual buildings were constructed on the basis of Vaastu guidelines. It is said that Lord Buddha from time to time delivered discourses on architecture and even told his disciples that supervising the construction of a building was one of the duties of the order. It is also mentioned that **monasteries (Viharas) or palatial temples** (Bhavya Mandirs), buildings which are **partly residential, and partly religious** (Ardhayogas), **four-five storied residential buildings** (Prasadas), **multi-storied buildings** (Harmyas and Guhas) or residential buildings for middle class people were built on the guidelines of Vaastu. The effect, while presenting a Vihar to a Buddhist mendicant, is decribed in a following Shloka.

20

सावत्थियं मयहं सखी भदन्ते सघंस्सकारेसि महाविहारं।
तत्थपसन्ना अहमानुमोदि दिस्वाअगारं च पियाच मेतं।।

Savtithayam Mayaham Sakhi Bhramadante Sanghaasskaresi Mahaviha |
Tatthapasanna Ahmanmodi Dishwaagaram Cha Piyach Metam ||

4. Excavations in the **ancient cultures of Harappa and Mohenjo-Daro** also indicate the influence of Vaastu on **Indus Valley Civilization**, which shows some specific guidelines in construction and planning very similar and comparable with the Vaastu Shastra of Vedic Origin.

The Vaastu, with word meaning 'peaceful dwelling', is believed to be the residing places or cohabitate/dwelling of God and man. According to its modern meaning it covers all buildings irrespective of their use like residences, industries, business establishments, lodges, hotels and so on. It is based on the five basic and essential elements, such as Vaayu (Air), Jal (Water), Agni (Fire), Bhumi (Earth) and Aakash (Space), which are known as **Panch-Bhutas**. Everything on earth is built from out of these Five Elements.

Our scholar Ramakrishna says about Origin of Vaastu Shastra: The Origin of Vaastu Shastra is difficult to be traced as it is lost in antiquity. The ancient Indian sages have divided the cosmic calendar into 4 broad stages, namely **Krityug, Tretayug, Dwaparyug, and Kaliyug**. Man came on the scene perhaps in **Tretayug** and the origin of Vaastu Shastra is traced to this period only. During this period of development, with its very limited communication facilities being this valuable Vaastu knowledge was restricted to ruling and elite class of this society only, thus depriving the large society, the benefits of this science. In course of time, things have drastically changed, and democracy has replaced the autocratic Government. Individual freedom has become the supreme possession of man. Further in the present information explosion the benefits of this valuable science have been available to one and all. Vaastu Shastra appears to be an abstract science until we delve into it deeply and come to know of its various aspects. The study of Vaastu Shastra starts with the knowledge of the basic five elements of creation Earth, Air, Water, Fire and Space.

Chapter
3
Basic Guidelines of Vaastu Shastra

Basic Guidelines of Vaastu in Nutshell

1. Vaastu is the science that **brings the harmony** among the five basic elements for the existence in the universe.
2. Vaastu Shastra helps us to understand the **effect of these five elements** on human life and also guides us to live in harmony with the law of nature for health, wealth, peace and over all prosperity.
3. Human body is made of the five elements i.e. **Earth, Air, Water, Fire and Space.**
4. The relationship between the **earth and the body is basic**. Our body through its presence in the form of muscles, bones and various other important minerals etc. is there to keep us healthy.
5. **Without air we are nowhere.** Air is essential for our healthy and peaceful living. It keeps our blood circulation positive for the better functioning of our body organs.
6. The **water on earth constitutes almost 73.7 % of the total mass**. Exactly the same way **our body too is composed 73.7 % water**. Life without water is unthinkable.
7. In order to live we all need to eat food. This food needs to get digested in our system so as to produce the energy. **The fire that helps break down the food,** burns the calories so that the energy required for living is adequately provided.
8. From **the moment we come on the earth, our body require space** and it continues to need space throughout the span of our life, without this space element the existence is not possible.
9. There is an **invisible and constant relation between all the five elements**. Therefore, while building or purchasing a house, it is advisable and beneficial to follow Vaastu suggestions which lend positivity to the human's symbiotic relationship with the five elements.

Vaastu is the Science of Harmony. It brings harmony among the five basic elements for the existence in the universe. The whole earth was an open space before the man started living on it. The open space is always having numerous energies flowing on it but the moment we construct any structure on it, the flow of energies gets distorted. Consequently, that starts affecting the occupant either in positive or negative manner. This disturbance compelled the man to look into the problem seriously and that very curiosity to know the power of energies, gave birth to the science of Vaastu Shastra. Vaastu Shastra helps us to understand the effect of these five elements on human life and also guides us to live in harmony with the law of nature for augmenting our health, wealth and over all prosperity.

The guidelines laid down in Vaastu Shastra were formulated keeping in view, the cosmic influence of the Sun, its light and heat, solar energy, directions of wind, the moon position, the earth's magnetic field and the influence of cosmos on our planet. The system is an amalgam of science of directions, astronomy and astrology.

Vaastu experts may have different views about certain aspects related to remedial measures but all of them have one single opinion about the origin of Vaastu. The origin of this great science of harmony is from origin of nature. Our Vedas and Shastras believe that what is nature inherent in each human being is **microcosmic part of macrocosm**. We all know that human body is made of the five elements i.e. **Earth, Air, Water, Fire and Space.** Each of these elements has a personality and internal environment that is connected with the bio mental spiritual aspects of humans. No aspect of the human body, functions as an independent and discrete entity. Each physical function is connected to an emotional aspect, each aspect governs an organ. There is an inter relationship between each and every emotional aspect, organ and its function. It is this that is responsible for the maintenance of balance between our physical and emotional relationship. Vaastu Shastra believes that all these elements are present everywhere both inside us as well as around us and these elements should be in a state of equilibirum.

Panch Bhootas (Five Elements)

1.   Bhumi (Earth) Magnetic field of the earth
The relationship between the earth and the body is basic and therefore the first reality of earth in our body through its presence in the form of muscles, bones and various other important minerals etc. keeps us healthy. Without the muscles and the bones, the body may not be able to function at all and the life may not be possible. Earth means its upper surface i.e. soil. It may be soft, stony, sandy, or in the form of lime, minerals etc. People like to construct houses/buildings where soil is soft and better for growing food products, availability of construction material and labor etc. in close proximity.

2.   Vayu (Air) Wind energy
Without air we are nowhere. It is essential and indispensable for our healthy and peaceful living. It keeps our blood circulation positive for the

better functioning of our body organs. Without the circulation of blood, the organs cannot function in our body. When we are breathing the flow of fresh Air inhaled during this process actually purifies the blood, inhaled during this process actually purifies the blood, imparts energy through this purified blood on to the heart and helps heart to pump the blood through our system and keeps us alive. However, moment there is any hindrance in the otherwise smooth process of inhalation that the disturbance is caused in the relationship of all the through our system and keeps us alive. However, moment there is any hindrance in the otherwise smooth process of inhalation disturbance is caused in the relationship of all the five elements and there occurs a disorder in the circulation of blood that becomes the cause of death. Our relationship with the element of air and its quality is vital. Therefore, the shape, size, construction and direction of house/building should be such that they provide sufficient supply of air. No part of house/building should remain without inlet for entry of fresh air.

Vaastu Purush and Five Elements

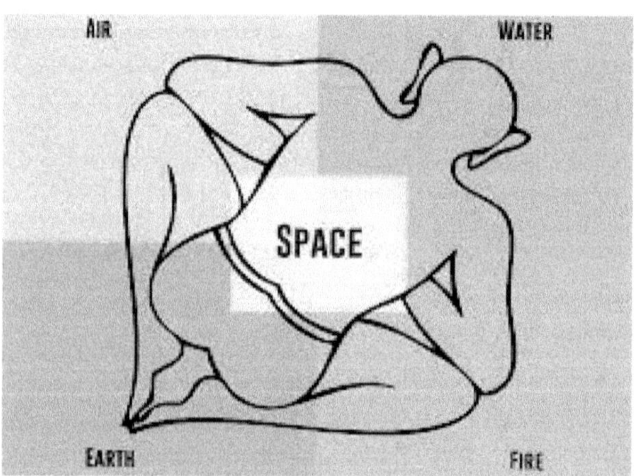

Figure-3

3.   Jal (Water) Gravitational attraction of the Earth

The water on earth constitutes almost 73.7 % of the total mass. Exactly the same way our body too is composed 73.7 % water. Life without water is unthinkable and in this respect our relationship with water is fundamental. It only goes to show the point that there is a great relationship of this element not only with the nature but also with the human survival. Water is such an element, which sustains life even without food for a limited period. It is first and foremost primary need for the construction of houses/buildings. It is the main reason most of the people constructs their houses and buildings near seas, lakes and rivers, where water is easily available. The villagers also dug out well near ponds to get clean and sweet water to protect their life.

4. Agni (Fire) Solar radiation

In order to live we all need to eat food. This food needs to get digested in our system so as to produce the energy for our upkeep and maintenance of essential body heat. Now, how this food is digested and assimilated in our system? Upon closer examination we will realize that it is the fire, for the sake of specific reference we refer to it as the 'digestive Fire' that helps break down the food and burns the calories so that the energy required for living is adequately provided for. Whenever there is a problem with our digestive system it automatically means there is a problem with the element of fire in our body and that it needs to be checked when we lose a balance of the element fire and our health tends to deteriorate and over a period of time it may even lead to a serious problem. You all know that the Sun is the main source of light and heat for us. The movement of our Earth in relation to the Sun causes day and night and changes seasons. Sometimes very hot i.e. in summer and sometimes cold i.e. winter season and sometimes rain all changes are due to Sun heat.

5. Akash (Space). Cosmic radiation

From the moment we come on the earth, our body require space and it continues to need space throughout the span of our life, without this element the existence is not possible in any from whatsoever. Space is widely spread over us and influences all other elements. In fact, all the other four elements prosper and flourish only within the ambience of congenial space, because of this our relationship with the element of space is crucial and essential. In the absence of space sound waves are not possible. Talking, singing, playing, weeping and all other manual activities cannot be done without the presence of space.

Note

There is an invisible and constant relation between all the five elements. Therefore, it is better to follow suggestions as described below while building a house on a plot for happy and peaceful living.
1. For people who are planning to buy a plot, make sure you get one that is in South, West and South-West directions. Theses plots are considered more favorable and advantageous than others.

2. Plots that are square or rectangular in shape are better than irregular cut ones. Also, the plot should be sloping towards the North and East/North-East.

3. A house which has a Peepal tree in the West side at some distance from the house and an Imli (Tamarind) tree in South-West direction of the house are considered auspicious. The Mango, Banana or a Jamun tree in the vicinity is not considered auspicious.

4. A house with Anaar, Ashoka, Chandan, Champa, Chameli, Gulaab, Nariyal and Keshar trees around is considered auspicious.

5. At the time of constructing a building, make sure that it has open space on all sides. The levels of open spaces should be higher in south and west sides and lower in north and east side.

6. In case you construct more than one floor, prepare the first floor on South-West. The height of first floor should not be more than the ground floor. Also, ensure that there is no storeroom on the first floor.

7. The entrance of the house should perfectly be in the North-East, East or North direction. This would bring in good luck, prosperity and harmony in the house.

8. In case you have a big house with an extra room, make the room in the North-West or North-East direction as guestroom.

9. Since center denotes Brahmasthan, make sure it is free from any sorts of obstructions. There should be no beam, pillar, fixture, toilet, staircase or even a wall or lift.

10. As for the shape and size of the gate, the width of the gate should be half to the height of the gate.

11. Paintings and statues in the house are also an important consideration to make when it comes to Vaastu. Picture depicting war, violence or any negativities of life like sorrow and struggle should not be in the house.

12. The Drawing room of the house should be in the East, North and North-East directions.

13. According to Vaastu, the bedroom should be positioned in South-West, South or West direction of the house.

14. The study room should be designed in such a way that you study facing East or North side. The ideal color for the study room is yellow.

15. The kitchen should be in the Aagnneya direction. Ideally, the best bet is to have the kitchen in the South-East. In case you cannot have it in the South-East direction, one in the North-West or East direction is also favorable.

Chapter
4
Birth of Vaastu Purush & Vaastu Mandal

Birth of Vaastu Purush and Vaastu Mandal in Nutshell

1. The **Vaastu Purush and Vaastu Mandal is the main base of Conventional Vaastu**. In Hindu mythology, there are two stories of origin of Vaastu Purush and Vaastu Mandal.
2. According to first story in Hindu mythology, in the beginning **Brahma, the creator of the Universe, created a large cosmic man.**
3. The Second story is that **one weird personality/monster emerged from a drop of Lord Shiva's sweat,** while Lord Shiva was fighting a war with one of Asuras namely Andhkasur.
4. Vaastu Purush was created/emerged in the **month of Bhadrapad,** Krishna Paksha, Tritya Tithi, Krittika Nakshtra, Vyatipat Yog, Vishti Karan, Bhadra on Saturday in Kulik Muhurta.
5. Indeed, cosmic man/weird person **devoured everything on his way**. He became very powerful. This terrified even all the Gods (Devtas) in heaven.
6. All the Gods went to Lord Shiva and with his consent they attacked on that new creature cosmic man/weird person/monster from all sides. **Total forty-five Deities including Lord Brahma collectively caught hold of Vaastu-Purush.** They laid it face down with his head to the North-East Corner (Eshaan direction) and his feet towards the South-West corner (Nairutya direction).
7. Thus, total forty-five Deities established Vaastu Mandal. 13 Devtas by name Apa, Savita, Indrajya, Rudra, Marichi, Savitri, Vivaswan, Vishnu, Mitra, Rudra, Prithvidhara, Apavatsa, Brahma sat inside Vaastu Purush and 32 Devtas by name Ish, Parjanya, Jayant, Indra, Surya, Satya, Bhrash, Akash, Agni, Pusha, Vitya, Gruhkshat, Yama, Gandharva, Bhrungraj, Mriga, Pittar, Dwarpal, Sugriv, Pushpadevta, Varun, Asur, Shesh, Yakshma, Rog, Nag,Mukhya, Bhallat, Kuber, Shail, Aditi and Diti on Outside Vaastu Purush.

The Vaastu Purush and Vaastu Purush Mandal is the main base of Conventional Vaastu. Birth of Vaastu Purush and Vaastu Purush Mandal has been interpreted in their own manner in various Epics and Puranas concerned with Vaastu Shastra. In Treta Yug two interesting stories about birth of Vaastu-Purush was noticed in Matasya Puran and the reason why is Vaastu-Purush worshipped before starting construction of any house or building.

Two Stories of Birth of Vaastu Purush

1.   According to **First story** in Hindu mythology, in the beginning Brahma, the creator of the Universe, experimented with a new creature. He created a large cosmic man in the month of Bhadrapad, Krishna Paksha, Tritya Tithi, Krittika Nakshtra, Vyatipat Yog, Vishti Karan, Bhadra on Saturday in Kulik Muhurta, who later on became extremely huge and with his size, his hunger also increased. He started to eat anything and everything that came in his way. In no time, he became so big that his shadow had cast an everlasting eclipse on the earth. The Gods Shiva and Vishnu begged Brahma to do something before everything was destroyed by this Creature. Lord Brahma requested the Gods of all the eight directions (Astha Dikpals) to come and help him. They gathered, overpowered the monster and held it flat against the Earth. Lord Brahma jumped over its Navel (Center part of Body). Then the Monster cried out and spoke to Lord Brahma, "You created me like this, so why am I being punished?" Lord Brahma offered him a compromise and made the Monster immortal with the boon that he would be worshiped by any mortal that builds a structure on earth. He was named as Vaastu Purush.

2. The **Second story** is that one weird personality/monster emerged from a drop of Lord Shiva's sweat in the month of Bhadrapad, Krishna Paksha, Tritya Tithi, Krittika Nakshtra, Vyatipat Yog, Vishti Karan, Bhadra on Saturday in Kulik Muhurta, when Lord Shiva was fighting a war with one of Asuras namely Andhkasur. This weird person/monster was cruel and felt always hungry. He prayed and appeased Lord Shiva to grant him a boon to meet his hunger. Lord Shiva granted him a boon for eating anything from all the three worlds i.e. Dharti, Aakash and Paatal.
At first, he consumed all the blood and flesh from the body of the demon Andhakasur. Then he occupied almost all the surface of the earth called Bhoolok, killing all the residents and destroying the nature of the earth. All the Five Elements of the galaxy namely Earth, Air, Water, Fire and Space suffered by the growth of this weird being and could not carry on their functions. Indeed, weird person devoured everything on his way. He became very powerful. This terrified even all the Gods (Devtas) in heaven. Then all the Gods in heaven grouped together planned to kill the new creature/weird person/monster that was grown up so huge.

Vaastu Mandal
All the Gods went to Lord Shiva and with his consent they attacked on that new creature/weird person/monster from all sides. Total forty-five Deities including Lord Brahma collectively caught hold of Vaastu-Purush. Out of Forty-five deities, thirteen held his body from within and thirty-two from outside. Lord Brahma touched his navel, the center of the house,

where the navel of Vaastu Purush is located is called as 'Brahmasthan'. They laid it face down with his head to the North-East Corner (Eshaan direction) and his feet towards the South-West corner (Nairutya direction). They then sat on different parts of its body and pressed it inside the earth. Lord Shiva named him this new creature/weird person/monster as **Vaastu-Purush** and all the deities as **Vaastu Mandal.**

Lord Shiva ordered Vaastu Purush that he would bless every occupant with health, wealth and prosperity and in return the occupant would worship him and make him lie down comfortably in the house. In this way, the Vaastu-Purush came in existence and all the forty-five Deities including Lord Brahma, those caught hold Vaastu Purush was named as Vaastu Purush-Mandal. It is the most
important spiritual aspect of Vaastu Evaluation. The body parts of Vaastu-Purush are given the names after those deities, who touched and caught hold there. The deities were-

Name of Devtas 13 Inside Vaastu Purush- Apa, Savita, Indrajya, Rudra, Marichi, Savitri, Vivaswan, Vishnu, Mitra, Rudra, Prithvidhara, Apavatsa, Brahma. **Name of Devtas 32 Outside Vaastu Purush** - Ish, Parjanya, Jayant, Indra, Surya, Satya, Bhrash, Akash, Agni, Pusha, Vitya, Gruhkshat, Yama, Gandharva, Bhrungraj, Mriga, Pittar, Dwarpal, Sugriv, Pushpadevta, Varun, Asur, Shesh, Yakshma, Rog, Nag,Mukhya, Bhallat, Kuber, Shail, Aditi and Diti. To know the actual position of Vaastu Purush and Vaastu Mandal, see the picture below.

Vaastu Purush and Vaastu Mandal

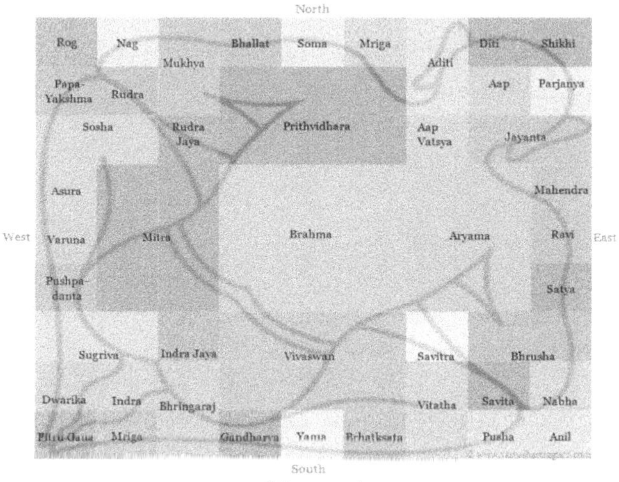

Figure-4

Vaastu Purush was quite satisfied. Since then, the worship of Vaastu Purush has been in practice and it has become compulsory to follow certain rules so as to make the Vaastu- Purush happy and comfortable. The Almighty ordered the Gods of heaven, who sat at key positions over the weird person, to safeguard the weird person and protect him from the people. Everyone shall pray and adopt the rules of Vaastu Shastra to live on the Earth having sound health, beautiful wife, healthy children, wealth, means of earning through business, profession or state service, high reputation in society and over all mental and spiritual peace without any disturbance and trouble.

Residents to Note
North-East indicates the Head of Vaastu Purush. One or the other person residing in that house may have some problem related to the head. Head related problems in the house will be such as headaches, brain hemorrhage, eye problems, educational problems, financial problems etc. South-West indicates feet of Vaastu Purush. One or the other person residing in that house may have some problem related feet such as instability in life, brings accidents, leg related problems etc. So always protect South-West and North-East of your place of living. Cuts in the North-West and South-East directions may give problems in the Knee and Elbow joints. So, the shape of an ideal house should be either square or rectangle. If it is not, there are either cuts or extensions which need to be taken care of through proper Vaastu corrections.

Chapter
5
The Scientific Values of Vaastu

The Scientific Values of Vaastu in Nutshell

1. **In Vaastu Purush Mandal two sources of energy or cosmic forces** are designated by symbolic categorization, which refers to the positive and negative influences.
2. **Cosmic Energy (Pranic Energy)** is ever changing. It moves through 360° degrees in relation to the Earth position. On the other hand, **Magnetic Field (Jaivic Energy)** is unidirectional from North Pole to South Pole.
3. **Pran and Jeev** is termed as one in life. Any inimical association of these two forces results in pain, hardship and sorrow. **Jeev** without **Pran** means Death.
4. **The Cosmic Energy (Pranic Energy)** comes in from the North-East direction, so there should be no obstruction along Eastern zone.
5. Bathroom, toilet, storeroom, staircase, master bedroom or even kitchen should not be placed there in North zone. Only prayer room or worship room (Pooja Ghar) is allowed there.
6. A Pessimist, gossiper and complainant type person means his **Pranik energy level** is low. If **Pranik Energy level of a person** is low, dogs can sense it and they may attack. Similarly North-East direction of a house is full of obstructions and South-West zone is open then the **Pranik Energy level** of a house will be low. If **Pranic energy level of a house is low**, thieves might sense it and burgle it.
7. If an individual's thinking is positive and feels happy with the environment, wherever he lives, his **Pranik energy level** will be high. He will always be full of energy and satisfied. In the same way if South-West direction is closed with heavy walls and fewer openings and North-East direction is open, then the **Pranik energy level** of a house will be high. Energy can be stored. Happiness and prosperity will be there.

Vaastu Purus Mandal

In Vaastu Purus Mandal there are two forces or sources of energies. These forces or sources of energies either lead to the positive, comfortable and lively results or negative, retrograde and destructive results. They are symbolized by the name of **Certain Deities** ruling various directions in Vaastu Purus Mandal. Their Positive influence is called **Priti Sangam,** and their negative influence is named **Vish Sanchar**, meaning to say the forces are turbulent and flow in opposite directions to annihilate each other.

Cosmic Energy (Pranic Energy) is ever changing. It moves through 360° degrees in relation to the Earth position. On the other hand, **Magnetic Field (Jaivic Energy)** is unidirectional from North pole to South pole. Union of these two forces is an ideal heavenly condition. In the same way oneness of **Pran and Jeev** is termed as life. Any inimical association of these two forces results in pain, hardship and sorrow. **Jeev** without **Pran** means Death. The Jeev is no more. There are different Granthas on Vaastu Shastra like Mansar, Vishwakarma Prakash, Samrangan Sutradhar, Vaastu-Ratnavali, Sthapatya Veda, etc. All these are based on the principle of cosmic energies. If the plot or flat is purchased in accordance with the guidelines of Vaastu Shastra, the all-round growth definitely occurs, and the owner gets peace and prosperity. However, if the selection goes wrong, it may lead to health problems and financial losses.

1.   Cosmic Energy (Pranic Energy)
At first, we discuss **Cosmic Energy (Pranic Energy).** As we know our Earth is tilted 23.5° degrees towards the North-East direction and it is moving from West to East direction. Here it is an example. When we run, we feel the air is coming against our direction. Similar thing happens to the movement of Earth towards the **North-East direction vis-à-vis the Cosmic Energy (Pranic Energy)**, which comes in from the North-East direction.

This is the reason that much focus is paid towards the North-East direction. If this zone is blocked, then the occupant will face many difficulties in life. No obstruction should be along the North-East direction such as bathroom, toilet, storeroom, staircase, master bedroom or even kitchen should not be placed there. Only prayer room or pooja room is allowed there.

This area must be kept clean and tidy and preferably light weight or no weight at all. Keep windows open here in the morning for the beneficial morning Sunrays. Use this place for meditation and prayers. Always keep your face towards North or East when praying. In addition, keep a bowl of clean water and place it at the corner of the North-East direction.

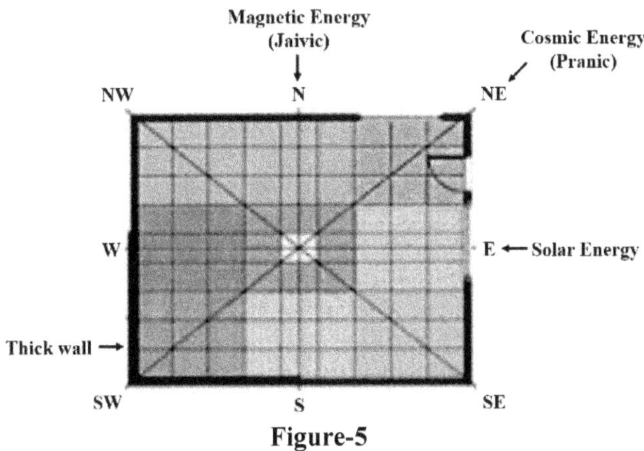

Figure-5

North-East zone represents the water element in Vaastu. Respect this zone, as if it is the heart of the house. This room can be used, if you are not well and wish to get well fast and to recharge yourself, when you are stressed out.

Why there are some cases of houses being burgled or robbed by thieves while some are not. Some people get robbed and some not. Similarly, some dogs attack people easily and some dogs don't and keep their distance? This may be connected to the energy level of people and their homes. When **Energy level or Pranik energy level** of a person is low, dogs can sense it and they may attack. Similarly, if **Energy level or Pranik energy level** of a house is low, thieves might sense it and burgle it. The question comes in our mind. How can they sense it? It comes down to their intuition and instinct and their feeling towards it. That is why that in some houses, we sense good feelings and, in some houses, we sense bad vibrations.

How do we know the Pranik energy level of a person, Is it high or low?
When you observe a person always talking pessimistically, gossiping and complaining about others and matters. He can never be happy with the environment. He will continue to attract negative things in his/her life. He will lose his energy and feel painful and unhappy. His **Pranik Energy level** will be low. If his thinking is positive and feels happy with the environment, his **Pranik energy level** will be high. He will always be full of energy and satisfied.

How do we measure the Pranik energy level of a house, Is it high or low?

At first observe the North-East direction of the house. If there are obstructions in North-East zone and South-West zone is open, then the **Pranik Energy level** of a house will be low. There will be no happiness. Next, observe the South-West direction. If South-West direction is closed with heavy walls and fewer openings, then the **Pranik energy level** of a house will be high. Energy can be stored. Happiness and prosperity will be there.

2.   Magnetic Field (Jaivic Energy)

Now we discuss **Magnetic Field (Jaivic Energy)** of Earth that flows from North to South. We as humans can only observe this energy, when we go to sleep on our beds. We see bad dreams; we cannot sleep at night, or we may sleep in excess. We may sleep with our heads towards North. Our body is receptive to the North-South **Magnetic flow (Jaivic Energy)** is due to Iron in our blood. Our head reacts as the North Pole and legs as South Pole. Our head and the North Pole repel each other. We get disturbed sleep. Sometimes we may even get acute migraine and headaches sleeping towards this direction.

The best direction to sleep is our heads towards South. When North and South Pole are opposite to each other, they attract, and we get sound and blissful sleep. We do not really have to sleep directly towards South. Our position of head can be South-East or South-West too but never towards North-East or North-West for getting the benefit of **Jaivik energy.**

Vaastu Shastra is not a belief or a superstition

Because of the above facts we can say, Vaastu Shastra is **not a belief or a superstition. It is a pure Science of the Cosmos.** Nothing is to be 'believed' or 'worshiped'. Every principle and technique have its scientific explanation behind it; and it can be observed regardless of religion or belief. Science is the concerted human effort to understand, or to understand better, the history of the natural world and how the natural world works, with observable physical evidence as the basis of that understanding. It is done through observation of natural phenomena, and/or through experimentation that tries to simulate natural processes under controlled conditions.

Characteristics of Science

On the basis of above features of science, we reach to the following six parameters that Science is based on **Cause and effect theory** i.e. Reasonable, **Capable of being put in to practice** i.e. Viable, **Not bound by barriers of time** i.e. Everlasting, **Codified and governed by**

guidelines i.e. Normative, **Beneficial to the society** i.e. Useful and **Acceptable and accessible to one and all** i.e. Universal.

The Science of Vaastu

Now we take all the above six parameters with relation to Vaastu to prove it to be a science. Is Vaastu based upon the laws of nature, and can it be predicted and established as Science? The equilibrium we observe in the nature is easily perceivable by us in all-moving bodies, but unfortunately, we are unable to notice this equilibrium in static bodies. The basic source of energy of the whole world is stored at North and South Pole. It flows uninterruptedly from North Pole to South Pole in the form of magnetic waves. Therefore, Southward portion of every building should be higher than the Northward portion so that there may not be any hindrance to the flow of magnetic waves. Similarly, when a building is constructed without observing the rules of Vaastu, various calamities, diseases, accidents can occur. This is the eternal rule of the nature, and it has no place for any logic, doubt or debate. It clarifies that the Science of Vaastu Shastra is believable. Indeed, Vaastu is like a magnetic effect and there is no known method to prove that it exists. It can only be proved and shown through examples and the experience of the people, who have followed Vaastu. Extensive research done worldwide by numerous Vaastu Scholars has established it as a science.

1. Reasonable

Vaastu is a systematic study of geological impact of Sunrays on earth. The geological conditions caused by the above impact prove to be favorable and suitable for construction of an ideal house/building. This is thoroughly proved by the fact that the residents of the houses/buildings possessing projections towards East, North and North-East likely lead a happy, healthy and prosperous life, while the residents of houses/buildings having wells and pits in South-East, South-West and North-West often face worries and troubles. Since Vaastu reads characteristics of the houses/buildings and explains their effects on the residents in a scientific manner, we can definitely say "Vaastu is a science".

2. Viable

Vaastu is Viable as it is capable of being experimented. Those, who want to construct a house, can follow the characteristics of an ideal house prescribed by Vaastu and lead carefree and happy lives there in. What all they have to do, is to follow the guidelines prescribed by Vaastu in providing gates, windows, flooring earth, water-well, bathroom and toilets. The above characteristics can be utilized for rectifying the existing houses, which are not built as per Vaastu, and such action will help to the house owner reap several advantages.

3. Everlasting

The effect of Vaastu is everlasting. This is also because of the binding between the Earth and Vaastu. The earth has been revolving around the Sun in a geostationary orbit for over 454 Crore years. The magnetic effect caused by earth rotation brings about the magnetic properties of earth, so the magnetic needle of compass always tends towards North. Since Vaastu is based on everlasting property of Earth, the effect of guidelines of Vaastu also becomes everlasting.

4. Normative

Vaastu prescribes certain rules and regulations which are governed by the guidelines based on geological conditions and the indisputable properties of the earth. For instance, sinking of a water-well in North-East, slope towards East, elevation of a plot in South, are certain norms prescribed by the science of Vaastu.

5. Useful

Any science which is not beneficial to the humanity becomes useless. Man continues to work for the invention of items which make his life happier and easier. Similarly, the sole aim of Vaastu happens to be useful i.e.to make the lives of the individuals on earth more and more comfortable and peaceful through conformance of the residence or abode to the Vaastu principles.

6. Universal

The origin of the science of Vaastu lies in the tie between Earth and Sun. Since these two cosmic bodies are of universal nature beyond religion, caste and nationality the science of Vaastu which studies their impact on human beings also becomes universal.

Role of Vaastu for Humanity

The system of Vaastu is an admixture of science, astronomy and astrology; it is based on the influence of the Sunlight and heat, Moonlight, the earth's atmosphere, wind direction, magnetic field and gravitation force on human beings. It gives practical guidelines on site selection, its contouring level, and orientation of the building in relation to climatology and micro weather, arrangements of areas/rooms in relation to the different activities of the proposed building, the proportions as well as rituals for successive stages of house building.

Vaastu also suggests the living condition in the house arrangements, and also plant & machinery layout in factory, business houses and also the location of different activities. The solar energy emanates only from the Sun. It is the source of Vitamin D as well. The morning Sun rays are very beneficial to our human bodies. It is best to get morning exposure during Sunrise Timings. As per the Hindu religion, praying the morning Sun God and chanting sacred 'Gayatri Mantra' facing East would be quite beneficial. Expose yourself towards the morning Sun as much as possible. Take a bath in the morning exposing to the beneficial morning Sun for better absorption of Vitamin D.

The best location for kitchen is in the South-East direction which is the fire zone, and which enables Cook facing East. The best time to cook is from 9am to 12 Noon. The Sun will be at the South-East zone this positioning of Sun facilitates us to benefit the Positive Ultra-Violet Sun Rays. After 12 Noon until Sunset, the immense heat of the Sun, which is not beneficial to us at all should be avoided. After 12pm, the position of the Sun will be at South then South-West then sets at West. This is the reason why our walls at home should be thicker along the Southern and Western zone. This is to prevent the harmful Ultraviolet rays of the Sun from entering into our living premises.

Chapter
6
The nature of Globe and Vaastu

The nature of Globe and Vaastu in Nutshell

1. The surface of the Globe is about 510100000 sq kms. According to Dr. Wagner's view **"Out of 510100000 sq kms. 71.7 % of the Globe is covered with water and the remaining 28.3 % is open Land/Earth.**
2. **It is only the Geographical position of India** as country, which made her subordinate to the alien powers.
3. If you look at Japan, the **"Land of the Rising Sun."** is a developed country. The reason for such growth is only its Geographical position.
4. If we look at the **map of Russia**, we find that the land on the West is more extensive than that on the East. Owning to this position, the people of Russia had to face untold difficulties.
5. There is Britain which used to claim that **"The Sun never sets on the British Empire."** Everybody knows that the British culture, civilization, industrial development, political strategy, religious supremacy and the popularity of the English language are seen, even today in each and every country in the world.
6. Let us have a look at the **geographical position of Africa**, Its North-East Portion was cut off. On the West and North-West side of the continent the extent of the land is bigger than that on the other sides. The East side is Dark because of the Indian Ocean, so African countries are backward, uneducated and poor.
7. **Capricorn line crosses in the middle of the continent** from east to west that made the three fourth part of the continent desert having goldmines. Foreigners came through sea route and became rich.

Surface of the Globe

Now it is a known fact that the surface of the Globe is about 510100000 sq km. According to Dr. Wagner's view "Out of 510100000 sq km. 71.7 % of the Globe is covered by water and the remaining 28.3 % is open Earth. Some of the countries that were formed on the earth are prosperous and progressive because of their directional position better on earth, while some others are in declining state owing to their unfavorable geographical position. If we consider a country, taking it as a separate unit, we can easily understand why that country is in rising position taking into consideration its religious, social, political, industrial and economic conditions. See some examples as under.

Example 1. India and its North and Other Sides

Now, we shall have a glance at our Motherland, India. When we read the History of our country, we find how big Empires rose and how they fell down. There were many attacks on this country by foreigners, who plundered the country many a time. It is only the Geographical position of this country, which made her subordinate to the alien powers. There is the Bay of Bengal on the East, the Indian Ocean on the South and the Arabian Sea on the West. It is surrounded by water on the South-East and South-West sides also. It is only owing to this reason that India became often a target of the foreign attacks. Of course, there are the Himalayas on the north of this sub-continent. Why to go far, let us discuss our own INDIA, we know we have the Himalayas in the North and North-East side of our country which is against Vaastu, thus there is lot of poverty in our country. The Himalayas, with its pristine glory, is called the King of the Mountains. A good feature in the Geographical position of this country is that it is a little bit bent towards East. This is the only reason for which our country dominates, even today, the whole world in religious, cultural, literary as well as philosophical field. Keeping in view the Geographical position of India, those who want to construct buildings, have to follow the guidelines laid down in the 'Vaastu-Shastra' so that the owner of the building might escape from evil powers.

Example 2. Japan and its East Side Islands

Look at Japan, the "Land of the Rising Sun.", you will have a different picture of the islands. It is a developed country. It was developed in a short period, sustaining the onslaughts of the Second World War. Though the area of the islands is not much, yet its all-round growth is praiseworthy. The reason for such growth is only its Geographical position. There is the Pacific Ocean on the East and North-East of the Islands. They are surrounded by water on the West and Southeast. This is the reason why Hiroshima and Nagasaki were much affected by the bomb attacks during the Second World War, as a result of which, they were destroyed. Besides facing the havoc, there is the danger of frequent earthquakes in this country. This is owing to the water flowing on the South-Eastern Side.

Example 3. Russia between Caspian and Arctic Ocean

In the map of Russia, we find that the land on the West is more extensive than that on the East. There is the Caspian Sea on the South-East side and Black-Sea on the South. Therefore, the water on the South-East is balanced with that on the North-East side. Owning to this position, the people of Russia had to face untold difficulties during the reign of the Czar and later on under the Communist Administration. It is also well-known that the Russian suffered a lot during the Second World War. So, to sum up the facts, one should know that the influence of water is seen on the countries which are surrounded by it.

Example 4. England and its West and North Side
There is Britain which used to claim that "The Sun never sets on the British Empire." Everybody knows that the British culture, civilization, industrial development, political strategy, religious supremacy and the popularity of the English language are seen, even today in each and every country in the world. The extent of this country is less; but its dominating power cannot be questioned. The reason for this importance is the Atlantic Ocean on the West, the North Sea spreading up to the Arctic Ocean is on the North. That is why this little country was able to lord over the whole world.

Example 5. Mediterranean Ocean and Africa
Let us have a look at the geographical position of Africa, Its North- East Portion was cut off. On the West and North-West side of the continent the extent of the land is bigger than that on the other sides. On the East of this ' Dark Continent' there is the Indian Ocean, on the North there is the Mediterranean Sea. These all conditions are inauspicious according to Vaastu, that's why African countries are backward, uneducated and poor. But on the contrary, in the North of this continent, there exists Mediterranean Sea, which is favorable according to Vaastu. In the eastern part, river Nile flows and that's why civilization developed in Egypt. Egypt got name and honor for its world-famous pyramids.

Example 6. Atlantic Ocean and its West Side
On the West the Atlantic Ocean. If the rules of "Vaastu Shastra" are applied to this continent, it is evident that the position of the land is quite erroneous. The whole world knows the ultimate result of this irregular position. There have always been civil wars, ethnical feuds and famine-stricken troubles. The people were treated as slaves by the white race for a long time, they were thirsty of blood.

Example 7. Australia and Bay of Carpentria
If we see the continent of Australia, it is surrounded by water, Pacific Ocean in the East direction and Hind Ocean towards all three directions i.e. North, West and South. There is a big Bay of Carpentaria on the North. Capricorn line crosses in the middle of the continent from East to West that made the three fourth part of the continent desert having goldmines. Foreigners came through sea route and became rich. Low pressure winds called Westerlies from North-West affect the land and keep area warm in the day and cold at night. South-East coastal region is better for happy and peaceful living. On both sides of Great Dividing Range, the maximum people live. Area around the big Bay of Carpentaria area on the North is also favorable for happy living.

Chapter
7
Geopathic Stress and Vaastu

Geopathic Stress and Vaastu in Nutshell

1. The word **Geopathic"** is derived from the Greek words, **"Geo"** means **"the Earth"**, and **"pathic" means "disease"** or "suffering", so literally "Suffering of the Earth".
2. Geopathic **stress occurs when the Earth Electromagnetic Forces becomes distorted**. It creates severe health problems, mental disorders and finally the major risk of cancer.
3. According to **WHO report, around 30% to 40% of the World houses are inducing sickness.** It is due to Geopathic stress that can harm us in a serious way.
4. The work on Geopathic Stress was **first started in 1920 by Winzer and Melzer in Germany.** They found that geological faults occurred in the area of Stuttgart city with the highest incidence of Cancer disease.
5. Geopathic stress reasons, effects and their treatment are defined later on.

What is Geopathic Stress?

The word Geopathic" is derived from the Greek words, "Geo" means "the Earth", and "pathic" means "disease" or "suffering", so literally "Suffering of the Earth". "The term "Geopathic Stress" is used to describe negative energies, also known as "Harmful Earth Rays," which originate from the earth and cause discomfort and ill health to those living above them. Geopathic energies pass through walls, windows, close gates. They do not recognize boundaries. They are not fixed and stable. They may change according to a season or time of a day.

Symptoms of Geopathic Stress

Geopathic stress occurs when the Earth Electro-magnetic Forces becomes distorted. Geopathic stress has been found to be the most common reason for many severe health problems, mental disorders and finally the major risk of cancer. If you are curious to know whether your house has Geopathic stress, you may find it by certain symptoms that may persist in your house –Long time to fall asleep, Wake up during night especially between 2-3 AM, Feeling tired in morning, Not well rested, Children restless sleep, Children nightmare, Baby crying for no reason, Appears Suicidal tendency, Chronic health issues to family members, Trees having abnormal growing pattern, Abnormal blood pressure and joint pains, Mental disorders, depression and at last Cancer.

Where was Geopathic Stress seen?

Initially, it was seen in an area of company office buildings. It was thought that inadequate ventilation and improper air conditioning as well as poor air quality were responsible for illness of the staff. But even after rectification of all these defects the problem in all company office buildings could not be traced. The view is slowly gaining ground that the Geopathic Stresses could be one of the factors resulting in imbalance in the energy field. These areas are purely natural, and we are not in danger, if we live in these areas for a short period. But the problem may arise, when we live continuously in these areas. In other words, when our home, office, workplace etc. are located in such areas, we may face this problem. Geopathic lines are produced due to irregularity in energy lines inside the Earth. These lines can be present in your house, office, workplace or anywhere. These lines may drain your energy thus making you sick. According to WHO report, around 30% to 40% of the World houses are sick. It is due to Geopathic stress that can harm you in a serious way.

Geopathic Stress has been accepted as a possible phenomenon. It has been acknowledged by several western thinkers that electromagnetic spectrum with the frequency of the earth waves can resonate. In turn they can affect certain energy fields inside a structure, which have a bearing on health and happiness of an individual. The western thinkers also believe that some other types of harmful radiations can pervade the building and can cause many unexplained diseases including Cancer. Though cancer is not the direct result of Geopathic stress, it can be held that Geopathic stress weakens the immune system and reduces our capacity to fight the cancer. Geopathic stress lines have also caused cardiovascular problems.

Geopathic stress afflicted area or a sick building polluted with harmful radiations causes various illnesses and persistent sickness among residents. Some of the illnesses that are being noted among people who have been living on Geopathic afflicted house are their Weak Immune system, Depression, Anxiety, Insomnia, Restlessness, Fatigue, Cancer, Tumour, Nightmares Fever Infertility, Behavioral problems, Miscarriage and so on.

The work First started on Geopathic Stress

The work on Geopathic Stress was first started in 1920 by Winzer and Melzer in Germany. They found that geological faults occurred in the area of Stuttgart city with the highest incidence of Cancer disease. **Gustav Freihherr Von Pohl** took up this work later on and he studied two other places **Vilsbiburg and Grafenau** where Cancer cases were found. He was able to show a link between cancer and Geopathic zones. The research in Germany and France was to identify the characteristics of Geopathic phenomena. Presence of Geopathic Stresses is inferred from its effect on humans, animals and plants.

Geopathic stress is the effect of negative earth energies. Some people use the term Geopathic stress only to describe Ley Lines or Man-Made Energy Lines or disturbance caused by underground water. But it is not correct. There are other factors responsible for the stress. Modernization, which has brought in tremendous amount of electromagnetic spectrum in the form of microwaves and other electronic transfer media, has contributed to Geopathic Stress. It may be one of the factors. The main factors are explained below.

1. The Earth Magnetic Field

Now we discuss **Magnetic Field** of Earth that flows from North to South. The rotation of the Earth creates electric currents in the molten metals found within in the earth's core thereby producing a magnetic field. This magnetic field is constantly changing. Sometimes the natural variations are due to changes in weather and other time in the Sun's activity. Geopathic stress effects only when the earth's magnetic field is disturbed either naturally or artificially. It occurs due to geological faults, underground masses and underground running water. Water is one of the few liquids that conduct electricity. The Combination of both water and electricity creates the disturbance to imbalance in the earth's energy that leads towards Geopathic stress. Man made disturbances to the Earth's magnetic field include mining, foundations for skyscrapers, tall buildings, underground transport system, public utility works such as sewer lines, drinking water pipes. Thus, both natural and man-made disturbances imbalance inside the earth's energy which affects animals and plants as well as humans adversely.

2. Water

When water flows fast in a bigger volume changing its levels, it imbalances inside the earth's energy that causes Geopathic stress. Geopathic stress is likely more intense, especially when two underground water streams cross each other in a considerable depth. Due to this animals and plants as well as human-beings are extremely affected. Here it is to be noted that Ground water of rivers and lakes does not usually create such problems.

3. Curry Grid

It was Dr. Manfed Curry and Dr. Writtman, who first hypothesized that there is a grid network of electrically charged lines of natural origin which encompasses the globe. These lines are flowing from North-East to South-

West and South-East to North-West at approximately 3 meters distance. Dr. Curry hypothesized that where the lines cross each other, there is a double positive or a double negative energy which can disturb the balance in a human body. The studies of Dr. Curry show that people who slept on positively charged ports got Cancer and those who slept on negatively charged ports got inflammatory diseases. Dr. Curry recommended that for best health one should sleep within the grid.

4. Hartmann lines
Dr. Ernst Hartman of Germany discovered another kind of flow of energy lines, which were running from north to south and east to west. These are called as the Hartman lines and again the study show that intersection points are dangerous for human health. Energy rays on North-South and East-West Lines. The super imposing of Hartman lines on the Curry lines leads to a plethora of possible errors of lines crisis crossing each other and are capable of creating ports, which are potentially more powerful than those that arise from the intersection of two lines in any one of the grids. It is always accepted that Geopathic Stress exists apart from the Curry and Hartman lines.

Curry Grid and Hartmann lines

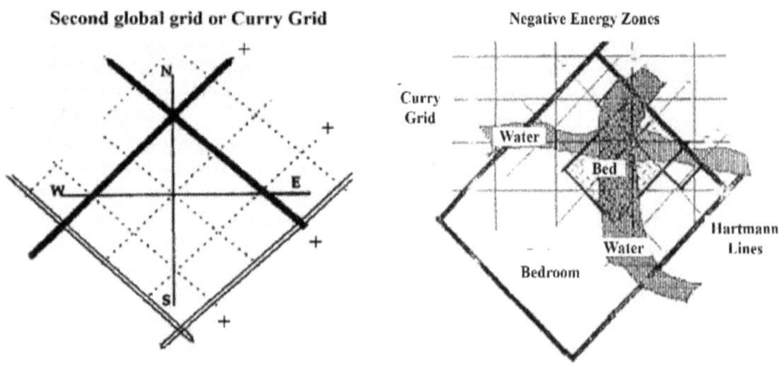

Figure-6

5. Black lines
Naturally generated certain lines called black lines can be straight or curved at ground level or even at higher level. These w ere noted on upper floor of buildings.

6. Spots and Spirals
Some geographic energies occur as spots and spirals. Spirals can have the energy flowing in towards the center or out towards the periphery. At

different spots the shape of the spiral may be same, but the energy effects are different. Spots are located randomly whereas spirals usually occur in pairs. It is not necessary that these are together. These may be far from each other and one of them may be found in a particular area and other may be a little away. Spirals of energy can be emanating from a single point of the earth's periphery or from inside a building, which are popularly called evolving sperm. An inward spiral can form when an energy from outside gets concentrated.

For example, we see while entering a narrow passage from a road which in turn leads to an open area. This makes the energy enter the building in a spiral form. Spirals are supposed to occur in pairs and a spiral when suspected can be corrected by using copper tube pyramids. Geopathic practitioners also believe that it is possible for negative energy to exist as a cloud and inadvertently it can move into a building where it is trapped. It is believed to be 1 ft. wider and most of the Geopathic clouds are formed when a structure is built in a wrong manner. You should suspect a cloud formation inside your structure if there are frequent accidents either in the bathroom or on the staircases.

7. Energy clouds

Energy clouds are found inside the building. Commonly they are created by constructing a building by loading positive zones like the North-East sector first and trying to advance towards the South-West sector. In this case, the weakened North-East sector allows negative energy to dominate the building. Subsequently, closure of this building by construction in south and west areas locks up the excessive negative energy and creates a cloud. You will notice a lock of this energy field in two stages. Firstly, the construction will be delayed there will be cost over runs and strained relationships between the builders and the owners. Sometimes there will be accidents of working personnel also.

However, there is another possibility of a negative cloud forming inside a structure. In this case a family could have lived in the structure for a number of years without any problem. The second person who occupies this structure could have the effect of the negative cloud if the earlier family had a member who was very much attached to the house and who reluctantly left it. Normally this happens in case of distress sale of residential or commercial building where the owner has developed sentimental feelings for the building. The same phenomenon could also surface where an older person suffers in humiliation and dies.

8. Shumann Waves

These were discovered by professor Shumann in 1952. These waves have the same frequency as the brain waves, and it is believed that these waves which occur on the surface of the earth and oscillate between the earth and the ionosphere regulate the human body mechanism. The importance of these waves has also been recognized by Nasa Research Center. Now all manned space aircrafts carry Schumann Wave generators as these waves are not present in outer space to protect the health of astronauts.

9. Subtle Energy

Ley lines or man-made horizontal lines are formed when stone like structures lie in a line. Any building contains stones which have been cut, hammered, dressed etc. In this sort of handling, the stone gets charged and the structure becomes an energy center. This energy is believed to radiate even up to 25 miles. When several structures like this are placed in a line, they can form a strong energy center with energy circulating in straight lines from one structure to other. They are called as by lines. Ley lines can be effectively used to block negative inference entering the building when such a phenomenon is suspected. On the same token dressed stone structures should never be used for dwelling purposes. A survey has revealed that people who live in dressed stones structures probably expose themselves to a wrong energy field and they suffer from ill health and ill luck. Dressed stones give negative energy and it is best to avoid them in construction. This does not apply to facade stones. This also does not apply to foundation stones as they lay buried under the earth.

above mentioned various types of subtle energy fields which exist can influence the functioning of an organism due to the vibrations it causes. As basically the human body is electrical in nature and as the energy fields mentioned above are electromagnetic radiations it is reasonable to suppose that the effect impacts the organism. However, nature builds a certain amount of immunity against these energy fields just like every human being enjoys certain amount of immunity from bacteria and viruses. However, if the immunity system is weak then the Geopathic Stresses can cause illnesses and can be responsible from simple fatigue to Cancer. Thus, we may have to examine a building where residents are distressed from various angles to arrive at a conclusion. The first factor to analyze is from the point of your Vaastu. Some people are under the impression that it is basically the science of designing structures in accordance with the local environment. They go so far as to say that the whole subject was designed keeping the prevailing wind conditions in India to take advantage of the rain and wind directions.

Figure-7

Effects
Geopathic stress afflicted area or a sick building polluted with harmful radiations causes various illnesses and persistent sickness among residents. Some of the illnesses that are being noted among people who have been living on Geopathic afflicted house. Their Weak Immune system, Depression, Anxiety, Insomnia, Restlessness, Fatigue, Cancer, Tumour, Nightmares Fever Infertility, Behavioral problems, Miscarriage and so on.

Treatment
Moving out the place or position in the house or blocking/neutralizing the negativity of the area. Blocking will be easier.

Chapter
8
Energy Level inside the Plot

Energy Level inside the Plot in Nutshell

1.   Open or High Energy Level inside the Plot is essential for better harmony and prosperity to the resident.
2.   For getting open or high energy and a better magnetic field, there should be a high thick compound wall in the West and South directions and a low-level thin wall or wire fencing in North and East directions.
3.   If Plot area length and width are equal or square in size and shape, Energy level will be open or high.
4.   If Plot is rectangular in size and shape i.e. length is more than width, Energy level will be tight or low inside the plot because of the reason that energy waves have to cover a long way.
5.   A square size Plot strengthens the magnetic field and high energy level inside the plot in comparison to a rectangular plot/house, which creates tight or low energy level.

Open Energy Level

Open Energy Level inside the Plot is essential for better harmony and prosperity to the resident. If a plot is covered with a compound wall, it creates a type of open and high energy level and a magnetic field inside the plot. For getting open and high energy level and a better magnetic field there should be a high thick compound wall in the West and South directions and a low-level thin wall or wire fencing in North and East sides. If North and East directions of a Plot are open, energy level will be more advantageous for harmony and prosperity to the resident. If Plot area length and width are equal or square in size and shape, Energy level will be open and high. If Plot is rectangular in size and shape i.e. length is more than width or double in comparison to width, there will be tight and low energy level inside the Plot because of the reason that energy waves have to cover a long way. So, to maintain the open and high energy level inside the Plot length and breadth should be equal in size and shape. This will strengthen the magnetic field also inside the plot. See ahead the square size/shape and the rectangular size/shape buildings and their energy level design. Square size/shape plot is strengthening the magnetic field inside the plot for harmony and prosperity to the resident.

A square size Plot/House

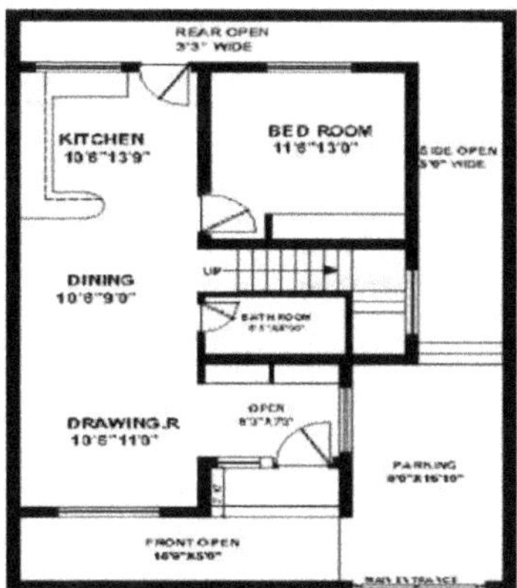

Figure-8

A rectangular size   Plot/House

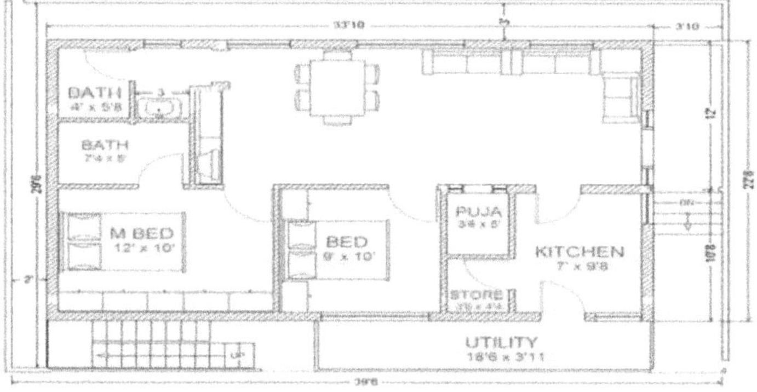

Figure-9

Note:

Now we can imagine the energy level open and high or tight and low difference between these two plots. One is a square size Plot and second is a rectangular size Plot. Square size/shape Plot is getting open and high energy in comparison to Rectangular plot.

Chapter
9
How to Check Directions of the Plot

How to Check Directions of the Plot in Nutshell

1. Right knowledge how to Check Directions of the plot is very important to make a House structure according to Vaastu guidelines.
2. Vaastu compass (**Pivotal compass)** is a device that every professional or Vaastu expert takes with himself to ascertain the concerned directions in a place.
3. **Pivotal compass** is commonly used by experts and even by laymen. **Floating compass** is an improvised version of former or pivotal compass and has an automatic system of working.
4. Find out the approximate center of the plot and stand there, keep the compass on the clean leveled surface of the floor.
5. If the deflection is found to be below 10 degrees, then plot is perfect in alignment. If deflection is higher or more than 10 degrees, then directions are needed to be calculated by making diagonal plots.
6. Though East and North facing plots have certain inherent advantages such as harmony, prosperity and peace, yet West and South facing plots can also beneficial and fruitful to the resident, if those are constructed as per Vaastu guidelines.

Note: See Vaastu Purush and all the eight directions map. Use compass and know direction.

Vaastu Purush and Directions

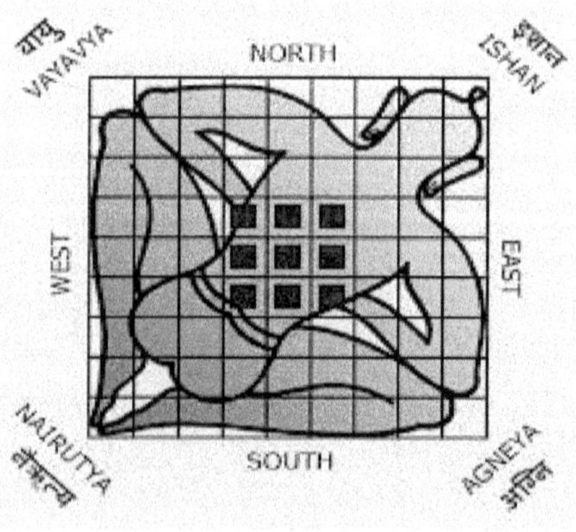

Figure-10

How to Check Directions in the Plot/house

Now we should check the directions of the plot, where is North from the center of our Plot? For this purpose, every Vaastu expert keeps with himself a Pivotal compass to ascertain the concerned directions of the plot. This tool is one of the prominent instruments to self-check the arrangements, location and directions. Directions play an important role in Vaastu. Right knowledge of direction is very important to make a house structure according to Vaastu guidelines. In the olden days people used to observe the shadow of Sun to check the directions.

In the modern technical world, a Magnetic Compass is used to check the directions. In all there are 10 directions but to check by Magnetic compass only 8 directions are available. Magnetic Compass has 360° degrees in total with its radius. Every direction is allotted 45° degrees. For every direction, checking the level of degree is very important.

Types of compasses used by Vaastu experts

There are two different types of compasses are used by a Vaastu expert to check the correct directions of the Plot.

1. **Pivotal compass**
2. **Floating compass**

1. Pivotal compass:

This type of compass is commonly used by experts and even by laymen to ascertain the exact direction. They usually have a red tip on one of the needles at the end and needle rotates itself as soon as it is kept on the leveled surface in the center. When the needle settles down, the red tip needle shows North direction. Now you can confirm other directions South, East, West and its corner directions North-East, South-East, South-West and North-West.

Pivotal Compass

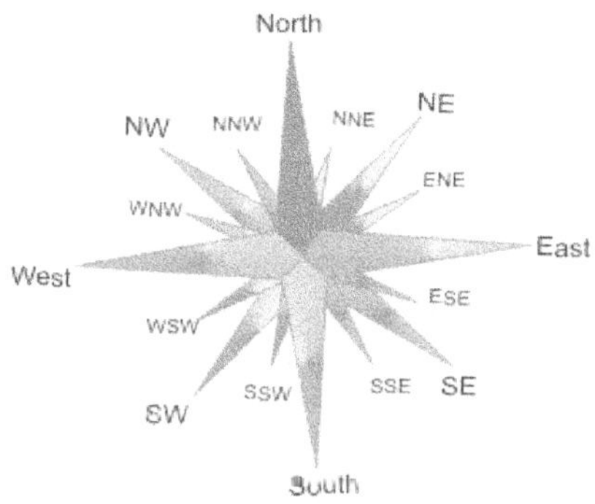

Figure-11

51

2. Floating compass:

Floating compass is an improvised version of former and has automatic system of working. In this compass there is no need to align the red tip towards North like in Pivotal because a disc is mounted on the top of needle. This device itself points towards North unlike pivotal compass. Now you can imagine the main gate direction and fix other positions as per Vaastu guidelines.

Floating Compass

Figure-12

How to use compass to know North and other directions

Pivotal compass can be used in a following way to know exact directions of the Plot/House.

1. Ascertain the approximate center of the plot and stand there, keep the compass on the clean leveled surface of the floor.

2. Don't have any magnetic device or mobile phone or high-tension wire nearby which can restrain you from ascertaining correct direction.

3. Let the needle rest on surface and then look at the needle pointing red. That pointed direction showing red is your North and difference in degrees between the red needle and letter 'N' provides the direction of the plot in degrees.

4. If the deflection is found to be below 10 degrees, then plot is perfect in alignment. If deflection is higher more than 10 degrees directions are needed to be calculated by making diagonal plots.

5. Do not come to the point immediately but one should calculate directions from different places for instance center, front or back.

<u>**Note about facing of a Plot/House**</u>

One should have the sound knowledge of directions in order to use Vaastu device to ascertain proper direction of an area. Though East and North facing plots have certain inherent advantages such as harmony, peace and prosperity, yet West and South facing plots can also be beneficial and fruitful to the resident, if those are constructed as per Vaastu guidelines. Thus, no direction is good or bad in itself. It is individual's thinking. Take expert's advice prior to constructing or purchasing a plot/house.

Chapter
10
Importance of Directions in the Plot

Importance of Directions in the Plot in Nutshell

1. **East** is the **first** direction in Vaastu. It stands for Sunrise. It is an auspicious direction. Planet Sun, the source of our energy, rules this direction. **It is the direction of harmony, happiness and prosperity.**
2. **West** is **opposite to the East**. West stands for Sunset. It is not considered very auspicious. Planet Saturn rules this direction.
3. **North** direction is ruled by the planet Mercury. **It is best for business** because of the fact that ultraviolet rays cast by Sun have the least negative effect. **It gives happy and peaceful life.**
4. **South** is quite a **contrary/divergent** direction. This direction is considered very **inauspicious** for any activity. Planet Mars rules this direction. **It reduces one's finances.**
5. **North-East** direction is called **Eshaan**. This is the **direction of Purity and divinity.** It is the most auspicious and Godly direction and **gives over all happiness.**
6. **South-West** direction is called **Nairutya** the residence of Demoness **Putna**. It **leads to mental agony and physical disabilities** in family life.
7. **South-East** direction is called **Aagneya**. It **stands for logics and reasons**. This direction **increases strength, determination and fame.**
8. **North-West** direction is called **Vayavya**. It governs **interpersonal relationship**. People of the family depend on each other.

A picture of Eight Directions

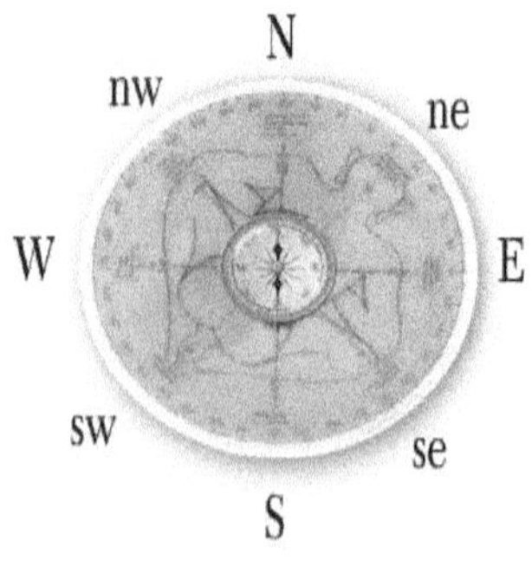

Figure-13

Directions in the Plot

There lies a co-relation between the rotational scenario of the planets and the house design and their different directions with respect of North. The house of any type and its construction meets the purpose, if proper orientation has been given using suitable local building material. It increases not only its life span but also improves the condition of occupants/residents.

There are instances, where houses were not planned according to required local orientation, those were lost or deteriorated much faster than the houses having built with proper studies of orientation. The proper orientation means the proper knowledge of all the eight directions. It is a common knowledge that the direction from where the Sun rises is known as **East (Poorav)** and where it sets as **West (Paschim)** and when one faces the East direction, towards one's left is **North (Uttar)** and towards one's right is **South (Dakshin).** The corner, where two directions meet obviously is more significant since it combines the forces emanating from both the directions. According to Vaastu guidelines, if we worship, revere and respect the lords of these eight directions, they will shower on us their blessings and benefits. Some Facts about all the eight directions are as under –

A Scene of Eight Directions

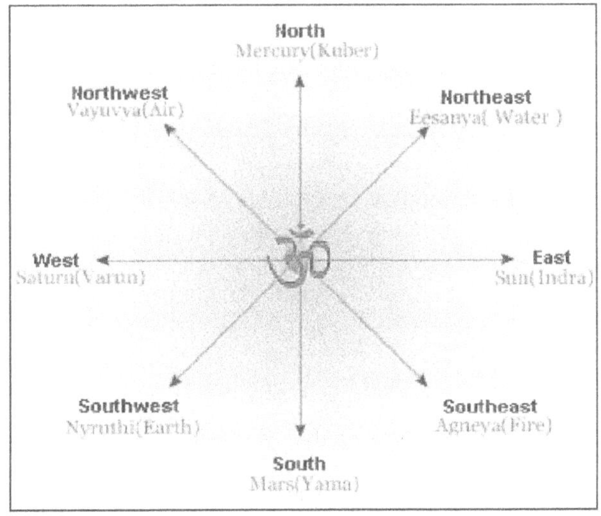

Figure-14

<h1 align="center">A Scene of Degree-wise Direction</h1>

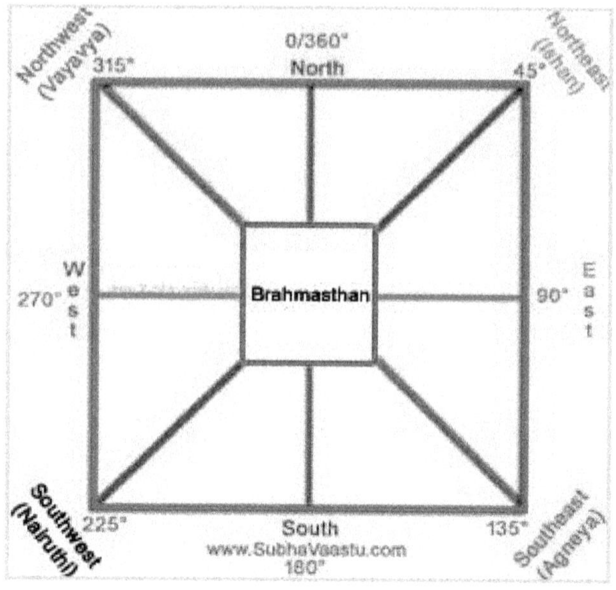

Figure-15

East (Poorav)

East is the best direction in Vaastu. Planet Sun, the source of our energy, rules this direction. East stands for Sunrise. It is very useful for people, who tries to end something bad and wants to start something good. **It is the direction of harmony, happiness and prosperity.** Following things in the house can be fixed in the east direction such as the main entrances of the house, Drawing room, study room, place of worship. Treasury boxes, lockers should open in the east. Eastern direction must be lower than the West, South-West and North-West. Mirrors put up in this direction double up the prosperity. **Indra,** The Lord of all Gods is the lord of this direction. It raises wealth and brings rain, whenever there is no rainfall. Other Eight Gods Ish, Parjanya, Jayant, Sun, Satya, Bharsh, Akash and Agni also lend power to this direction.

South (Dakshin)

South is quite a contrary/divergent direction. This direction is considered **very inauspicious** for any activity. Planet Mars rules this direction. If someone builds a house with a South facing entrance, he will face a painful future. Financially he will be loser after first few years. His money will start decreasing. However, he should keep the South direction elevated compared to rest of the house, putting overhead tank and staircase. No basement and kitchen should be in south direction. It has been noted that Persons living in the South Facing Gate House face wealth Problems after seven or eight Years of Staying in that Place. **Yama**, the lord of Death is the lord of this direction. Other six Gods Pusha, Vitya, Gundharva, Gandharva, Bhrungraj and Mriga ban all auspicious functions to this direction.

West (Paschim)

West direction is the opposite direction to the East. West stands for Sunset so West direction are less desirable than East. It is not considered very auspicious. Planet Saturn rules this direction. People, who are living in the Western part of the house or having entrances towards West, **lead an unhappy and unlucky life.** This direction spoils the prospects of income. Women lose every success and happiness in such houses. But in most cases, it has also been noted that the West direction is more beneficial to women. It is better to have Staircase or a Water Tank or an Office or a Garage or a Garbage store in the West. **Varun**, the Lord of Water is Lord of the West direction. Other Eight Gods Rog, Pap, Asur, Dwarpal, Pittar (the cruel in power), Shesh, Pushpdevta and Sugreev (the caring in nature) also give their powers to west direction.

North (Uttar)

North direction is ruled by the planet Mercury. It is best for business because of the fact that ultraviolet rays cast by Sun have the least negative effect in the Northern parts. **Open space to this side gives advantages of better happy and healthy life.** Northern parts of the house bring maximum success. Minimum construction is required this side so as to maintain efficiency. Slope or elevation is better to this direction. Do not have Staircase or Toilet or Garbage store or Kitchen to this direction. Fixing of Mirrors is auspicious here. They are supposed to double up your wealth. **Kuber,** the treasurer of all the Gods is the Lord of the North direction. Other six Gods Diti, Aditi, Shail, Bhalat, Mukhya and Nag bring happiness and prosperity to this direction.

Northeast (Uttar-Poorav)

North East direction is called **Eshaan** direction. It is the direction of Purity and divinity. The Sun's powerful Ultraviolet rays fall on this direction. Planet Jupiter rules this direction and gives **over all happiness**

and prosperity in life. It is the most auspicious and Godly direction called **Eshaan** and promotes positive aspects to men and women both. Open space and slope are essential towards this direction. It will be better, if there is a street outside the entrance. **Hindu Lord Shiva** is the supreme deity of this direction. It is the best Direction to Place a Temple (Mandir) or worshipping place (Pooja Sthan). Underground tank, Boring and well also give auspicious results to this direction.

Southeast (Dakshin-Poorav)

Southeast direction is called **Aagneya** direction for logics and reasons. This direction **stands for strength, determination and fame.** Planet Venus rules this direction. It is very beneficial to have a kitchen in this direction. Electric instruments such as Televisions, Motor batteries, Inverters, Home theatre and so on should be placed or fixed on the South-East side of the room/rooms. There should be no toilet and water tank in this direction. People doing **Homa-Havans** (Oblations by Fire to the Deity) at homes are blessed by **Agni Dev,** the lord of fire. Residents enjoy wealth, prosperity and fame.

Southwest (Dakshin-Paschim)

Southwest direction is called **Nairutya** direction. It is the residence of **Putna,** the Demoness. It leads to mental and physical disabilities in family life. Planet **Rahu** rules this direction. Therefore, **this is the most inauspicious and evil direction**. Gates here many times bring misfortunes. This space should be filled with heavy stuff to pull down the negativity of this direction. **The Lord of the demons** is the lord of this direction. It bans all auspicious functions to this direction.

Northwest (Uttar-Paschim)

Northwest direction is called **Vayavya** direction. It **governs interpersonal relationship.** People of the family depend on each other. Moon rules this direction. For total happiness of the family no basement, underground water tank, kitchen, dining room and master bedroom should be in this direction. Any type of extension in the house/building should also be avoided in this direction. **Lord Hanuman** is also symbolic of this direction. This is the Direction of Movement. Thus, according to Vaastu Girls, who are not Getting married after reaching a marriageable age, generally get married Soon. **Vayu Devta**, the lord of Air is the lord of this direction.

Disha and Vidisha Chart

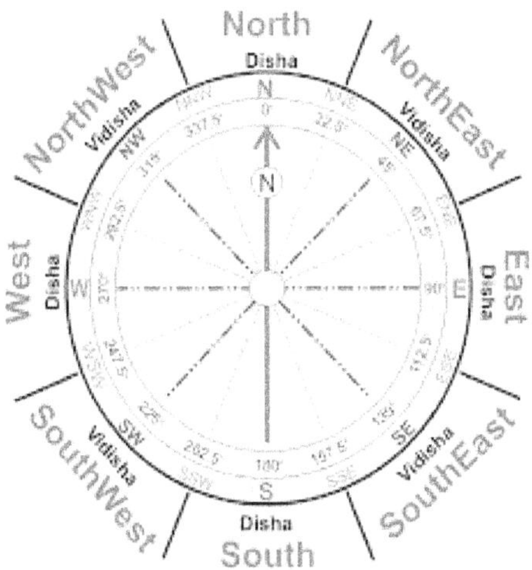

Figure-16

Note: Above is a Disha (Direction) and Vidisha (Corner Direction) Chart of all the eight directions North, East, South and West Four Dishas, North-East, South-East, Southwest and North- West Four Vidisha.

Chapter
11
Selection of Site for the Plot

Selection of Site for the Plot

While going for construction of a dream house, we need careful consideration. The first and foremost consideration is the selection of the site of the plot. It is advisable to follow Vaastu guidelines, while selecting a site of the plot to make sure that the site becomes a healthful, energetic, cheerful and prosperous residence. The following considerations are useful for selection of site for the plot.

1.   The site is good for construction having fertile land, where fruit trees, flower plants, grassy area and so on exist.
2.   The site is having a very good source of ground water.
3.   If the site of the plot is having big building area about 500 square yards or more that should be far away from the big trees.
4.   If the plot is having small area about 100 square yards, there may be small trees nearby.
5.   The site should be far away from temple, ashram, school, college, hospital, graveyard, garbage dump site etc.

(i) Quality of Soil

The soil of the plot should also be checked. In the famous scriptures of Vaastu Shastra, soil is classified according to its color, smell and taste. Therefore, one should give special importance to the type of soil as per Vaastu. One must take care of this fact that a good/auspicious soil gives peace, happiness and prosperity in life of the occupant.

Good/Auspicious soil
1.   Only the white color soil, having lotus smell, sweet taste and which contains greenery is considered very good for the site of the plot.
2.   The soil is treated good/auspicious, where the cereals germinate and gives more production.
3.   While digging for the foundation, if cow's horns, conch, shells, turtles etc. are obtained, the soil of the land is considered good/auspicious.
4.   While digging for the foundation, if one finds gravel and bricks in the soil, it indicates acquiring of gold and wealth for the occupant from unexpected sources.
5.   While digging for the foundation, if one obtains copper, he gets all kinds of luxuries in life.

Bad/Inauspicious soil

1.Black, red, yellow, pale-green and clayey soil is not treated good/auspicious for peace, happiness and prosperity.

2.While digging, if things like coal, iron, lead, gold, gems and stones, crude oil etc. are obtained, the site is not good/auspicious. It indicates disturbed dwelling for the resident.

3.While digging, if things like cowries, tiles and tattered clothes are obtained, the site is bad/inauspicious. It also indicates disturbed dwelling. There will be no peace and happiness in the life of the occupant.

4.While digging, if the soil contains anthills, bones, skeletons, the site is bad/inauspicious. It also indicates disturbed dwelling. There will be no peace and happiness in life of the occupant.

(ii) Size and Slope of Plot

There are two sizes of the plots. One is square size and the second is rectangular size. Size extension of plot (Figure ahead) is also beneficial for growth and prosperity of the resident.

1.Square Size of Plot

If the ratio of two adjacent sides of a plot is 1:1 and every corner is 90° angle, then other two remaining sides will also be equal on 90° angle, it is called square size plot. It is the best for overall growth of the resident in life.

2.Rectangular Size of Plot

If the ratio of width and length of a plot is 1:1.5 and all corners are of 90° angle, it is called Rectangular size plot. It is also good for growth of the resident.

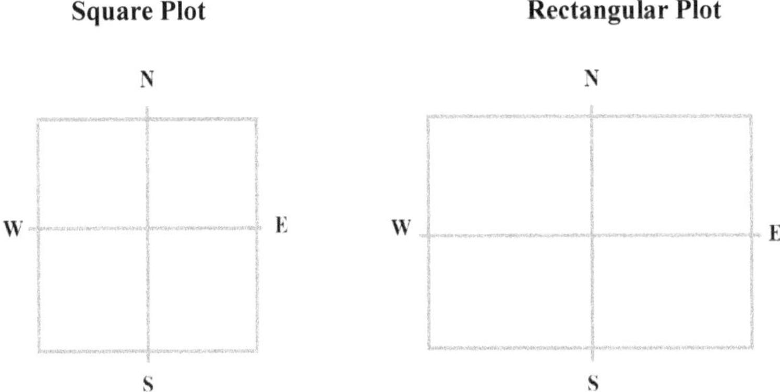

Figure-17

3.Extended Plots Quality:

i)If Plot Area is at Northeast and East North— Good for growth and Good for Growth of Wealth for Resident.

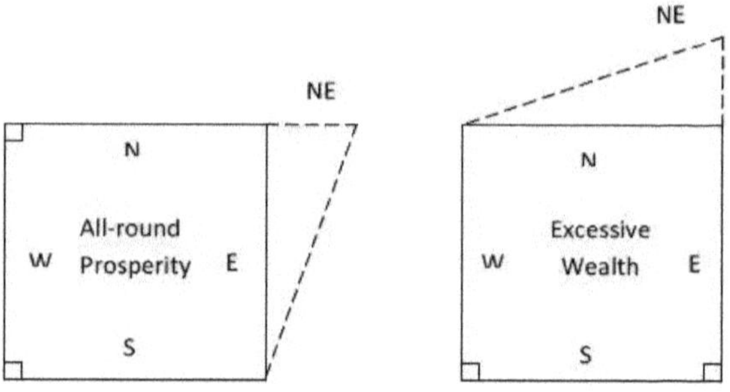

ii)If plot area extension is at Southeast and East-South --- It is Harmful for resident. Quarrel, Litigation, Illness, Financial Loss an unwanted Expenses, Poor Growth of Children.

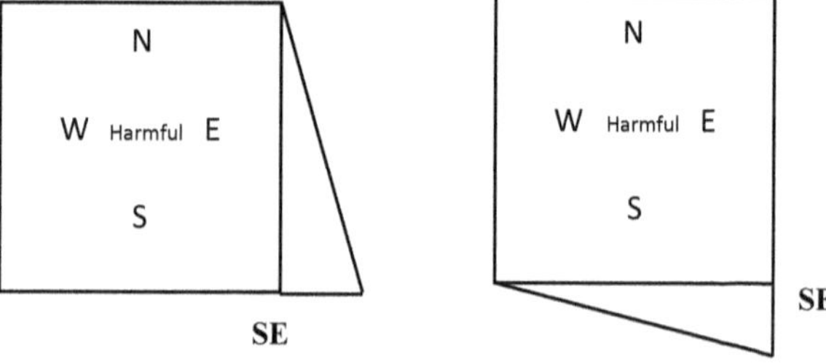

iii)If plot area extension is at West South and Southwest--- It is Harmful for resident. Accident, Financial Loss, Defamation, Displeasure and Accidental Injury, Ill Health, No Prosperity.

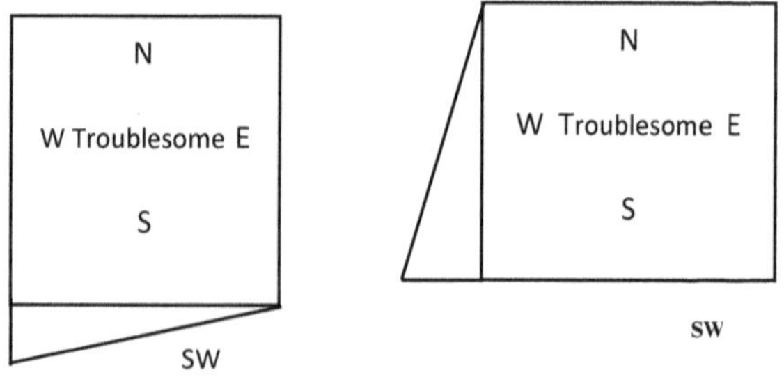

iv)If plot area extension is at Northwest and West North --- It is Harmful for resident. Poor Financial Position, Vehicle Loss, Mental Unrest, No Human Growth and Loss of Business and Wealth, Theft, Unhappiness.

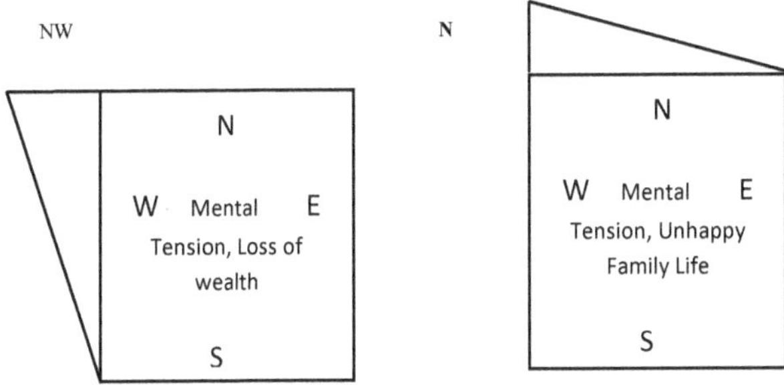

Figure-18

Slope of the Plot

When we see the size of the plot site, please note it can be divided in to two halves the North-East half and the South-West half. The North-East half of the plot is called the Solar half, and the South-West half is called the Lunar half. Vaastu suggests that the Solar half should be lower, and the Lunar half should be higher. This ensures the ideal flow of light, solar energy and polar energy. This type of plot brings happiness, good children and all the success in life to the resident of the house built on it. One should avoid a depressed at the center. The plot should either slope down towards the North or East, but never towards the South or West. From the appearance of the surface Plot can be divided into following four categories

1. Elephant's back: The Plot, which is somewhat elevated in South, West, South-West and North-West and sloping towards North-East is called **Elephant's back** (Gaja Prishtha). **Elephant's back** (Gaja Prishtha) Plot is very auspicious and provides health, prosperity and good longevity. Lakshmi, the Goddess of wealth is said to occupy such plot/house. The occupants, naturally, grow rich and enjoy long life on such a plot/house.

2. Turtle's back: The Plot, which is elevated in the middle and shallow in all four directions is called Turtle's back (Koorma Prishtha) Plot. In Hindu Mythology, tortoise (Koorma) is a very auspicious symbol. A tortoise is an animal which can survive both on land and water, has a very long life and has a tough shield provided by nature. Turtle's back (Koorma Prishtha) Plot is very beneficial and provides happiness and prosperity to the occupant. Dwelling in such a Plot/house leads to greater enthusiasm, luxuries and accumulation of wealth.

3. Demon's back: The Plot, which is elevated in North-East, East and South-West directions is known as Demon's back (Daitya prishtha). As the name suggests this kind of Plot has inauspicious results like loss of wealth and unhappiness and is harmful for sons of the house owner.

4. Serpent's back: The Plot/house, which is extended in East-West directions and elevated in North and South directions is known as Serpent's back (Naga Prishtha). Dwelling in such a Plot/house the occupant meets untimely death, loss of wife and sons. He has lot of enemies.

(iii) Shape of the Plot

Vaastu has a great significance on the geometrical shapes of Plots. Different shapes have different corners. Some are good and brings growth and prosperity for the residents. Some are bad for its residents and gives mental tensions, defame, disputes and losses. If all the four angles/corners are of 90° degree, it is very good plot. The South-West angle/corner should be 90° exact, but never more or less. Keep in mind that this is very important. The North-West angle/corner must be close to 90° degree or more, but never less than 90° degree. The North-East angle/corner must be close to 90° degree or less in degree, but never more than 90° degree. In concluding words, the distance between North-East corners to South-West corners should always be more than the distance from North-West corners to South –East corners. Following are some of the Shapes of the Plots/houses with their relative effects on its residents. Some are auspicious and some inauspicious.

<u>Auspicious shapes</u>
<u>Square/Rectangular:</u> A square or a rectangular plot is always very good. A Square or a rectangular plot provides overall growth in all spheres of life.

Square shape/size Plot   **Rectangular shape/size Plot**

Figure-19

<u>**Circular plot:**</u> Circular plots are rare. These might be in the middle of a circular road. Only a circular building should be built here. This is beneficial for growth of wealth and knowledge.

<u>**Hexagon:**</u> Six sided plots with almost equal sides is called Hexagon plot. It brings progress to the family members and prosperity.

<u>**Octagon:**</u> This shape has 8 sides and 8 angles. The People, who reside in octagon houses, get prosperity.

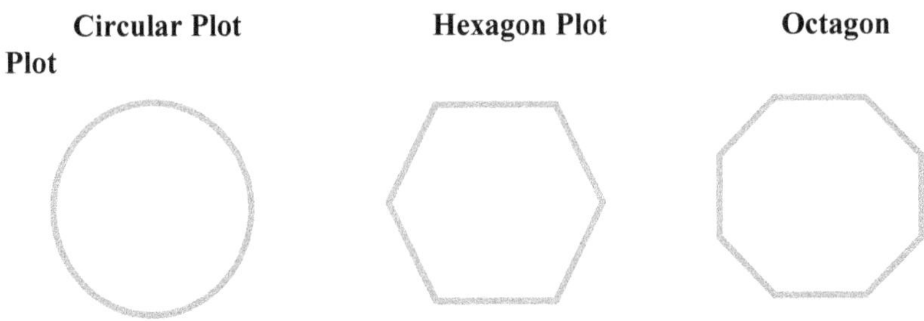

Figure-20

<u>**Shermukhi:**</u> It means a plot, which is wider in front than the back (like a face of a lion). It is good for business and industry.

<u>**Gaumukhi:**</u> It means a plot, which is wider in back than the front (like a face of a cow). It is good for residential purpose.

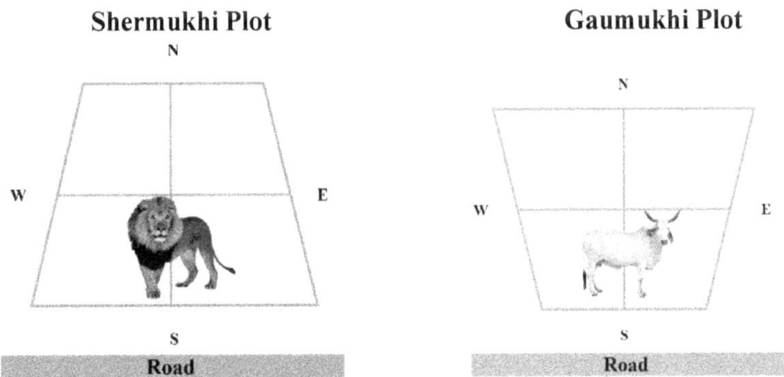

Figure-21

<u>**Inauspicious shapes**</u>
<u>**Oval/Elliptical:**</u> The oval plot is bad for commerce as well as for living. It causes loss in many ways.

Oval/Elliptical Plot

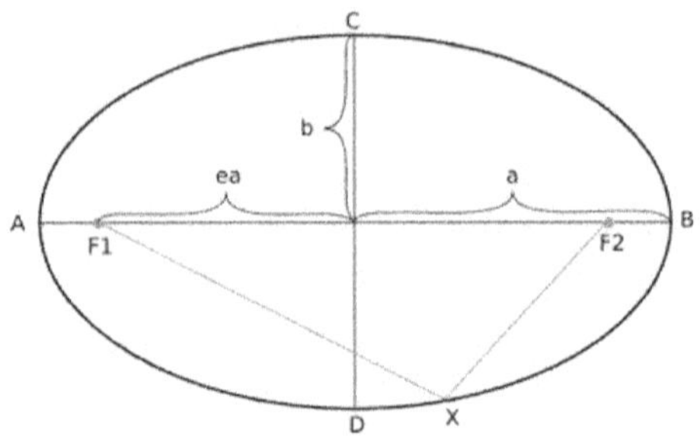

Figure-22

Parallelogram: Financial losses and quarrels, discord in the family is indicated, if the plot is so shaped.

Triangular: Three sides and three corners plot are called Triangular. This plot is considered very bad and inauspicious. This plot leads to mental tensions, defame, disputes and losses.

Parallelogram and **Triangular Plot**

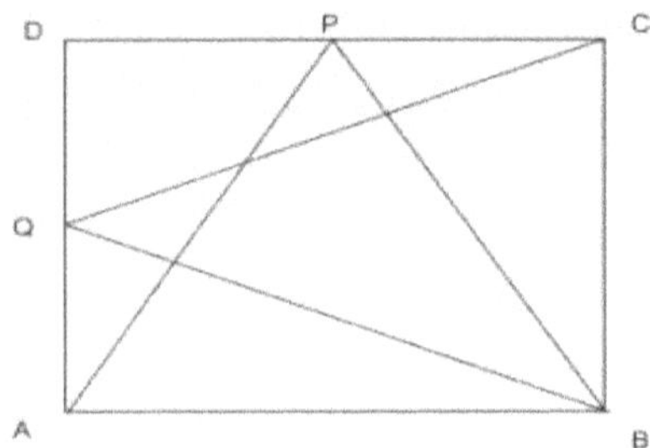

Figure-23

(iv) Road around the Plot

While selecting a plot for building a house or buying a built-up house, it is necessary to see the road around the plot/house. One should see the road around the plot/house, if the road is one side or two sides or three sides or all the four sides.

If the road around the plot/house is one side

Following are its results-

1. North or East facing road plot/house is auspicious. It brings reputation and prosperity, gives a very good business and lot of wealth.

2. If Road is in South is average for residence. It is beneficial for female articles, cosmetics, hospitals, surgery, bass items, disco, casino etc.

3. If Road is in West is not good for residence. It is good for business.

If the roads around the plot/house are two sides

Two roads may be corner sides or opposite sides. Corner sides mean North-East Sides or South-East Sides or North-West Sides or South-West Sides. Opposite sides roads mean East and West or North and South. Following are its results-

Opposite Roads

1.If the roads are East and West of the plot /house, it comes in medium category. It may be auspicious to have main gate on East side.

2.If the roads are North and South of the plot /house, it will be very auspicious. It brings a good business, wealth and prosperity. The condition is that main gate should be in North.

Corner Roads

1.If the roads are North and East directions (Ishaan Corner) of the plot /house, it gives new opportunities of the business to become prosperous.

2. If the roads are South and East directions (Agneya Corner) of the plot/house, it is inauspicious.

3. If the roads are North and West directions (Vayavya Corner) of the plot /house, it brings in wealth.

4. If the roads are South and West directions (Nairatya Corner) of the plot /house, it weakens health and loss of wealth.

If the roads around the plot/house are three sides

Roads on three sides of Plots/house mean one side or direction will be closed. It may be East or West or North or South side.

1.If South direction road is closed and roads are on West-North-East directions, the plot/house

is very good for business.

2.If West direction road is closed and roads are on North-East-South directions, the plot/house   is auspicious for commercial purposes.

3.If North direction road is closed and roads are on East-South-West directions, the plot/house is very good for commercial purposes.

4.If East direction road is closed and roads are on South-West-North directions, the plot/house   is very good for commercial purposes.

If the roads around the plot/house are four sides

The plot/house having roads on all the four sides (East-West-North-South directions), it is most auspicious. It gives, health, wealth, prosperity, peace and all happiness to the owner in life.

(v) Other Surroundings

Before buying a plot, one must study the nearby surroundings and resources. According to Vaastu guidelines the certain other surroundings (structures or natural resources) affect directly and indirectly on its resident. Surroundings and resources must be beneficial to the resident.

What to follow
1. If any natural resource of water such as Ocean, River, Lake is near the plot that should be in the East or North direction of the plot.
2. If Mountains or High-rise buildings or Multistoried Apartments exist near the plot that should be in the South or West direction of the plot.
What to avoid
1. If larger plots are on both the sides of the site for the plot that site should be ignored. It is not good and beneficial for the resident.
2. If plot site is opposite or next to a hospital that site should be ignored. It is not beneficial to the resident.
3. If a temple/church/mosque is in front of the site of the house, it should also be ignored. Its falling shadows bring undesirable problems of sickness.
4. If Plot site is nearby graveyards, cemeteries, crematoria, garbage dump, it should also be avoided. Residents in that house will always live in fear and will never have the peace of mind.
5. One should ignore to buy such a plot/house from the people suffering from prolonged sickness or who have become insolvent, distressed or unfortunate.
6. One should avoid buying such a plot/house, which is damaged due to fire/lighting/rain/storm etc. It is not good for living.
7. The plot/house at the T- junction should also be avoided. It is not good for living.

(vi) Green Belt

Green belts are a shield between towns and also between town and countryside. The green belt designation is a planning tool, and the aim of green belt policy is to prevent urban slump by keeping land permanently open for more energy. However, there is not necessarily a right of access there. There are green belts everywhere in the cities and countryside. Having a green area in the vicinity of any house or around its axis has been known to cast a positive effect on the residents of the house. Rapid construction has made life in urban forests quite painful and distressful with Mother Nature. Nowadays Green belts are coming under increasing threat to meet the need for housing. It is not good for the happiness and peace of the residents. The National Green Tribunal contains specific reference to the protection of green belt everywhere in the cities and countryside. The plants and their surrounding aura not only help in overall beatification but also churn out healthy vibes that allow us to maintain a healthy emotional quotient. Some traditionally important plants like Tulsi and Neem have immensely beneficial medicinal properties and their placement in one's house can help in creating a positive aura. Plain green lawns or green belts with grass are best suited in the eastern direction as well as the north depending on the availability of empty space in the plot design. Water bodies between the North-East and South-West axis along with the green lawn enhances the positive flow of energy. Usually, most people leave an empty area near the entrance of their plot for a green belt or a small garden. Planting of trees and plants in and around the house can promote the positive energies entering the house enhancing the health, spiritual and monetary aspects on then residents.

Chapter
12
Location of the House inside the Plot

The People, who have bigger plots, want to construct a house/building inside the plots. What type of location of the house/building should be there inside the plot to lead a better life? Location of the house/building inside the plot depends on the plan. It should be good looking and attractive. It may be in shape/size either square or rectangular. More open space towards North and East is essential. Its angles/corners must be closed to 90° degree from all sides. It may be in shape/size either square or rectangular as per the square or rectangular plot. Placement of the house/building may be in different sizes as per Vaastu guidelines.

1. The house/building can be either square in shape/size or rectangular in shape/size as per plot location with equally open space towards all directions from the compound wall. It will be auspicious and bring happiness, peace and prosperity to the resident and family.
2. If road or front is in the South or West of a square plot, one can construct rectangular shape/size house/building with a double space towards East side, shorter in North side and very short in both South and West directions. It will be auspicious, and the resident will be happy, healthy and wealthy.
3. If road or front is in the South or West of a rectangular plot, one can construct square shape/size house/building with a double space towards North side and half of the North space in East side and shorter in both South and West directions. It may also be somewhat auspicious, and the resident may feel happy.
4. In case of either square or rectangular plot with almost square shape house/building with a double space towards North side, shorter space than North in East side and very short space in South or West direction. It may also be auspicious, and the resident may feel happy.
5. The house can be either square in shape/size or rectangular in shape/size as per plot location with open space more or double towards North in comparison to remaining three directions. The open space towards remaining East, South and West directions will be equally shorter in distance, but all corners to 90° degrees. Such a house/building will be inauspicious and give mental tensions to the resident and family.

What to do

1. More open space towards North and East is better than South and West so first choice should be given priority. It brings happiness, peace and prosperity to the resident.
2. The 2nd, 3rd and 4th choices are also auspicious, and the resident may feel happy.

What not to do

1. Fifth choice is not good. It should be left out while constructing a house/building inside a plot. The resident may be mentally tensed in future.
2. In case of a square plot in shape and size or a rectangular plot in shape and size the house/building South or West space should not be more open than North or East. It will stop positivity inside and good luck to the resident.

Chapter
13
Open area planning of the Plot/House

There are nine properties come in the **Open area planning** of a big Farmhouse. These are (i) Main Gate of the Plot/House (ii) Compound Wall of the Plot/House (iii) Water Bodies-Well/Tube well/Water supply Tap/Underground water tank (iv) Swimming pool (v) Overhead Tank (vi) Septic tank (vii) Cattle shed (viii) Garage and (ix) Garden (Trees and Plants). We take them as under:

(i) Main Gate of the Plot/House

The main gate is the only entry point, which indicates life in a house. If it is built according to the Vaastu Guidelines, it gives best of health, happiness and prosperity to the resident and his family. It shows resident's approach to the life. Therefore, Main Gate should be attractive and welcoming. There should be no obstruction such as a big tree or a temple or a high raised multistoried building or a water-well up to twice height of the house distance in front of the Main Gate. The Main Gate of the house should be good looking better in a Grid form so that energy remains continued to flow in every portion of the house. Following things are also to be kept in mind regarding main Gate of the house.

Do's

1. Main Gate should be fixed in an auspicious Muhurta.
2. Main Gate position should be on the road facing wall.
3. The length and breadth of the gate should have 2:1 proportion.
4. It should be bigger than other gates inside the house.
5. There should be a threshold on the main gate and a slope towards road.
6. It should be decorated with attractive colors and symbols.
7. Place a pious symbol on the main gate.
8. Main Gate of the house in the North/East/North-East is always better for harmony, peace and prosperity.
9. Stone sculptures, if any like Jain caves/Ajanta caves or gardens like Moughal gardens/Rock gardens should be in South-West of the main gate of the house.

Don'ts

1. No garbage or old waste should be in front of Main Gate.
2. Any type of blockings such as Trees, rocks, pillars, electricity or telephone poles should not be in front of Main Gate of the house.

3. There should be no shadow of any religious monument such as a temple or a mosque or a church or a gurudwara on the Main Gate of the house.
4. Hospitals and mortuaries should not be near main gate.
5. Graveyards, cemeteries, crematories should not be near main gate.
6. A high raised multistoried building should not be in a distance less than 100 meters from the main gate.
7. A main gate should not be rough.

We have already indicated about directions (Dishas) and Corner directions (Vidisha) i.e. all eight directions of the plot/house in Chapter-10. Now we will examine the impact of Main Gate facing direction - wise.

Impact of Main Gate facing direction - wise

Sr. No.	Main Gate facing	Advantages	Disadvantages
1	East	Prosperity, Government favor, Female growth	Financial loss due to theft/fire, Cruelty, Lack of peace.
2	West	Human growth, financial growth.	Unwanted expenses, Government harassment, Accidents.
3	North	All types of gains, financial gains, Human growth, Happiness.	Loss due to fire, Imprisonment, accidents,
4	South	Prosperity, Human growth.	Meanness, Insubordination, Financial loss due to fire.
5	North-East	All types of gains, Government favor, Female growth.	Enmity with son, Loss due to fire, Lack of peace.
6	North-West	Financial growth, All types of gains, Happiness, Human growth.	Government harassment, Sickness, Accidents, Tragic death.
7	South-East	Government favor.	Lack of peace due to Insubordination, False accusation, Cruelty.
8	South-West	Good position, financial growth, Human growth, mental peace.	Financial loss due to unwanted expenses, Enmity, Trouble to son.

(ii) Compound Wall of the Plot/House

Before starting the construction of the dwelling unit, it is essential to build a compound wall on all four sides of the plot. As per Vaastu guidelines the Compound wall should be symmetrical in both the sides at the same height. If the North and East walls are lower than South and West walls, it is considered better and more beneficial. Main Gate may also be fixed with compound wall for the safety and security of material and man force working there. According to the principles of Vaastu South and West side wall should be thicker and higher than North and East side wall to have more energy inside the house.

Do's

1. Before constructing house, build a compound wall on all four sides of the plot.
2. Compound wall should be symmetrical to both the axis of the same height.
3. South and West side wall should be thicker and higher than North and East side walls.
4. North and East walls must be lower than South and West side walls.
5. Main Gate may also be fixed with compound wall.

Don'ts

1. Avoid house construction before building a compound wall on all four sides of the plot.
2. Northern and Eastern compound walls should not be thicker and higher.
3. Do not forget to fix the Main gate while constructing compound wall.

A Scene of Compound Walls

Figure-24

(iii) Water Bodies-Well/Tube well/Underground tank

There are many more public utilities. Water, electricity and roads are most essential. Water system is the first primary necessity for the resident. Water is always needed for drinking, cooking, bathing, washing clothes and lastly for the house sanitation. If there is no water supply Tap on your plot/house area, you are to manage your own system. For water you need a well or a tube well or a water supply tap or an underground water storage tank. For well or a bore well or a water supply tap or a water storage tank the owner should adopt the Vaastu Guidelines. As already stated, there are eight directions, and one is to see the proper direction for this task. While digging or boring well or constructing underground water storage tank an axis is to be drawn to all the sides of the plot/house. If these bodies are made in the North-East, they are very good for overall growth, if made in the North, they are good for health and happiness and if made in the East or West increases wealth/prosperity.

There are four corners (1) North-East corner, (2) South-East corner, (3) South-West corner and (4) North-West corner of the plot/house and thus axis can also be four, (1) North-East to South-West, (2) South-East to North-West, (3) South-West to North-East and (4) North-West to South-East.

Do's
1. The best position for digging or boring well or constructing underground water storage tank is the North-East corner on both the sides of North-East and South-West axis. It results all kinds of happiness and overall growth. This leads to further knowledge, wealth, prosperity, family members and up to some extent the reputation of the house owner.
2. For digging well or boring tube well or constructing underground water storage tank works should start in an auspicious Muhurta for happy, peaceful and bright future.

Don'ts
1. Avoid digging or boring well or constructing underground water storage tank on the South-West corner on both the sides of the South and West direction, the owner may suffer certain problems. Differences may break out in the family. Children may be affected. Family may suffer health and loss of wealth.
2. Avoid digging or boring well or constructing underground water storage tank towards the North-West corner on South-East and North-West axis on both the sides of the line. This position will increase owner's difficulties and hardships. Accidents may occur.

3. Avoid digging or boring well or constructing underground water storage tank towards the South-East corner on South-East and North-West axis on both the sides of the line, enemies and thieves may hurt the inhabitant.
4. Avoid digging or boring well or constructing underground water storage tank in center of the plot/house so called Brahamsthan. It results life unstable to the resident and lacks wealth.

Note:

For construction of Well/Tube well/Underground/water supply tap/Water Storage Tank, if one wants to use other directions or center there may be following effects. See below a table.

Table of Effects of Well/Tube well/Underground Water Storage Tank

Sr. No.	Direction	Effects
1	East	Wealth and prosperity
2	West	Acquisition of wealth and good health
3	North	Good for health, acquisition of wealth and happiness
4	South	Ill health and mental worries
5	North-East Corner	All kinds of happiness and overall growth
6	North-West Corner	Enmity, theft and loss of wealth
7	South-East Corner	Loss of wealth and downfall of name and fame
8	South-West Corner	Accidents
9	Center	Inauspicious

(iv) Swimming pool

Swimming is a good habit for sound health. It needs a swimming pool. The North-East corner (**Eshaan**) direction is the best place and very auspicious for swimming pool. Thus, Swimming pool should be constructed exactly in the North-East restricting some walking area around the swimming pool. Though construction of Swimming pool is very difficult inside houses, yet it is a very good option for building a Swimming pool inside houses. In some cases, if North-East corner may not be possible for the Swimming pool, then another suggestion is to construct the swimming pool at East side or at North side i.e. North-East to East side or North-East to North side. It brings good luck, pocket full of money, raising of their position in their fields, good name and fame, life-long cash flows, bank balances, having credit in the society etc. for the residents. The slope inside the Swimming pool should start from West side to East side.

In the states of West Bengal and Kerala, we still find swimming pool in old houses. Swimming pool can be made on ground floor or upper floors. An industrialist named Mukesh Ambani has made a swimming pool on an upper floor of the house. Swimming pool should be built towards North-East direction (Eshaan) or on both the sides of North-East corner i.e. in the North or East. North-East direction (Eshaan) Swimming pool is the best source of good health, immense happiness, peace and prosperity.

A Scene of a Swimming Pool

Swimming Pool

Figure-25

Do's
1. The ideal location for a swimming pool in the house is towards North-East corner, the Eshaan direction. This location brings luck and fortune to the residents of the house. East or North area is also good.
2. The location should be closest to the underground water tank or other water source bore-well etc.
3. Swimming pool needs to be built in such a specific location that can balance the energies and offer some privacy.

Don'ts
1. Avoid construction of Swimming pool in the South or West directions. This position gives health problems.

2. Avoid modern day concept having a swimming pool at the upper floors or at a terrace. It is against Vaastu guidelines. It stops energies and privacy.

3. Avoid Swimming pool construction towards the North-West corner. It brings accidents for the resident.

(v) Overhead Water Tank

Constructing or fixing of overhead water tank is essential. The water is always required for drinking and cooking in kitchen, cleanliness, taking bath and flow of waste in toilets. Therefore, the water that is stored in the well or the bore-well has to be pumped into the overhead tank, in order to be able to flow down into different places of the house. As per Vaastu guidelines founded by our ancient sages should be followed during the construction of overhead water tank in a house. If the overhead water tank is placed in the right area, it would definitely lead to an increase in wealth, prosperity and knowledge. Now-a-days plastic overhead water tanks of 500 to 2500 liters water capacity are used. These tanks are not good for drinking and cooking. They affect one's health. If used, only black or blue color plastic tanks should be used so that that they may absorb maximum Sunrays. West side i.e. North-West/West/South-West is good for placing overhead tanks. It can also be fixed in the middle of South side.

Do's

1. Overhead tank placement should be in the West or South-West direction because West side belongs to Lord Varuna, the lord of rains. It would be extremely beneficial.

2. North-West, South-West and South direction are also good.

3. Overhead tank placed in the South-West direction, should be at least two feet over the uppermost slab to make sure that there is no dampness.

4. Overhead tanks placed in the house should be small size. Those may be more than two.

5. It is advisable to place different tanks for different purpose. One water tank can be used for drinking and cooking and other one for toilets and bathrooms.

Don'ts

1. Avoid placing Overhead tank in the South-East corner. It results in loss of wealth and accidents.

2. Avoid placing the overhead tank in the center so called Bramhasthan. If there is load on the Brahma, life of the individuals living in the house would be uneasy. One would also not like staying in the house for a long time as overhead tank just above Bramhasthan is not conducive or helpful to the life of inhabitants.

3. Avoid overhead tanks made out of plastic. If you were to get one, make sure it is blue or black in color, as darker shades absorb Sunrays.

Overhead Tank   **Septic Tank**

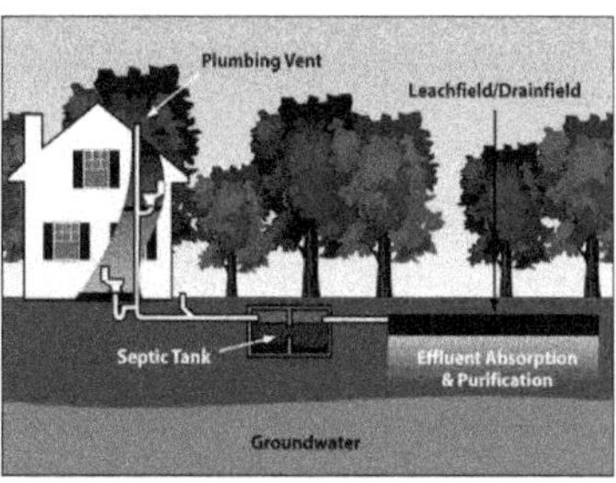

Figure-26   **Figure-27**

(vi) Septic tank

The evolutionary transition of our society from 'traditional' to 'modern' has led to some drastic changes in house structures and designing. One of such changes is the invention of septic tanks. Septic tanks are economical, environmentally friendly and effective private sewage treatment plants. However, like every other component of a house structure, they too must build Septic tank as per Vaastu guidelines.

The location of septic tank is very important in the house. It carries house owner and his family members physical waste to the sewer line or in a deep pit made in the right place. Septic tank or pit should be made in the North-West corner. Middle of the West and East may also be used for Septic tank or pit, but in no case septic tank should be in the South-West and North-East because of environmental reasons.

Do's

1. Septic tank must be at least two feet away from the compound wall.
2. Septic tank must be in the North side of West wall, if there is a scarcity of space.
3. Septic tank length must be in the East-West side and the breadth in the South-North side.
4. Septic tank outlets must be in the West or North.
5. Septic tank must fall in the third part from North-West, if disvide North side in nine parts,
6. Septic tank has three parts. The water must be in the East and the outlet in the West.

7.   Septic tank gutter can be in any other direction except South.

Don'ts
1.   Avoid Septic tank facing North-East/South-East/West corner.
2.   Avoid Septic tank placement touching the compound wall.
3.   Avoid placing outlets in the South.
4.   Avoid construction of the tank higher than the level of the house.
5.   Avoid pipes from upper floor down to the South-West corner.

Direction-wise bad effects

It is noticed-

1. If **a Septic Tank** is fixed in North direction, it brings **monetary loss**.

2. If **a Septic Tank** is fixed in North-East direction **business loss**.

3. If **a Septic Tank** is fixed in East direction **loss of fame**.

4. If **a Septic Tank** is fixed in South-East direction **wealth loss**.

5. If **a Septic Tank** is fixed in South direction **loss of wife**.

6. If **a Septic Tank** is fixed in South-West direction **loss of life**.

7. And if **a Septic Tank** is fixed in West direction **loss of mental peace**.

(vii) Cattle Shed

Ancient texts on Vaastu, such as "Vrahamihir Samhita" give very specific guidelines as to the direction in which one should provide space to the animals like dogs, cats, cows, buffaloes, horses, elephants, parrots, pigeons etc. Mind it that animals are quite scared of fire. So Cattle shed is to be built on the North-West/West/South-West sides of the plot. The lots of dry grass may also be stored towards South/West/North-West corners. We have to take all the precautions to maintain cleanliness on the portion of site in which cattle shed is built. Waste material may be placed on the South-East/South/West/South-West corner without digging a pit. It may also be placed in the North and East sides digging a pit to make it "Compost Khaad". Number of times, it is found that the animals fall sick, and the reason remains a puzzle. During those times, it can be very vital for you if you just check the direction, where they usually rest. If their sitting direction is not good as per Vaastu guidelines, they might feel lazy, dull and less energetic. So, we should be more careful about the direction. It is most important to keep the area neat and clean, where the animals stay. No negativity because this will have bad effects for the health of animals.

A Scene of Cattle Shed

Figure-28

Cattle sheds/Cow sheds should be made in the North-West side of the house. The reason is that it is closed and safe for animals. The center place in North/West/East direction can also be used for animals. Our religious books say that cows are the best animal for milk and reducing Methane gas, which negate pollution of carbon-di-oxide released by human beings.

Do's

1. Cattle-shed is to be built on the North-West/West/South-West side along with compound wall.
2. Cows are the best animal for milk and reducing Methane gas. They negate pollution of carbon-di-oxide released by human beings.
3. Fodder or dry grass may also be stored towards South/West/North-West corners.
4. Waste material may be placed on the South-East/South/West/South-West corner in an open area without digging a pit.
5. It may also be placed in the North and East sides digging a pit to convert it into "Compost Khaad".
6. It is most important to keep the area neat and clean, where the animals stay. A water pipeline may be fixed.
7. Check their health every week and take doctor's advice.

Don'ts

1. Avoid South-East side (Aagneya direction) for animal-shed. They are quite scared of fire.
2. Avoid place of negativity for animals because this affects adversely on their health.
3. Avoid change of placement direction, if they are healthy.
4. Avoid unhealthy fodder or dry grass.

(viii) Garage

Garage is used for tractors, cars, motorcycles, scooters. It should be built either in North-West or South-East on a little distance from the compound wall. Mind it that vehicles face should be either in the North or in the East. Now Due to lack of space some people also park their vehicles out of the main gate. This is not good for vehicle's safety.

These days a concept of parking below ground floor is developing day by day. Car, Motorcycle and Scooter are a necessity. Do you know that a garage is just as important as your house? Therefore, it should be designed as per Vaastu guidelines so that positivity is continued in abundance, and it might prove lucky trouble-free long life for the resident and the vehicles.

Do's

1. The garage must always be built in the South-East or North-West direction in the house.
2. When designing a garage three feet of walking space is left inside after the car is parked.
3. Ensure free movement of air and light inside garage.
4. The garage gate should face East/North and must open freely without any obstruction.
5. The garage floor should slope towards the East/North direction.

Don'ts

1. Avoid touching of vehicle to the compound wall or house building.
2. Garage height should not be more than the height of the main gate of the house.
3. Trash or inflammable material must never be stored inside a garage.

A Scene of Car Garage

Figure-29

(ix) Garden (Trees, Plants and Grass)

In so far as Contribution to the balance and harmony of the house is concerned, Garden is most effective. Trees, plants and Grassy land give proper and positive energy to the house resident and his family. These are better for good health and happiness. Similar height of trees or plants and the grassy area attract everyone. So specific trees, interesting plants and country evergreen grass should be planted. If possible, garden should be nearby water bodies and fountains are fixed in the center of the garden, it will increase the beauty of the garden. Atmosphere will be healthy, and the resident will get happiness and peace.

Trees and Plants facing houses or inside the plots
1. **East direction** - Bargad, Bamboo
2. **South-East direction** - Panax, Mango, Pomegranates
3. **South direction** - Maulsiri, Rose, Goolar
4. **South-West direction** - Black berry (Jamun)
5. **West direction** - Khair, Peepal
6. **North-West direction** - Bel
7. **North direction** - Kaith, Shami, Pakad
8. **North-East direction** – Anwla

Do's
Other trees and plants, which can also be placed in the plots/houses mainly are Basil (Tulsi), Punnag, Neem, Ashoka, Jatinag, Jayanti, Aprajita, Coconut, Jackfruit, Mangolia (Champa), Jasmine (Chameli), Draksha, Ketki, Creepers and Grapes.

Don'ts
Peepal, Red color flowers, Scmal, Kadam, Milky plants, Vatvriksha, Thorney plants should not be placed in a happy house.

A Scene of Trees and Plants

Figure-30

Note:
Increasing population and decreasing land made plots/houses smaller in area so all above items can't be adjusted such as puja room, cattle shed, car garage. Big trees may also not be planted. This planning can only be successful in big farmhouses having acers of land.

Chapter
14
Inner Area Planning of a Plot/House

When we think for Inner Area Planning of a Plot/House facing main road direction of the plot/ house, eleven portions of the house have to be studied separately. First comes Basement, then Pooja room, Kitchen, Drawing room, Dining room, Guest room, Study room, Master bedroom with other bedrooms, Storeroom, Toilet and Staircase. Now we examine them one by one. See a chart below:

A Scene of Internal Planning of House

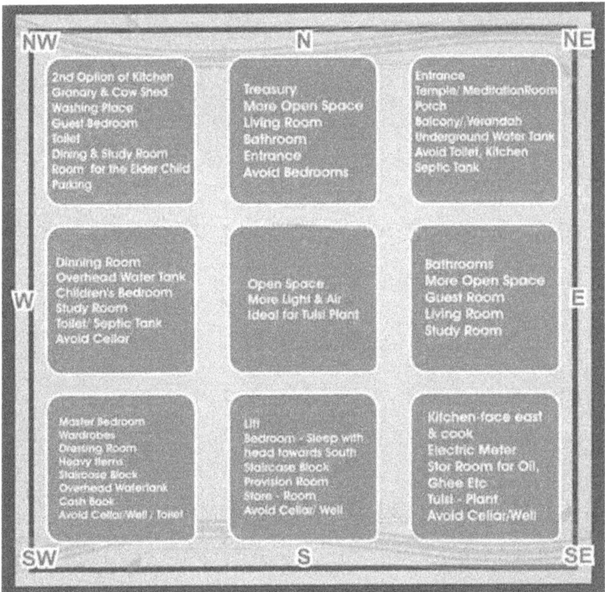

Figure-31

(i) What is a Basement?

Basement is an underground room. It may be smaller or bigger in area as per space and house owner's necessity. According to Vaastu guidelines basement should be avoided in residential house, because empty space under the house is not considered auspicious. It brings negativity in the house and affects the house owner's peace and prosperity. However, if basement is constructed in a house, some of the basic guidelines should be followed.

Basement-Why?

The construction of basement has now become a trend. Maximum Plot owners are constructing basement to use it as Godown or an Office or a Place of recreational activities. It is also necessary in the present time for those plot owners, who have limited space available for residence. Basement can only be built in North-East (Eshaan) direction up to middle of North and East side of the house according to Vaastu guidelines. Basement can be built in the direction. See the picture ahead for placement of basement.

Place Position of Basement

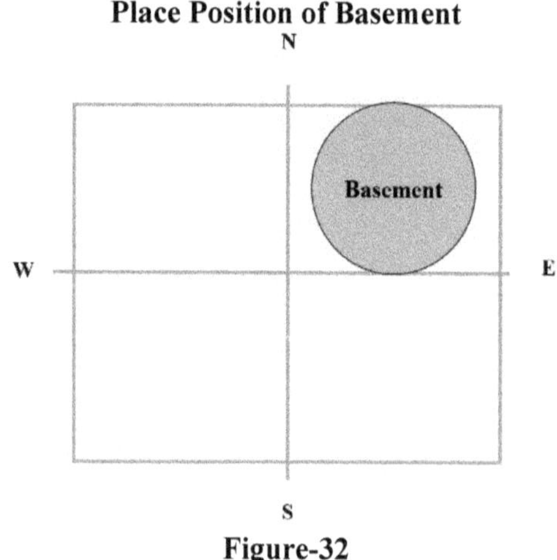

Figure-32

Do's

1. The basement is beneficial only, when it is built in North- East direction (Eshaan Vidisha) of the house according to Vaastu guidelines.
2. It should be built only in ¼th portion of the plot and in North and East direction (Eshaan Vidisha). See the positional figure-32 above.
3. The shape of basement may be square or rectangular, but the basement slope should be in the North-East direction.
4. Proper height of a basement should be at least 9 feet, but it should be at least 2 feet more than ground floor.
5. Paint your basement with light and faint colors.

6.   The purpose of basement should be either for storage or an office or for recreational purposes/activities.
7.   The basement shape should be made at 90° from East to all directions or corners.

Don'ts
1.   The basement should not be built under entire house and if built, it can cause bad health.
2.   The basement should not be made other than square/rectangular as per size and shape, otherwise it can cause loss of wealth.
3.   The level of the height of basement should not be more than 9 feet.
4.   Avoid blue, black dark colors/paintings in the basement.
5.   Avoid heavy stuff to be kept in North or East side of the basement.

(ii) What is a Pooja Room?

Pooja room is one the most auspicious and sacred rooms in the house, where we worship God for peace and prosperity. Pooja room can be used for meditation also. We need to construct this room according to Vaastu guidelines.

Pooja Room -Why?

For worshipping one should keep religious texts, idols and images of deity's and other Godly belongings. Worshipping God increases our positive energy. Meditation controls our worries and gives us happiness. We get peace of mind.

Pooja Room -Where?

North-East direction so called **Eshaan** is the Godly direction. This is the direction of Purity and divinity. It is the most auspicious for Pooja room. Second and third Positions in figure-33 given below are also good for Pooja room. North-West corner (Vayavya) is also good for Pooja room. Once you have made a pooja or prayer in the room then the room automatically starts to attract positivity and harmony. However, if the pooja room is left unprotected then this attracted positivity and harmony starts to weaken due to influence of negative energies.

Location for Pooja Room

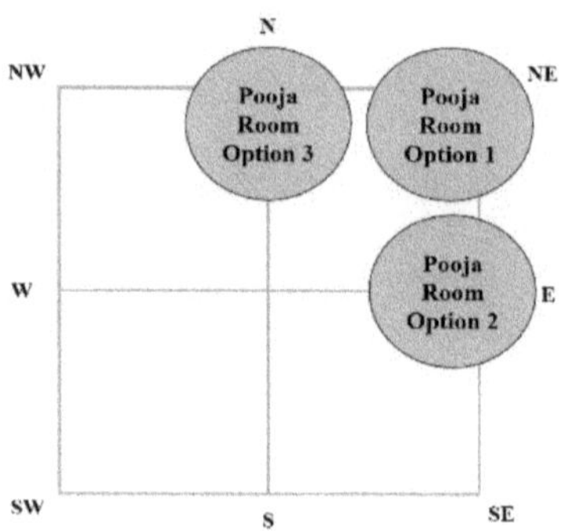

Figure-33

Do's

1. The best place of Pooja room is North-East direction (Eshaan) or both sides of Eshaan in North or in East. North-West corner (Vayavya) is also good for Pooja room.
2. Keep the Pooja place preferably on ground floor with a threshold on the entrance.
3. In 500 Square yards or bigger plots or in factories or in other institutions auspicious place for Pooja room is the center. Pyramid shape Pooja room is said to be very auspicious.
4. Place the Godly idols perfect in condition in the East and West of the Pooja room a few inches away from wall.
5. Have two shutter doors of high-quality wood for Pooja room in North or East walls.
6. White or light yellow colored marble work in Pooja room makes it luckier.
7. Place a lamp stand in the Pooja room in South-East or East side.
8. Place an Agnikund or Hawankund in the Pooja room in South-East (Aagneya) direction.
9. Keep showcases and almirahs towards West or South walls.

Don'ts

1. The Pooja room should never be in South, South-West or West direction.
2. Do not use basement or store as Pooja place.
3. Mind it while sleeping or lying on bed feet should not be toward North-East corner.
4. Pooja place should not be below or next to any toilet or kitchen or under a staircase.
5. Idols should never be fixed directly.

6. Idols should never face South direction and not in front of the main door of prayer room.

7. Women should not enter the prayer room during menses.

8. Do not fix photos of crime, battles or of negative emotions, photos of dead people.

9. Never keep a dustbin in the Pooja room, because it reduces positive energy of the room.

(iii) What is a Kitchen?

Kitchen is the place where healthy and nutritious food is cooked. Kitchen is the place of transformation. It is the kitchen where all the raw and uncooked food is transformed into delicious meals. The same food then provides energy to the house owner and his family members. The energy that we receive by consuming the food, if it is positive one it makes us feel good, happy and satisfied and if it is negative we start to have bodily sufferings. It will make us physically and mentally sick and we start to lose our position, respect and dignity in society. It is therefore very important for us to make our kitchen as per Vaastu guidelines so that the kitchen might generate and enhance positive energy, suppressing and even eliminating negative energy. We will prosper, become more and more joyous, successful and will continue to have peace of mind.

Kitchen-Why

Kitchen is an important place for a house lady. From morning to late night, she is to enter the kitchen for preparing tea, breakfast, lunch, brunch, dinner etc. Kitchen represents the Fire element so the best place for kitchen is South-East (Aagneya) direction. In the middle part of East and North-West (Vayavya) directions are also good for Kitchen. Remaining directions should be discarded. See the best and good directions for kitchen below:

Location of Kitchen in the House

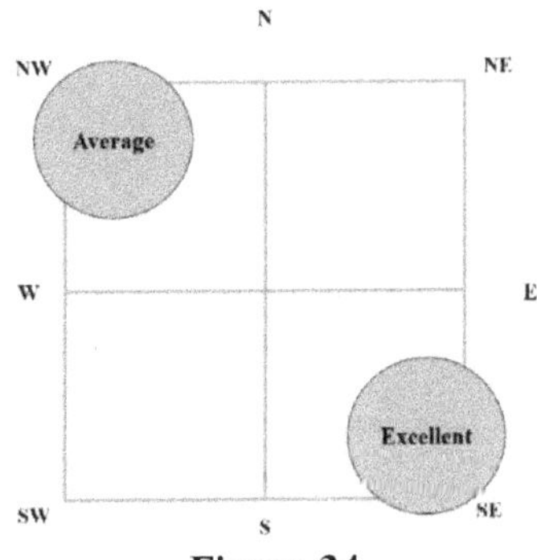

Figure-34

Do's

1. Place main platform of the kitchen in East or South-East direction for putting cooking gas so that the cooking lady may face East direction. East brings prosperity in the house.
2. Next to the kitchen's main platform there should be a "L" shaped platform, near South wall for keeping and operating microwave ovens, mixer/grinder etc.
3. Wash-basin or Sink must be fixed in the North-East direction. Keep drinking water and utensils for drinking water in the North-East or North direction.
4. Keep grain boxes, pulses, various spices, salt etc. in South or West direction.
5. Have two windows in East and place an exhaust fan in any of the windows.
6. Place a refrigerator in South-East/South/West/North of Kitchen a foot away from wall.
7. Before sleeping at night clean all the utensils, kitchen platform and kitchen daily.
8. Place a dining table in North-West or West side of kitchen.
9. While preparing food in kitchen, give sacred offering to the fire first. It ensures family members peace and prosperity.

Don'ts

1. Kitchen should not be under or above Pooja room, Bedrooms and Toilets
2. The main door of kitchen should not be in the corners of East/North/West wall.
3. A kitchen in North-East causes mental tension among family members.
4. A Kitchen in South-West leads to differences among family members.
5. A kitchen in North-West direction or lord Kubera's North direction increases expenditure.
6. While cooking, the cooking lady should never face West as this leads to health problems.
7. While cooking, the cooking lady should never face South as this brings monetary loss.
8. Do not use black color for kitchen walls and flooring.
9. Do not keep refrigerator in North-East direction.

(iv) What is a Dining room?

Dining room is a place, where cooked food is served to eat. The House owner and his family members enjoy it here comfortably. Sometimes friends and visitors also enjoy food here. This collective eating creates an environment of positive energy, and they all feel easy, relaxed and stress free. Therefore, this should be near Kitchen and Drawing room.

Dining room-Where?

According to Vaastu guidelines and regulations the best location for Dining room is either in the East/South/West direction or North-West corner (Vayavya) direction. Dining room should always be spacious, hospitable and comfy. Window should be placed in North or East side as per location of entrance i.e. North or East. The color of dining room should be light green or pink or yellow or cream. Scenery and paintings give positive effect in dining room. This position brings happiness and peace among family and friends. See the positional figure of dining room ahead.

Best locations for Dining

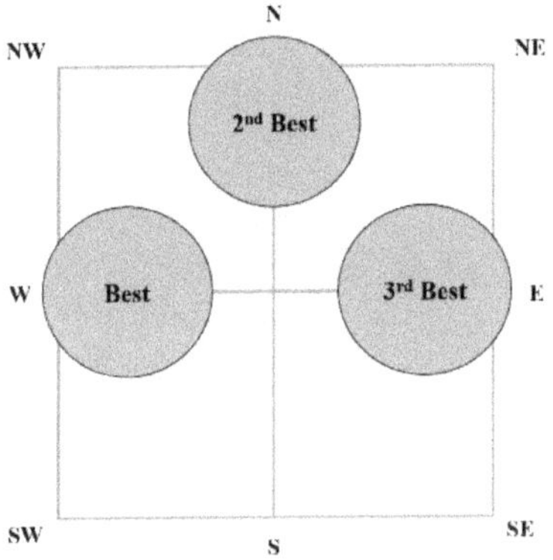

Figure-35

Do's

1. Dining table should be placed with even number of chairs six/eight.
2. Dining table shape and size should be Square or rectangular.
3. Chandelier in ceiling should be fixed just above the center of the table.
4. While eating food, the house owner's face must be in the East.
5. Water arrangement should be in North-East direction.
6. Wash-basin should be provided in North or East direction.
7. Hang a mirror in East or North wall of D.

Don'ts

1. Dining table should not be placed in front of the gate.
2. Dining table should not be placed below and above the toilet.
3. Dining table should not be kept below the beam.
4. Dining table should not be in round shape, egg shape, and oval shape.

5. Faces should not be in South direction as it creates quarrels among family members.
6. Family members must speak politely to each other while eating.
7. Family members should not make fun about inadequacy of anyone.

(v) What is a Drawing room?

A Drawing room/Drawing room/Family room is a place, where the family members, friends, visitors meet and talk on social and business matters and sometimes enjoy pictures on TV and replenish their energies. Drawing room should be spacious, well ventilated, decorated and electrified. White or sky blue color is good for drawing room. Pleasant sceneries and paintings may be displayed on North and East wall. Heavy furniture, sofa, table thus arranged in the South or West or South-West corner direction, that people move freely and feel easy, comfortable and relaxed.

Drawing room – Where?

A Drawing room can be constructed in the North-East corner direction (Eshaan) or North-West corner direction (Vayavya). East or North side is also good for a Drawing room. For South facing plot/house Drawing room can be constructed in South-East corner direction (Aagneya). Mind it that Sofa or chairs should not be underneath of the beam. While sitting, face of the House owner should be in front of the Main gate. It is almost built in the straight line of Main gate. It enhances the energy of the house owner and his family. They get mental peace.

Position of Drawing room

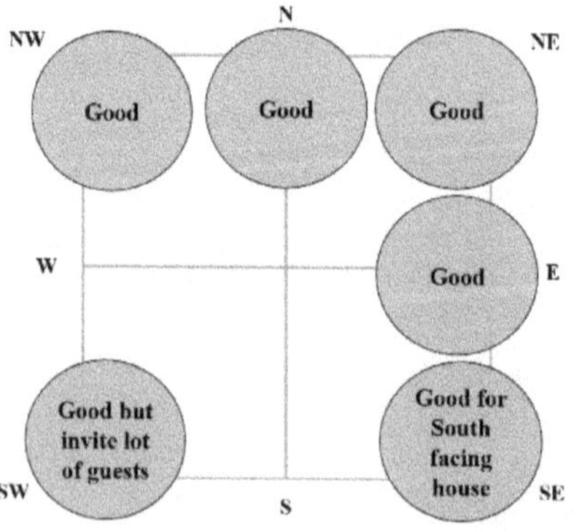

Figure-36

Do's

1. Construct a Drawing room in North/East direction. North direction is more beneficial to get more energy. North-West (Vayavya) side is also good to enhance energy.
2. North-East side of the house is Godly direction. This is an ideal location for a Drawing room. North brings lot of wealth and health for entire family.
3. Drawing room's entrance should be in North-East/South-East/South and slope towards East or North. It indicates all success.
4. Fixing of the door of the Drawing room in East/North direction is very auspicious and brings wealth, health and overall progress.
5. Drawing room's West/North-West entrance is good for scholars and researchers.
6. Keep Square size or rectangular size furniture, articles and heavy things in West/South side of the Drawing room.
7. The House owner in living area should sit facing East or North so that he remains in command and guests are not able to dominate him.
8. Place TV in South-East corner, telephone in East, South-East or North, air conditioner in West/North-West/East and hang of Gods portraits/paintings in the North-East wall.
9. Put light curtains on North-East windows and doors and heavy curtains in South-West.
10. Use white, light yellow, blue or green colors for Drawing room walls.
11. Hang a chandelier and soothing lights in South or West of living area.

Don'ts

1. Drawing room should not be in South-East (Aagneya) corner. It brings negative energy.
2. Do not use drawing-room for late night parties and get-together.
3. South-West located Drawing room is not favorable for house owner.
4. Do not keep TV and telephone and fish aquarium box in South-West.
5. Avoid hanging any portrait depicting negative energy e.g. war, crime, weeping etc.
6. Never keep artificial flowers/dried flowers/cactus/cacti/bonsai plants in the Drawing room. They give negative influence on finance and career. They bring misfortune,

(vi) What is a Guest room?

A guest room is the place where guest stay and just like other rooms in the house. Our guest room should be neat and clean and that too nearby the main gate. It will help the guest completely enjoy their stay and at the same time, spread happiness and warmth in the entire house. This needs to follow Vaastu guidelines.

Guest room-Why?

Indian culture has always been based on practices for respecting of guests. A Shloka in Sanskrit "Atithi Devo Bhavah" hints at it. We regard our guest as God. We welcome guests with great warmth and treat them as a part of family. Thus, there should be a Guest room. North-West or North or North-East or East are the best directions for Guest room. Remaining directions should be left out. See the position of Guest room in the diagram below.

A location of a Guest room

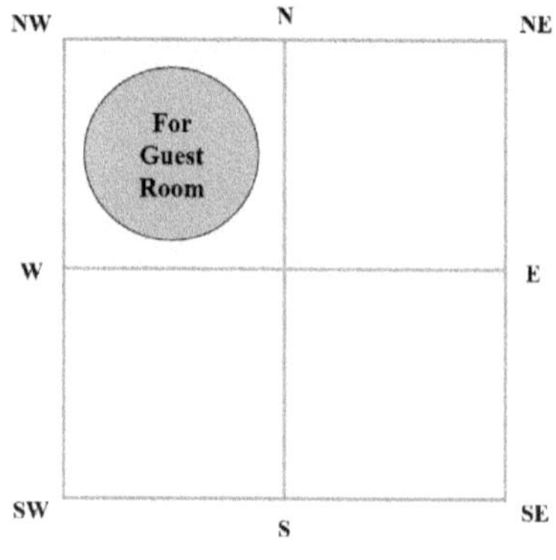

Figure-37

Do'

1. The guest room is best in North-West (Vayavya) direction. It is most unstable corner of the house.
2. The bed should be placed in the South or West part of the room. While sleeping Guest head must be towards South direction.
3. All the electronic items should be on the South-East wall of the room.
4. The cabinets should be designed on the South or West wall.
5. The electrical equipment should be placed in the South-East corner of the room.
6. The door of the bathroom should be exactly towards bedside.

Don'ts

1. The guest room should not be constructed in the South-West direction of the house.
2. The door of the bathroom should not be exactly opposite to the bed.
3. There should not be any beam running over the bed.
4. Avoid guest room items placement to North/East side wall.

(vii) What is a Study room?

Study room is a place for the welfare of children as they are the best source of energy in the house. The children sit here peacefully to concentrate on studies. It should be clean, clutter free and noise free. According to Vaastu guidelines, the study room should be located in the auspicious directions for studies such as East/North/North-East of the house. These directions improve the power of concentration while studying. South-West and West directions are also good for studies.

Study table and Books-Where?

The study table is also important for concentration. Place a square or rectangular study table far from the wall facing East/North so that the children should face East/North while studying. There should be open space in front of children. It augments fresh ideas. There should be a solid wall behind the children to support. Shelves and cabinets should be placed in the East, North, and North-East directions. The walls should be painted in light colors. It should have proper light. Windows should be in the East. How much they have gained and what more they can attain in competing with their classmates or friends will depend on how far positioning of the study room is in consonance with Vaastu principles. Have a look at the best study room in the diagram below. If the West portion of the house is unavailable, then We can make the study room in North-East corner or East side of the house.

Study Room Position in the house

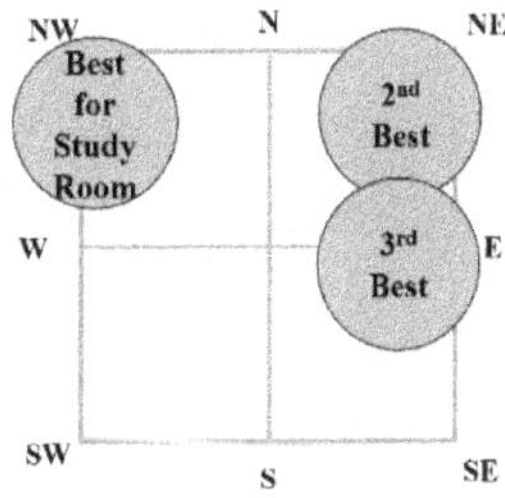

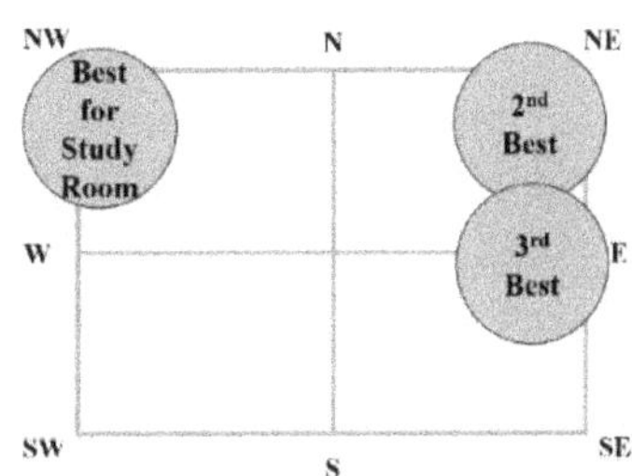

Figure-38

Do's

1. The study room should be built either in the West/North-East/East side of the house.
2. Doors of study room should be in North-East/North/East/West.
3. The windows should be larger on the East side and smaller on the West side of the Study room.
4. Place computer in South-East and fix a pendulum watch on the North wall of the room.
5. A pyramid can be kept near study table to balance the energy and increase the memory.
6. If the learner uses Table lamp, then it should be kept in the South-East corner of the desk.
7. Use light and soothing color scheme for better learning power.
8. Keep the study place clutter and noise free.
9. A photo of Vidhyadevi Saraswati and Budhideva Ganesh can be fixed in the North or East side wall to enhance registration, retention and recovery of knowledge.

Don'ts

1. Avoid doors in South-East, North-West and South-West corners of Study Room.
2. Avoid bed in study room as it may make children lazy.
3. Avoid TV in study room, because it interrupts concentration of students.
4. Avoid toilets in study place as far as possible.
5. Avoid sitting of the children for study under a beam.
6. Avoid study table from sticking to the wall.

(viii) What is a Bedroom?

A bedroom is the place for privacy and total relaxation. According to ancient science of directions, a bedroom is the place, where we relax after strenuous day's work to have a sound sleep to regain energy for the next day. There are two types of bedrooms-(1) Master bedroom (2) Other bedrooms-Son's bedroom, Daughter's bedroom, Parent's bedroom and Children bedroom. As per Vaastu guidelines and regulations bedrooms are acceptable in a square or rectangular shape. All the bedrooms should be safe, secure and comfortable. Tension free and peaceful environment in the bedrooms is must.

(a)Master bedroom and other bedrooms

The master bedroom relates with the house owner or resident. The master bedroom should always be bigger than other rooms of the house. The master bedroom should be in the South-West (Nairutya) direction or in the South direction. While sleeping head of the house resident should be towards South and feet towards North. Keep heavy Cupboards and Almirahs in South and West sides. Cupboards with valuable item should open towards North. Dressing table should be kept in the North or East. Attached toilet/bathroom can be in the North-West (Vayavya direction) or South-East (Aagneya) direction. Walls of the room may be painted in any one white/blue/pink light and soothing color.

(b) Bedroom for married/unmarried Son

This bedroom may be comfortable in center of South direction attached with Master bedroom. Teen or adolescent son should have his bedroom in North-West direction. This will be comfortable for him. His bedroom should not be constructed in central portion of the house or in basement as it may lead to mental tension.

(c) Bedroom for married/unmarried Daughter

Teen or adolescent daughter should have her bedroom in North-West (Vayavya) direction. This will be comfortable for the daughter of a marriageable age or for newly married couple.

(d)Parent's bedroom

Parent's bedroom may be in the North-East. It will give them energy and better health. They will always feel happy and peaceful.

(e)Children's bedroom

A West side bedroom is good for children. East side bedroom can also be made for children. A newly wedded couple should not use this room, because it can cause unnecessary quarrel between the couple. Room in the North-West direction is good them.

Do's

1. The master bedroom should be in the South-West direction to be used only by house owner/resident or married couples.
2. If the house is multi-story, then master bedroom in the South-West corner of the top floor is best. Master bedroom windows are beneficial only in the East and North walls.
3. Unmarried children or guests can use a bedroom in the East.
4. An attached bathroom can be made in North-West or South-East of bedroom.
5. The box beds should be of good quality wood. The bed should be placed in such a way that the user's legs/feet should be in North and East. It will increase prosperity and opulence.
6. While sleeping, if legs/feet stretch towards the East, it gives name, reputation and richness and if legs/feet towards the West it gives mental harmony and augments fondness for spiritualism.
7. Light colors rose, pink, blue, yellow and green are better than dark colors.
8. Cabinet /Almirah should be placed in South-West of the room opening towards North.
9. Electrical appliances should be kept in South-East of the room.

Don'ts

1. Avoid bedrooms in the center or above porch and kitchen or under the beam of the house.
2. Avoid bedroom in the North-East Kuber's direction. It brings many mishaps and illness in the family and for a married couple long-term several diseases.
3. Avoid sleeping legs towards South. It indicates bad dreams, bad thoughts in the mind and heaviness in the chest. It is the direction of Yama (the Lord of Death). It will lessen the life span.
4. Avoid having bedroom in the South-East. It leads to unnecessary quarrels between husband and wife. They face lot of difficulties and unnecessary expenditure increases.
5. Avoid TV, PC or laptops keeping/using in a bedroom and placing a dressing table not good for health.
6. Avoid placing pictures of war, cruelty, sadness, single bird, any animal and wild animals.
7. Avoid black and red color in bedroom as it affects our mind and changes the mood.

Position of Bedrooms

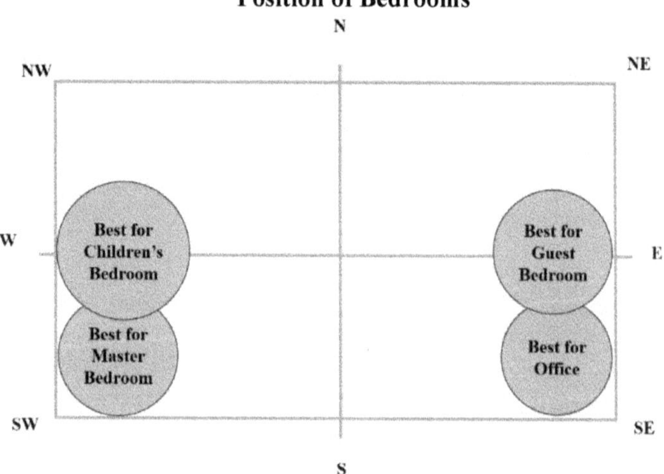

Figure-39

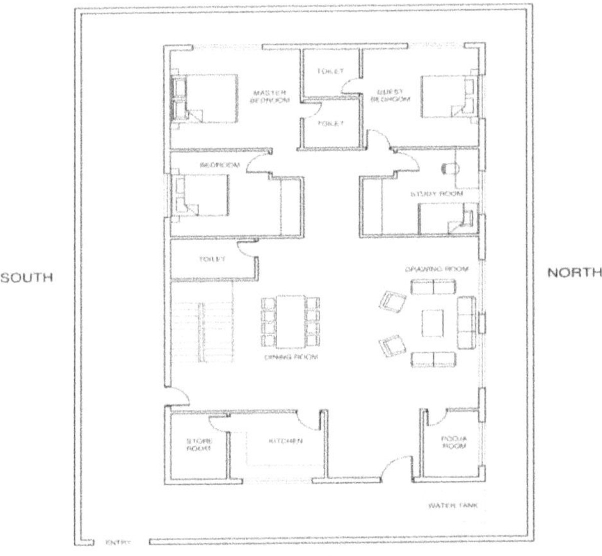

Figure-40

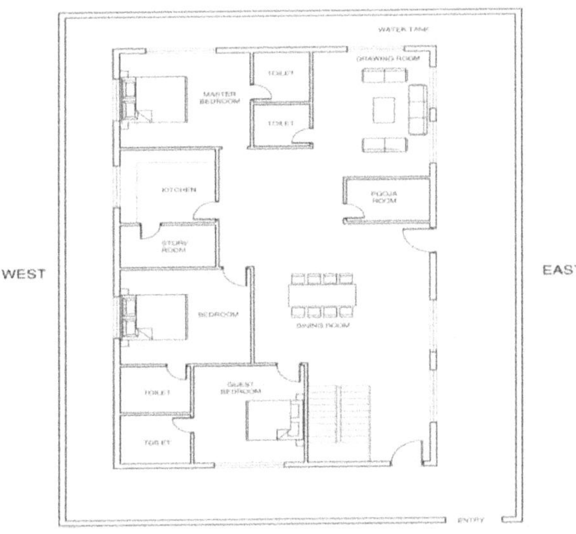

Figure-41

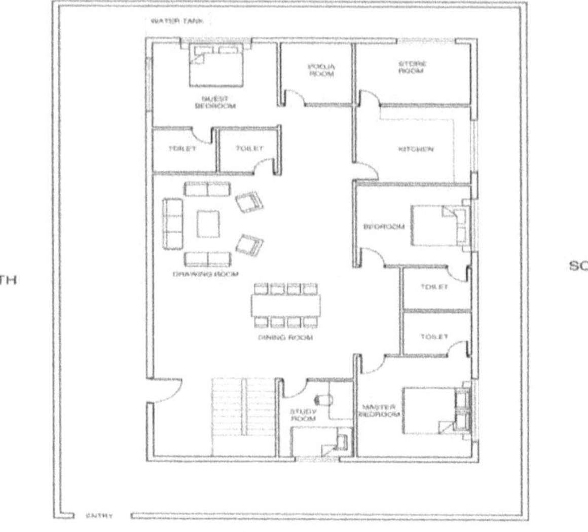

Figure-42

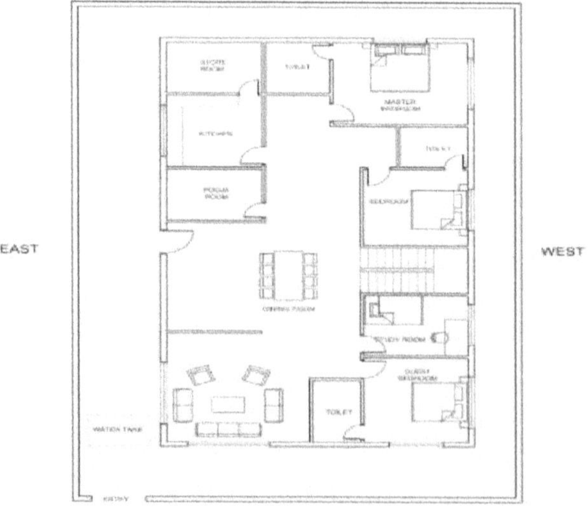

Figure-43

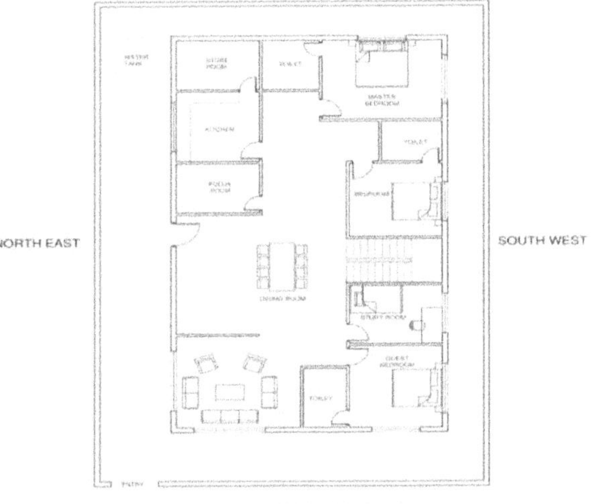

Figure-44

Figure-45

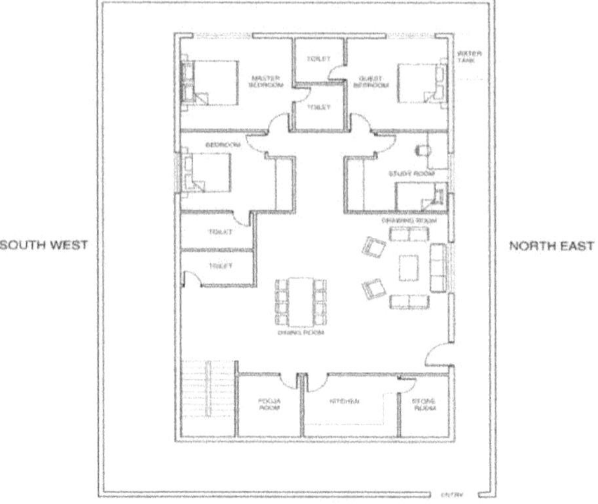

Figure-46

Figure-47

(ix) What is a Storeroom?

The storeroom is the place to keep unused goods such as grains, provisions and other items such as machines, machinery parts, tools etc., which can be used in future. Storeroom should be built in the North-West and South-West corner directions or in the center of South or West direction. According to Vaastu some essential principles indicating what to follow and what to avoid are as below.

Position of Storeroom

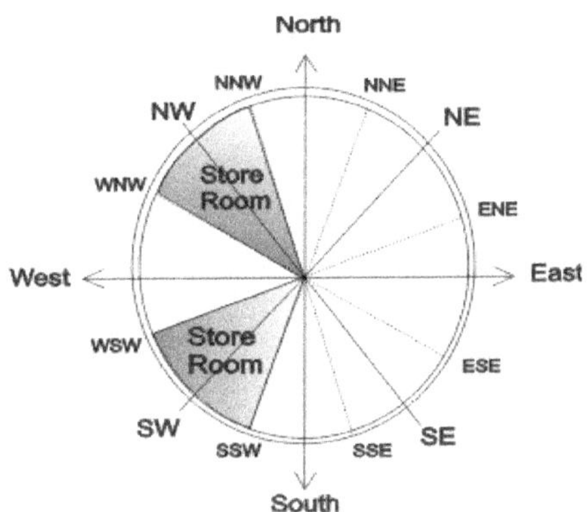

Figure-48

Do's

1. The storerooms should be placed in North-west part of building as it is beneficial for providing good provision of storage with minimum chances of shortage.
2. Store annual stock of granary in South-West corner while daily use grains must be stored in North-West direction.
3. Door in this room can be constructed in any direction except South-west direction with two shutters and a picture of Lord Vishnu must be placed on the Eastern wall.
4. Keep in mind that the height of granary room should be more than other rooms. The   windows in this room should be made on Eastern or Western sides.
5. The color chosen in storeroom should be tints of white, yellow or blue.
6. Things like oil, ghee, refined and gas cylinder etc. should be stored in South-East corner.
7. Drinking water in storeroom must be kept in pitchers or vessels.

Don'ts

1. Avoid fixing main door of storeroom in South-west direction.
2. Never sleep in storage room as the vibrations tends to obstruct people.
3. Avoid any kind of empty container in storage room.

(x) Toilet cum bath- Where?

In olden days toilet and bathrooms were built separately outside the bedrooms even outside the house. Nowadays concept has changed. New concept is to build a toilet cum bath attached with bedrooms. As per Vaastu guidelines, the best place for the toilet cum bath is North-West direction (Vayavya) of the house. The second option would be the South-West direction (Nairutya). North-West side is the best place for building a toilet cum bath. The slope of toilet cum bath should be in the East or North or North-East direction. Wash basin and shower should be on the East/North wall.

Position of Toilet cum Bath

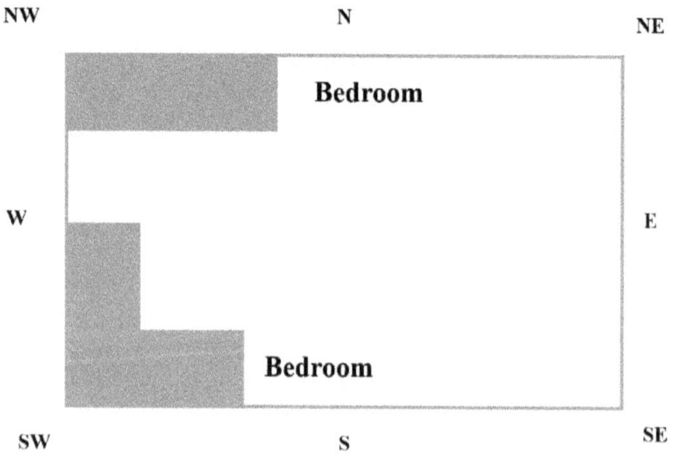

Figure-49

Do's

1. Toilet seats should ideally be placed in South to North directions or less preferably West to East direction.
2. The person, who is using toilet cum bath, must face towards North or South.
3. Bath taps should be in the East or North side wall.

4.   Mirrors in toilets should be placed on the North or East walls only.

5.   Washing machine can be put in North-West/West/South-East/East side only.

6.   The toilet cum bath walls should be painted in lighter shades such as white or light grey.

Don'ts

1.   Toilets should not be designed in North-East (Eshaan). It creates health problems and brings unnecessary tensions and problems in progeny of family. It may cause accidents also.

2.   Avoid toilet cum bath construction in the South-East (Agneya). It will bring sudden problems, legal issues, excise problems, unexpected losses, electricity gadgets failure and accidents.

3.   Avoid toilet cum bath construction in the South-West direction (Nairutya). The residents will have to face unexpected expenses and loss of finances.

4.   Avoid toilet cum bath construction under the stairs or in center area or near Pooja room and kitchen.

5.   Avoid red and black color in toilet cum bath walls.

(xi) Staircase-Why?

Many houses consist of more than one floor or multiple floors. They need staircase to connect one floor to another floor in the house. Staircase is a heavy structure. Therefore, the construction of staircase should touch the West/South-West/South walls. A staircase in other directions is believed to lead to financial losses. Staircase steps should begin from East to West direction or North direction. Mind it that Stairs should turn clockwise and not anti-clockwise. The steps should always be in odd numbers such as 9-11-13-17-21 etc.

Position of staircase in the house

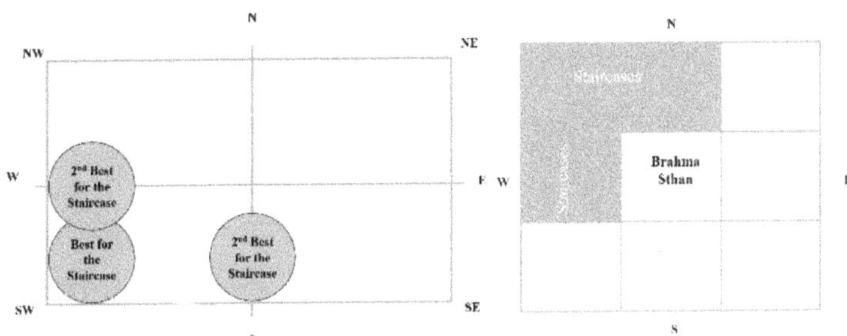

Figure-50

Do's

1. Build staircase of the house in South or Western portion of the house as these directions are heavy and beneficial.
2. If the staircase is outside the house, build staircase in South-East in East, North-West in North, South-West in West and South-West in South.
3. Steps should begin from East to West direction or North to South direction.
4. The steps should always be in odd numbers such as 9-11-13-17-21 etc.
5. Paint staircase in light colors such as white or light gray.
6. If stairs have suddenly broken, repair broken stairs immediately, otherwise it may cause accidents or mental tension due to clashes.

Don'ts

1. Avoid staircase in North-East and in center of the house as it will cause loss of wealth.
2. Avoid circular staircase in the house as it may cause ill effects on health.
3. Avoid building Pooja' room, kitchen and bathroom under staircase.
4. Do not use common staircase for going upstairs and basement.
5. Avoid paint red or black color on staircase.

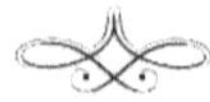

Chapter
15
Auspicious Moment(Muhurata) for a Happy House

Auspicious Moment (Muhurata) for Happy House

1. The purification of the place is mandatory before its occupation.
2. For this purpose, four rituals (Poojas) are conducted.
3. The first is performed before the construction is actually commences.
4. The second is performed on positioning the main gate.
5. The third is to ensure that the new occupants have happy and peaceful lives.
6. The fourth ritual is associated with moving in the new house.

Note:

There are five following essential items required for this Pooja, because they represent all five elements.

(1) Water or Milk - It represents the Water element.
(2) Incense - It is the symbolic of the Air element.
(3) Flowers - Flowers represents the Earth element.
(4) Light - It symbolizes the fire element.
(5) A bell - A bell sound represents space element.

Since all living spaces are said to be filled with unseen entities, so certain rituals (Poojas) are conducted for the house. The first is performed before the construction is actually commenced, the second on positioning the main gate, the third to ensure that the new occupants have happy and peaceful lives, and the fourth set of rituals are associated with moving in the new house. Before entering a new house, a Vaastu Pooja is performed to the imaginary Vaastu Purush. The place is scrupulously cleaned, and a light is carried to the center of the house, where a jug of water, white flowers and burning incense have already been placed. Milk is then boiled until it overflows, or food is cooked and offered to the Gods, then follows a prayer for health, wealth and happiness. Finally holy water mixed with sandalwood oil is sprinkled into each corner of the property to purify it. The food, which has been cooked, is then offered to the Gods and given to the guests as Prasadam.

Figure-51

Figure-52

Conclusion: Thus, all the items related to five elements are brought together and offered to the Gods of the space directions to ensure the protection and prosperity of the house and occupants.

Chapter
16
Residential House

Vaastu Shastra is based on Solar energy, cosmic energy, lunar energy, thermal energy, magnetic energy, light energy and wind energy. If the Residential house is constructed according to Vaastu guidelines and is getting much more energies, the house owner/resident will be healthy and happy. These energies of atmosphere balance to enhance him peace, prosperity and success. He may roll in wealth and enjoy all the happiness in life. If a house is made against Vaastu guidelines and it is not getting above mentioned energies, it will be a place for all sorts of problems and worries. There will be no peace and no prosperity in the life of resident. Indeed, the above-mentioned planning in Chapter-13 and 14 is at least for a 500/1000 sq. yards area plot or a big farmhouse plot. One can adjust almost all the rooms, kitchen, toilets, water bodies, staircase, trees and plants etc. for the comfortable and peaceful living. According to "Vishwakarma Prakash" Chapter- 2nd following Shlokas 94 to 97 also indicate the same beneficial house plan-

ईशान्यां देवतागेहं पूर्वस्यां स्नानमन्दिरम् ।
आग्नेयां पाकसदनं भाण्डारागारमुत्तरे ।।
आग्नेयपूर्वयोर्मध्ये दधिमन्थनमन्दिरम् ।
अग्निप्रेतेशयोर्मध्ये आज्यगेहं प्रशस्यते ।।
याम्यनैर्ऋत्ययोर्मध्ये पुरीषत्यागमन्दिरम् ।
नैर्ऋत्याम्बुपयोर्मध्ये विद्याभ्यासस्य मन्दिरम् ।।
पश्चिमानिलयोर्मध्येरोदनार्थं गृहं स्मृतम् ।
वायव्योत्तरयोर्मध्ये रतिगेहं प्रशस्यते ।।

Eshanyam devtageham poorvasya snanmandiram |
Aagneyam paksadnam bhadaragarmuttre ||
Aagneypoorvyor madhye dadhimanthan mandiram |
Agnipretesh yormadhye aajaygeham prashsyte ||
Yaamyneraty yormadhye purishtyag mandiram |
Neratyambu payormadhye vidhyabhasasya mandiram ||
Paschimanil yormadhye rodnartham grahamsmratam |
Vayavyoter yormadhye ratigeham prasasyate ||

Meaning to say that the Pooja room should be in North-East (Eshaan) direction, bathroom in the East, kitchen in South-East (Aagneya) direction, store room in North direction, other activities related to Milk and curd in the middle of South-East (Aagneya) direction and in East/South direction, Study room in South direction or in between South and South-West (Nairutya) direction or West direction, Drawing/Family room in West or North-West direction and Dining room also in West, Master bedroom in North direction, Other bedroom in South, Cattle shed in North-West, Weapons if any in South-West and Garage in North-West direction.

If someone has a small plot of 100 Sq. yards area, then he is to sacrifice on some rooms. On a small plot all above rooms and other facilities can't be adjusted. He is to plan the house in a different way according to Vaastu guidelines so that he gets maximum energies to lead a comfortable and peaceful life.

The Main gate of the house comes in **Open area planning of the House,** indicates the internal beauty of the house. It can be in any Disha (Direction) or Vidisha (Corner Direction) as per position of the main or front road i.e.in North/East/South/West direction or North-East/South-East/South-West/North-West corner direction. Main Road facing is the way of main gate. Now we will take main gate of the house on facing each direction of the road. What type of **open area planning and inner area planning** is required for each direction? Following picture is a scene of a good residential house built in the center of a 500 square yards area plot facing East direction. All essential rooms i.e. drawing room, dining room, kitchen, master bedroom, guest room, pooja room, water bodies, overhead tank, septic tank, toilet cum baths, trees, plants and garden almost seen in this house. We may call it a happy and comfortable dwelling place. Direction-wise eight houses plan is given ahead. First see a picture of good Residential house.

A Scene of a good Residential House

Figure-53

(1) House Plan for East Facing (Poorav Disha) Plot

This is an East facing **(Poorav disha)** plot. The main road or front is in the East. Its main gate entry is in the East direction. East stands for Sunrise. Planet Sun, the source of our energy, rules this direction. It is very useful for people, who try to end something bad and wants to start something good. This direction gives strength, vigor, courage and a brilliant son. Planet Venus resides in this direction. It is the direction of harmony, happiness and prosperity. Following things in the house can be fixed in the East direction such as drawing room, study room, pooja room. Treasury boxes, lockers should open in the East. East direction must be lower than the West, South-West and North-West. Put up mirrors in this direction double up the prosperity of the resident. Indra, the Lord of all Gods, is the lord of this direction. It raises wealth. It brings rain, whenever there is no rainfall. Other Eight Gods Ish, Parjanya, Jayant, Sun, Satya, Bharsh, Akash and Agni also give power to this direction. See the following house plan Figure-54 along with inner portions such as pooja room, master bedroom, other bedrooms, toilet cum bath, drawing, dinning, store/service room, kitchen, staircase etc. with certain area measurement of each portion.

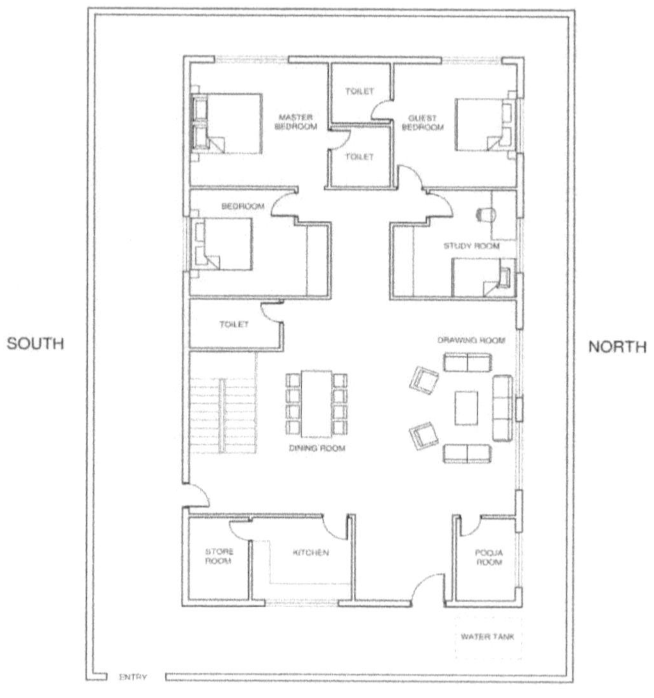

Main Road

Figure-54

<u>Open area planning of the Plot/House in 500/1000 Sq. Yard</u>

(1) Main Gate of the Plot/House

This is an East facing (Poorav disha) plot. The main road or front is in the East. So, the Main gate will be in the East direction. See the above house plan. According to Vaastu guidelines, Main gate should be on the upper side of the East direction. There should be no hindrance in front of the Main gate. Hindrances may be troublesome for the house owner or the resident. The East facing Main gate entry gives Prosperity, Government favor and Female growth in the house, but sometimes it changes in to Lack of peace, False accusation, Cruelty, Money loss due to theft/fire.

(2) Compound Wall of the Plot/House

Before starting the construction of the dwelling unit, it is essential to build a compound wall on all the four sides of the plot for the safety and security of material and men force working there. As per Vaastu guidelines the Compound wall should be symmetrical to both the axis of the same height. It will be very good and beneficial, if the North and East walls are lower than the South and West walls. Resident will lead a comfortable and peaceful life.

(3) Water Bodies-Well/Tube well/Underground tank

Water Bodies i.e. boring and underground water tank should be in the North or East side wall nearby main entrance of the house. The used water and rainwater should flow towards East. This will give the resident healthy atmosphere. He will be happy and healthy.

(4) Swimming pool

If open area of the plot/house allows construction of swimming pool, it can be constructed exactly in the North-East restricting some walking area around. If North-East corner construction is not possible, then construct the swimming pool at North-East to East side or North-East to North side. It makes healthy and brings good luck, pocket full of money, raising of their position in their fields, good name and fame, life-long cash flows, bank balances, having credit in the society etc. for the residents. But in India most of the houses have no swimming pool.

(5) Overhead Tank

It can be fixed on the roof of the Toilets cum baths, which are on the center along with the West side wall. Water flow will be normal. This situation will make you healthy, wealthy and happy.

(6) Septic tank

A Septic tank can be built towards upper side of North and East wall to protect from dirty air and unhealthy environment. Thus, house owner and his family member's health will be free from diseases and they will enjoy healthy, peaceful and happy life.

(7) Cattle Shed

Cattle shed should be built in an open area. The West and South sides of the plot are better for Cattle shed. The lots of dry grass may also be stored towards South/West/North-West corners. Water is essential for them, so a pipeline for the Cattle shed and for Cattle must be fixed from the boring or underground water tank. It will protect them from bad health and sanitation. Resident's health will also be protected.

(8) Garage

Garage should be built either in North-West or South-East on a little distance from the wall. Mind it that vehicles face should be either in the North or in the East. Nowadays there is a verandah along with Main gate. People keep their vehicle or car in verandah or sometimes outside main gate. It is an easy access to resident and time is saved. But the vehicle will be unsafe.

(9) Trees, Plants, Garden and Small Playgrounds

Trees and plants are planted outside the South side wall of the house. Bargad, Bamboo trees are good for East facing plot. Grassy area should be made nearby Pooja room. Resident can walk freely and peacefully with family. Kids can also play. This will provide the house owner healthy, happy and peaceful atmosphere. Small playgrounds such as Volleyball, Basketball, Badminton, Table tennis grounds are to be developed here. For self and family members these games are necessary for good health and happiness.

Inner area planning of the Plot/House

(1) Basement

Now the plot area of houses in town or cities is becoming smaller day by day because of increasing population and decreasing land. This is the main reason that people are constructing basements in the houses. A Basement can only be built in the North or East or North-East direction according to house plan measurement. North/East/North-East direction basement is beneficial for only storage of domestic items, office work and recreational activities. No bedroom should be built on basement floor. If it is built, the resident will always be moving in the world of dreams.

(2) Pooja room

North-East direction so called **Eshaan** is the Godly direction. This is the direction of Purity and divinity. It is the most auspicious for Pooja room. Pooja room should be made nearby main entry of the house in the East. It can also be built in the middle of North or East wall of the house. This increases positive energy and gives spirituality, happiness, peace of mind and prosperity to the house owner and family.

(3) Kitchen and Dining

The kitchen is built in the lower side of the South or South-East (Aagneya) direction. It generates and enhances positive energy, suppressing and even eliminating negative energy in the house. It can also be built in the North-West (Vayavya) direction of the house. The house owner and family feel joyous and peaceful and succeed in every field of life. Soon they will become prosperous.

Dining room is made in between kitchen and the drawing room almost in the center of the house so that food items can easily be served. Such situation brings happiness, peace and unity in the house. It also creates respects to elders.

(4) Drawing room and Guest room

Now drawing room is constructed in the North side or East side wall i.e. in the North-West side wall or in the middle of North side wall or North-

East side wall or in the middle of East side wall or South-East side wall of the house. Such situation brings happiness and peace in the house. Family gets a new baby. Guest room is specially built in the North-West corner of the East facing plot/house. Guest stays there for a short period and feels good. Soon they leave the room. It favors the resident to continue his business.

(5) Study room

For encouraging children study room is essential. They can read books and think independently.   It can be built nearby West side of Pooja room. It gives them healthy atmosphere for studies and thoughts of bright future. The children get energy and feel happy.

(6) Bedrooms-Master bedroom and other bedrooms

Master bedroom and other bedrooms are built nearby South-West direction because of the fact, if any problem comes with the children that can be solved immediately and easily. Other bedroom may be on North-West side. If bedrooms gates are in the direction of Plot's Main gate direction, the house owner and his family rise with health, wealth and prosperity.

(7) Storeroom

This room should be in the South-West corner nearby or above kitchen in the South to store food items such as grains, pulses, ghee, vegetables and other items to cater the family needs. It makes the house owner cconomically sound.

(8) Toilets cum bath

Toilets nowadays are attached to the bedrooms. Toilets and bath are at one place. This position saves time and area of the house. It is an easy access especially to parents and grandparents to entertain rest room and smooth bath.

(9) Staircase

It will be better that Stairs may be built in the middle of South side wall to reach to the roof. It will be easy approach from Master bedroom and Drawing room. This position is good for safety purposes for all the members of family.

(2) House Plan for South facing (Dakshin disha) Plot

This is a South facing **(Dakshin disha)** plot. The main road or front is in the South. Its main gate entry is on the upper side of the South direction towards East. Planet Mars rules this direction. **Yama**, the lord of Death is the lord of this direction. Other six Gods Pusha, Vitya, Gundharva, Gandharva, Bhrungraj and Mriga ban all auspicious functions to this direction. So, this is the reason, people dislike South facing plots. If nearby houses are facing South direction, then there is no harm to construct a house with a South facing entrance. But the construction should be according to Vaastu guidelines. It will bring opportunities for increasing wealth and influence the longevity and employment of resident. The plot owner should keep the South direction elevated compared to rest of the house, putting overhead tank and staircase nearby. No basement and kitchen should be in South direction. See the following house plan Figure-55 along with inner portions such as pooja room, master bedroom, other bedrooms, toilet cum bath, drawing, dinning, store/service room, kitchen, staircase etc. with certain area measurement of each portion.

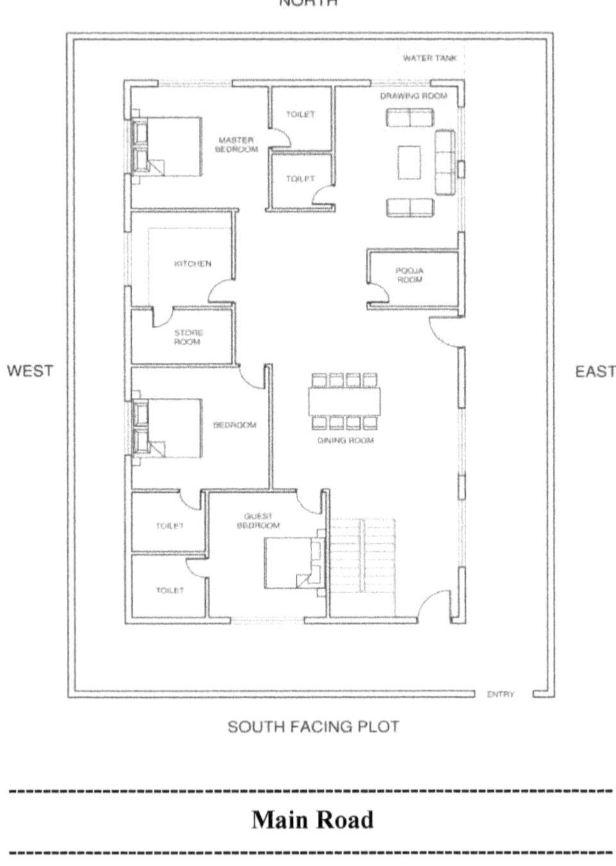

Main Road

Figure-55

<u>**Open area planning of the Plot/House**</u>

(1) Main Gate of the Plot/House
Main entrance of the house will be on the upper side of the South direction towards East, as the main road or front is in the South. According to

116

Vaastu guidelines the impact of South facing Main Gate will be such as **Advantages**-Prosperity and Human growth and **Disadvantages**-Meanness, Insubordination, Ungratefulness, Financial loss due to fire, Unwanted expenses, Trouble to son and Loss of male child. There should be no well/bore well in South direction. The resident should be careful about wealth and prosperity.

(2) Compound Wall of the Plot/House

Before starting the construction of the dwelling unit, it is essential to build a compound wall on all the four sides of the plot for the safety and security of material and man force working there. As per Vaastu guidelines the Compound wall should be symmetrical to both the axis of the same height. South and West walls should be higher than the North and East walls to receive more Solar energy. Resident will feel comfortable and peaceful.

(3) Water Bodies-Well/Tube well/Underground tank

Water Bodies i.e. boring and underground water tank will be in the North side wall or North-East (Eshaan) direction. The used water and rainwater should flow towards East. If it is not possible then pipeline first towards East, then turn it towards the correct direction. This will provide a good environment to the resident. He will be healthy and happy.

(4) Swimming Pool

If open area of the plot/house allows construction of swimming pool, it can be constructed exactly in the North-East restricting some walking area around. It makes healthy and brings good luck, good name and fame, bank balances, credit in the society and so on for the residents. But in India most of the houses have no swimming pool.

(5) Overhead Tank

It can be fixed on the roof of the Toilets, which are in the lower side of North side wall. This side water flow will be normal. This situation will make you healthy, wealthy and happy.

(6) Septic tank

A Septic tank can be built in the upper side of the West or North-West direction wall. It will protect from dirty air and unhealthy environment. Thus, house owner and his family member's health will be free from diseases and they will feel healthy, peaceful and happy.

(7) Cattle Shed

Cattle shed should be in an open area and toward North side. Water is essential for them, so boring or underground water tank is must nearby the cattle shed or cattle shed nearby boring or underground water tank. It will protect them from bad health and sanitation.

(8) Garage

Garage should be nearby the main gate towards South or West side wall. Nowadays there is a verandah along with Main gate. People keep their car in verandah or outside main gate. For safety and security measures it is not good for the resident.

(9) Trees, Plants, Garden and Small Playgrounds
Trees and plants are planted outside the South side/West side wall of the house. Grassy area should be nearby Pooja room or near cattle shed. This will provide the house owner healthy and happy atmosphere. Small playgrounds such as Volleyball, Basketball, Badminton, Table tennis are to be developed here. For self and family members these games are necessary for good health and happiness.

Inner area planning of the Plot/House

(1) Basement
Now the plots are small or very small because of shortage of land. This is the reason; the people are constructing basements in the houses. A Basement can only be built in the North direction or East direction or North-East direction as per house plan measurement. But basement is denied to be constructed in a South facing plot. It will harm resident's health and happiness.
(2) Pooja room (Place of worship)
Pooja room should be made in the center of North side wall or in the East side after main entry of the house. Worshipping and meditation will provide the resident peace and prosperity.
(3) Kitchen and Dining
The kitchen should be built attached to the West side wall. It will generate and enhance positive energy, suppressing and even eliminating negative energy in the house. The house owner and family will enjoy joyful and peaceful life and succeed in every field of life. Soon they will be wealthy and prosperous. Dining room should be built in the center of the house opposite kitchen. From the bedroom the Dining room should be in North-East side down to the drawing room or in the Northwest from the main gate. Such situation brings happiness, peace and unity in the house. It also creates respects to elders.
(4) Drawing room and Guest room
A Drawing room can be constructed in the North-East corner direction (Eshaan) or North-West corner direction (Vayavya). East or North side is also good for a Drawing room. It should be constructed in the middle of East and West wall far from main entry of the house. Such situation brings happiness and peace in the house. New baby entry is possible in the family. Guest room is especially built in the North-West side wall nearby Pooja room. Guest will stay there for a short period and feel good. It favors and comforts the resident and brings happiness.
(5) Study room
For encouraging children study room is essential. A table with chairs should be there. They can sit, read books and think independently. It can

be built nearby West wall with bedroom. It gives them healthy atmosphere for studies and thoughts of bright future.

(6) Bedrooms-Master bedroom & other bedrooms

Master bedroom & other bedrooms are built nearby South-West and North-West direction because of the fact, if any problem comes with the children that may be solved immediately and easily. The children will feel happy and safe.

(7) Storeroom

This room should be attached to the West side wall or South side wall nearest to the kitchen to store food items such as grains, pulses, ghee, vegetables and other items to cater the family needs. It makes the house owner economically sound.

(8) Toilets

Toilets nowadays are attached to the bedrooms. Toilets and bath are at one place. This position saves time and area of the house. It is an easy access especially to parents and grandparents for using rest room and taking bath.

(9) Staircase

It will be better that Stairs may be built on South side wall with the Main entrance of the plot/house to reach to the roof. It will be easy approach for Master bedroom and Drawing room. This position is good for safety purposes and healthy atmosphere.

(3) House Plan for West facing (Paschim disha) Plot

This is a West facing plot. The main road or front is in the West. So, the main entrance will be in the West direction. West is opposite to East direction. West stands for Sunset so West direction are more pitiable than East. It is not considered very auspicious. Planet Saturn rules this direction. People, those are living in the West part of the house or having entrances towards West, lead an unhappy and unlucky life. This direction spoils the prospects of income. But in most of the cases it has also been noted that the West direction is more beneficial to women. They get success and happiness in such houses. **Varun**, the Lord of Water is Lord of the West direction. Other Eight Gods Rog, Pap, Asur, Dwarpal, Pittar (the cruel in power), Shesh, Pushpdevta and Sugreev (the caring in nature) also give their powers to West direction. See the following house plan Figure-56 along with inner portions such as pooja room, master bedroom, other bedrooms, toilet cum bath, drawing, dinning, store/service room, kitchen, staircase etc. with certain area measurement of each portion.

Main Road

Figure-56

<u>Open area planning of the Plot/House</u>

(1) Main Gate of the Plot/House

Main entrance of the house will be on the upper side of the West direction towards North as the main road is in the West. According to Vaastu guidelines the impact of West facing Main Gate will be such as **Advantages**-Financial and Human growth and **Disadvantages**-Government harassment, Imprisonment, Enmity, Sickness, Accidental injury or Tragic death, Unwanted expenses, Trouble to son.

(2) Compound Wall of the Plot/House
Before starting the construction of the dwelling unit, it is essential to build a compound wall on all the four sides of the plot for the safety and security of material and man force working there. As per Vaastu guidelines the Compound wall should be symmetrical to both the axis of the same height. South and West walls should be higher than the North and East walls to receive more Solar energy. Resident will feel comfortable and peaceful.

(3) Water Bodies-Well/Tube well/Underground tank
Water Bodies i.e. boring and underground water tank will be near North side compound wall or North-East (Eshaan) direction. The used water and rainwater should flow towards East. If it is not possible then pipeline first towards East, then turn it towards the correct direction. This will provide a good environment to the resident. He will be healthy and happy.

(4) Swimming Pool
If open area of the plot/house allows construction of swimming pool, it can be constructed exactly in the North-East compound wall restricting some walking area around and at some distance from boring. It makes healthy and brings good luck, good name and fame, bank balances, credit in the society and so on for the residents. But in India most of the houses have no swimming pool.

(5) Overhead Tank
It can be fixed on the roof of the Toilets, which are near bedrooms in South-West direction. Here water flow will be normal. This situation will make the resident healthy, wealthy and happy.

(6) Septic tank
A Septic tank can be built in the outside center of the house in the West direction by the side of Main gate. It will protect from dirty air and unhealthy environment. Thus, house owner and his family member's health will be free from diseases and they will feel healthy, peaceful and happy.

(7) Cattle Shed
Cattle shed should be in an open area and toward boring near the North-East compound wall. Water is essential for them, so boring or underground water tank is must nearby the cattle shed or cattle shed nearby boring or underground water tank. It will protect them from bad health and sanitation. Resident's health will also be protected.

(8) Garage
Garage should be near to the Main gate towards West side wall. Nowadays there is a verandah along with Main gate. People keep their car in verandah or outside Main gate. It is an easy approach, but not a safe one.

(9) Trees, Plants, Garden and Small Playgrounds
Trees and plants are planted outside the South side wall of the house. Grassy area should be nearby Pooja room or near cattle shed. This will provide the house owner healthy and happy atmosphere. Small

playgrounds such as Volleyball, Basketball, Badminton, Table tennis are to be developed here. For self and family members these games are necessary for good health and happiness.

Inner area planning of the Plot/House

(1) Basement

Now the plots are small or very small because of shortage of land. This is the reason that people are constructing basements in the houses. A Basement can only be built in the North direction or East direction or North-East direction as per house plan measurement. North/East/North-East direction basement is beneficial for only storage of domestic items, office work and recreational activities. No bedroom should be built over it.

(2) Pooja room (Place of worship)

Pooja room is made nearby Main entry of the house i.e. on the lower side of North side wall or in the East nearby main entry of the house. Worshipping and meditation will provide the resident peace and prosperity.

(3) Kitchen and Dining

It is built in the lower side of the South or South-East (Aagneya) direction. It will generate and enhance positive energy, suppressing and even eliminating negative energy in the house. The house owner and family will enjoy joyful and peaceful life and succeed in every field of life. Soon they will be wealthy and prosperous. Dining room should be built in the center of the house opposite kitchen. From the bedroom the Dining room should be in North-East side down to the drawing room or in the Northwest from the main gate. Such situation brings happiness, peace and unity in the house. It also creates respects to elders.

(4) Drawing room

A Drawing room/Drawing room can be constructed in the North-East corner direction (Eshaan) or North-West corner direction (Vayavya). East or North side is also good for a Drawing room. It should be constructed in the middle of East and West wall far from main entry of the house. Such situation brings happiness and peace in the house. New baby entry is possible in the family. Guest room is especially built in the lower portion of the North side wall. Guest will stay there for a short period and feel good. It favors and leads to comfort the resident and family.

(5) Study room

For encouraging children study room is essential. A table with chairs should be there. They can sit and study books independently. It should be built nearby West wall with bedroom. It will give them healthy atmosphere for studies and thoughts of bright future.

(6) Bedrooms-Master bedroom & other bedrooms
Master bedroom & other bedrooms are built nearby South-West and West direction because of the fact, if any problem comes with the children that may be solved immediately and easily. The children will be safe and secure. They will enjoy good time.

(7) Storeroom
This room should be in the South-East corner by the side of kitchen in the South. It is essential to store food items such as grains, pulses, ghee, vegetables and other items to cater the family needs. It makes the house owner economically sound.

(8) Toilets
Toilets nowadays are attached to the bedrooms. Toilets and bath are at one place towards South side wall. This position saves time and area of the house. It is an easy access especially to parents and grandparents for using rest room and taking bath.

(9) Staircase
It will be better that Stairs may be built on West side wall along with the Main entrance of the plot/house to reach to the roof. It will be easy approach for Master bedroom and Drawing room. This position is good for safety purposes and healthy atmosphere.

(4) House Plan for North facing (Uttar disha) Plot

This is a North facing plot. The main road or front is in the North. So, the main entrance will be in the North direction. See the house plan. Its main gate entry is on the upper side of the North direction. The internal parts of the house i.e. the position of master bedroom, other bedrooms, toilet or bath, drawing and dinning, store/service room, kitchen, pooja room, staircase etc. will be as shown in the plan follows. North direction is ruled by the planet Mercury. It is best for business because of the fact that ultraviolet rays cast by Sun have the least negative effect in the Northern portions. Open space to this side gives advantages of better happy and healthy life. Northern portions of the house bring maximum success. Minimum construction is required this side so as to maintain efficiency. Slope or elevation is better to this direction. Do not have Staircase or Toilet or Garbage store or Kitchen to this direction. Fixing of Mirrors is auspicious here. They are supposed to double up your wealth. **Kuber,** the treasurer of all the Gods is the Lord of the North direction. Other six Gods Diti, Aditi, Shail, Bhalat, Mukhya and Nag bring happiness and prosperity to this direction. See the following house plan Figure-57 along with inner portions such as pooja room, master bedroom, other bedrooms, toilet cum bath, drawing, dinning, store/service room, kitchen, staircase etc. with certain area measurement of each portion.

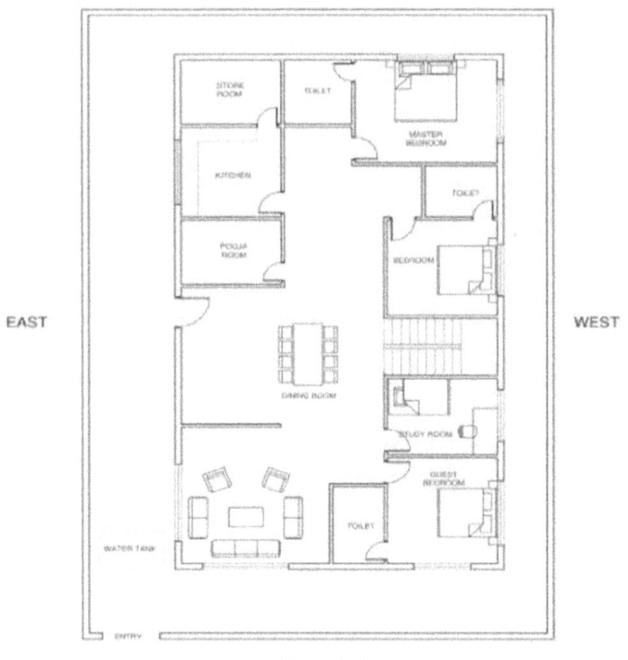

Main Road

Figure-57

Open area planning of the Plot/House

(1) Main Gate of the Plot/House
Main entrance of the house will be on the upper side of the North-East direction as the main road is in the North. According to Vaastu guidelines this entrance is resulted for the resident such as advantages-All types of gain, prosperity, Government favor, Female growth and disadvantages-Enmity with son, Unsuccessful, Defect in female, Loss due to fire, Lack of peace.

(2) Compound Wall of the plot/house
Before starting the construction of the dwelling unit, it is essential to build a compound wall on all the four sides of the plot for the safety and security of material and man force working there. As per Vaastu guidelines the

Compound wall should be symmetrical to both the axis of the same height. South and West walls should be higher than the North and East walls to receive more Solar energy. Resident will feel comfortable and peaceful.

(3) Water Bodies-Well/Tube well/Underground tank

Water Bodies i.e. boring and underground water tank will be near East side compound wall or North-East (Eshaan) direction. The used water and rainwater should flow towards East. If it is not possible then pipeline first towards East, then turn it towards the correct direction. This will provide a good environment to the resident. He will be healthy and happy.

(4) Swimming Pool

If open area of the plot/house allows construction of swimming pool, it can be constructed exactly in the North-East compound wall restricting some walking area around and at some distance from boring. It makes healthy and brings good luck, good name and fame, bank balances, credit in the society and so on for the residents. But in India most of the houses have no swimming pool.

(5) Overhead Tank

It can be fixed on the roof of the Toilets, which are near bedrooms in South-West direction. Here water flow will be normal. This situation will make the resident healthy, wealthy and happy.

(6) Septic tank

A Septic tank can be built in the outside center of the house in the North-West direction by the side of Main gate. It will protect from dirty air and unhealthy environment. Thus, house owner and his family member's health will be free from diseases and they will feel healthy, peaceful and happy.

(7) Cattle Shed

Cattle shed should be in an open area and toward East side. Water is essential for them, so boring or underground water tank is must nearby the cattle shed or cattle shed nearby boring or underground water tank. It will protect them from bad health and sanitation. Resident's health will also be protected.

(8) Garage

Garage should be near Main gate. Nowadays there is a verandah along with Main gate. People keep their car in verandah or outside Main gate. It is an easy approach, but not a safe one.

(9) Trees, Plants, Garden and Small Playgrounds

Trees and plants are planted outside the South side wall of the house. Grassy area should be nearby cattle shed or Pooja room. Small playgrounds such as Volleyball, Basketball, Badminton, Table tennis are to be developed here. For self and family members these games are necessary for good health and happiness.

Inner area planning of the Plot/House

(1) Basement

Now the plots are small or very small because of shortage of land. This is the reason that people are constructing basements in the houses. A Basement can only be built in the North direction or East direction or North-East direction as per house plan measurement. North/East/North-East direction basement is beneficial for only storage of domestic items, office work and recreational activities. No bedroom should be built over it.

(2) Pooja room (Place of worship)

Pooja room is made nearby Main entry of the house i.e. on the lower side of East side wall of the house. Worshipping and meditation will provide the resident peace and prosperity.

(3) Kitchen and Dining

It is built in the lower side of the South or South-East (Aagneya) direction. It will generate and enhance positive energy, suppressing and even eliminating negative energy in the house. The house owner and family will enjoy joyful and peaceful life and succeed in every field of life. Soon they will be wealthy and prosperous. Dining room should be built in the center of the house opposite kitchen. From the bedroom the Dining room should be in North-East side down to the drawing room or in the Northwest from the main gate. Such situation brings happiness, peace and unity in the house. It also creates respects to elders.

(4) Drawing room

A Drawing room/Drawing room can be constructed in the North-East corner direction (Eshaan) or North-West corner direction (Vayavya). East or North side is also good for a Drawing room. It should be constructed in the middle of East and West wall far from main entry of the house. Such situation brings happiness and peace in the house. New baby entry is possible in the family. Guest room is especially built in the lower portion of the North side wall or North-West wall. Guest will stay there for a short period and feel good. It favors the resident and family. They will feel comfortable.

(5) Study room

For encouraging children study room is essential. A table with chairs should be there. They can sit and study books independently. It should be built nearby West wall with bedroom. It will give them healthy atmosphere for studies and thoughts of bright future.

(6) Bedrooms-Master bedroom & other bedrooms

Master bedroom & other bedrooms are built nearby South-West and West direction because of the fact, if any problem comes with the children that may be solved immediately and easily. The children will be safe and secure. They will enjoy good time.

(7) Storeroom

This room should be in the South-East corner by the side of kitchen in the South. It is essential to store food items such as grains, pulses, ghee, vegetables and other items to cater the family needs. It makes the house owner economically sound.

(8) Toilets

Toilets nowadays are attached to the bedrooms. Toilets and bath are at one place towards South side wall. This position saves time and area of the house. It is an easy access especially to parents and grandparents for using rest room and taking bath.

(9) Staircase

It will be better that Stairs may be built on West side wall along with the Main entrance of the plot/house to reach to the roof. It will be easy approach for Master bedroom and Drawing room. This position is good for safety purposes and healthy atmosphere.

Note:

Now you have gone through all the four directions (dishas) plot plans, the main entry of the house and inner portions i.e. master bedroom, other bedroom, toilet-bath, hall-drawing room-dinning-lobby, staircase, service room or store, kitchen, pooja room etc. If you want to add more portions such as, swimming pool, cattle-shed, garden, trees and Plants, you can get prepared another house plan according to your desires. It all depends on the size and facing of the plot. In the above manner house plans for four Corner directions facing plots the North-East facing (Eshaan direction) plot, the South-East facing (Aagneya direction) plot, the South-West facing (Nairutya direction) plot and the North-West facing (Vayavya direction) plot can easily be prepared with the help of a Vaastu expert as per Vaastu guidelines.

(5) House Plan for North-East (Uttar-Poorav Disha) facing Plot

This is a **North-East direction (Uttar-Poorav Disha) facing plot.** It is called "Eshaan" direction. The Main Road or front of this plot/house is in the North-East (Eshaan) direction. The North-East (Eshaan) direction is regarded the best and sacred direction out of all the eight directions for residence. It is the direction of Purity and divinity. It is believed that God resides in this direction. Moreover, Sun's powerful Ultraviolet rays fall on this direction. Auspicious planet Jupiter rules this direction and gives over all happiness i.e. reputation, wealth, prosperity and intelligent children for the house owner in life. The Main gate entry is on the upper side of the North-East (Eshaan) direction. It is treated favorable and beneficial to the resident. It is the most auspicious Godly direction. It promotes positive aspects to men and women both. Open space and slope are essential towards this direction. Hindu Lord Shiva is the supreme deity of this direction. It is the best direction to build a worshipping place (Pooja room). Underground tank, Boring and well also give auspicious results to this direction. See house plan in Figure-58 on next page along with inner portions such as pooja room, master bedroom, other bedrooms, toilet cum bath, drawing, dinning, store/service room, kitchen, staircase etc. with certain area measurement of each portion.

Open area planning of the Plot/House

(1) Main Gate of the Plot/House

Main entrance of the house will be on the upper side of the North-East direction as the Main Road is in the North-East direction. According to Vaastu guidelines this North-East (Eshaan) direction results some Advantages such as All types of gain, Prosperity, Government favor, Female growth for the resident. This also brings some disadvantages such as Enmity with son, Unsuccessfulness, Defect in female, Loss due to fire and Lack of peace.

(2) Compound Wall of the plot/house

Before starting the construction of the dwelling unit, it is essential to build a compound wall on all the four sides of the plot for the safety and security of material and man force working there. As per Vaastu guidelines the Compound wall should be symmetrical to both the axis of the same height. South and West walls should be higher than the North and East walls to receive more Solar energy. Resident will feel comfortable and peaceful.

(3) Water Bodies-Well/Tube well/Underground tank

Water Bodies boring and underground water tank will be ahead of Main gate in the North-East (Eshaan) direction touched with compound wall. The used water and rainwater should flow towards East. This will provide a good atmosphere to the resident. He will be healthy and happy.

(4) Swimming Pool

If open area of the plot/house allows construction of swimming pool, it can be constructed exactly in the North-East compound wall restricting some walking area around and at some distance from boring. This makes healthy and brings good luck, good name, fame, bank balances, credit in the society for the residents. But in India most of the houses have no swimming pool.

(5) Overhead Tank

It can be fixed on the roof of the Toilets, which are near bedrooms in South-West direction. Here water flow will be normal. This situation will make the resident healthy, wealthy and happy.

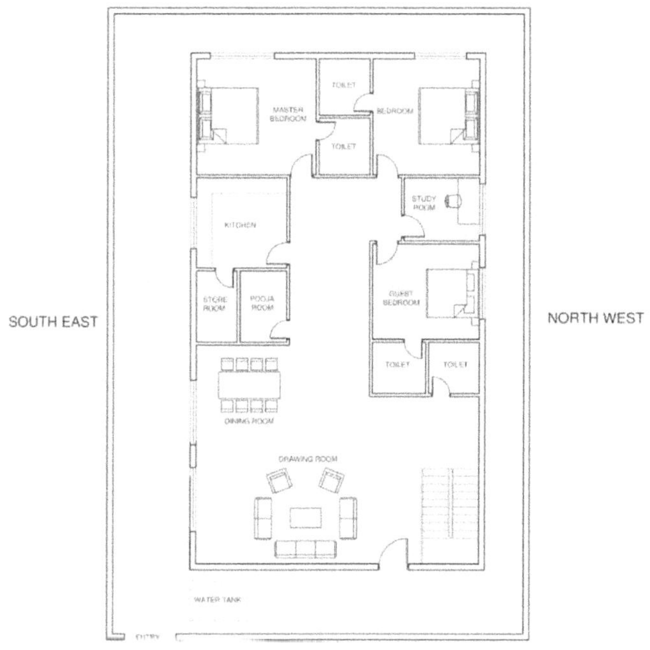

Main Road

Figure-58

(6) Septic tank

A Septic tank can be built in the outside center of the house in the South-East direction along with compound wall. It will protect from dirty air and unhealthy environment. Thus, house owner and his family member's health will be free from diseases and they will feel healthy, peaceful and happy.

(7) Cattle Shed

Cattle shed should be in an open area and toward West side. Water is essential for them, so boring or underground water tank is must nearby the cattle shed or cattle shed nearby boring or underground water tank. It will protect them from bad health and sanitation. Resident's health will also be protected.

(8) Garage

Garage should be near Main gate along with East side compound wall. Now-a-days there is a verandah along with Main gate. People keep their car in verandah or outside Main gate. It is an easy approach, but not a safe one.

(9) Trees, Plants, Garden and small Playgrounds

Trees and plants are planted outside the South-West side wall of the house. Grassy area should be nearby cattle shed or pooja room. Small playgrounds such as Volleyball, Basketball, Badminton, Table tennis grounds are to be developed here. For self and family members these games are necessary for good health and happiness.

Inner area planning of the Plot/House

(1) Basement

Now the plots are small or very small because of shortage of land. This is the reason that people are constructing basements in the houses. A Basement can only be built in the North-East or East or North direction as per house plan measurement. North-East/North/East direction basement is beneficial for only storage of domestic items, office work and recreational activities. The condition is that no bedroom should be built over it.

(2) Pooja room (Place of worship)

Pooja room is made on the upper side of South-East side wall of the house. Here worshipping and meditation will provide the resident peace and prosperity.

(3) Kitchen and Dining

It is built in the lower side of the South or South-East (Aagneya) direction. It will generate and enhance positive energy, suppressing and even eliminating negative energy in the house. The house owner and family will enjoy joyful and peaceful life and succeed in every field of life. Soon they will be wealthy and prosperous Dining room should be built in the center of the house down to the kitchen. From the bedroom the Dining room should be in North-East side down to the drawing room or in the North-West from the main gate. Such situation brings happiness, peace and unity in the house. It also creates respects to elders.

(4) Drawing room

A Drawing room/Drawing room can be constructed in the North-East corner direction (Eshaan) or North-West corner direction (Vayavya). East or North side is also good for a Drawing room. It should be constructed in the middle of East and West wall far from main entry of the house. Such situation brings happiness and peace in the house. New baby entry is possible in the family. Guest room is especially built in the lower portion of the North side wall or North-West wall. Guest will stay there for a short period and feel good. It favors the resident and family. They will feel comfortable.

(5) Storeroom

This room should be in the South-East corner down to the kitchen in the South. It is essential to store food items such as grains, pulses, ghee, vegetables and other items to cater the family needs. It makes the house owner economically sound.

(5) Study room

For encouraging children study room is essential. A table with chairs should be there. They can sit and study books independently. It should be built nearby West wall with bedroom. It will give them healthy atmosphere for studies and thoughts of bright future.

(6) Bedrooms-Master bedroom & other bedrooms

Master bedroom & other bedrooms are built nearby South-West and West direction because of the fact, if any problem comes with the children that may be solved immediately and easily. The children will be safe and secure. They will enjoy good time.

(7) Storeroom

This room should be in the South-East corner by the side of kitchen in the South. It is essential to store food items such as grains, pulses, ghee, vegetables and other items to cater the family needs. It makes the house owner economically sound.

(8) Toilets

Toilets nowadays are attached to the bedrooms. Toilets and bath are at one place towards South side wall. This position saves time and area of the house. It is an easy access especially to parents and grandparents for using rest room and taking bath.

(9) Staircase

It will be better that Stairs may be built on West side wall along with the Main entrance of the plot/house to reach to the roof. It will be easy approach for Master bedroom and Drawing room. This position is good for safety purposes and healthy atmosphere.

(6) House Plan for South-East (Dakshin-Poorav) facing Plot

This is a **South-East direction (Dakshin-Poorav Disha) facing plot.** It is called **Aagneya** direction for logics and reasons. The main road or front is in the South-East (Aagneya) direction. So, the main entrance will be in the South-East (Aagneya) direction. This direction stands for strength, determination and fame. Planet Venus rules this direction. It is very beneficial to have a kitchen in this direction. Electric instruments such as Televisions, Motor batteries, Inverters, Home theatre and so on should be placed or fixed on the South-East side of the room/rooms. There should be no toilet and water tank in this direction. People doing **Homa-Havans**

(Oblations by Fire to the Deity) at homes are blessed by **Agni Dev,** the lord of fire.   Residents enjoy wealth, prosperity and fame. See the following house plan Figure-59 along with the inner portions of the house i.e. the position of basement, pooja room, master bedroom, other bedrooms, toilet and bath, drawing and dinning, store/service room, kitchen, staircase etc. with certain area measurement of each portion.

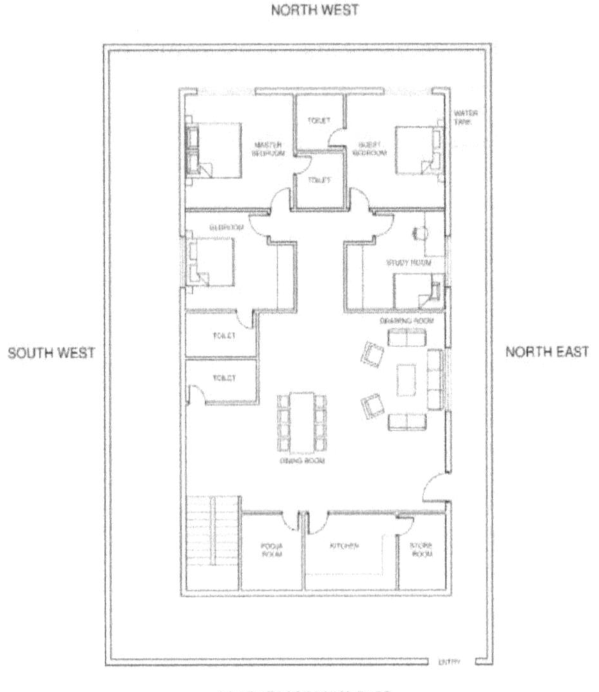

Main Road

Figure-59

<u>Open area planning of the Plot/House</u>

(1) Main Gate of the Plot/House
Main entrance of the house will be on the upper side of the South-East direction as the Main Road is in the South-East direction. According to Vaastu guidelines this South-East (Aagneya) direction results some

advantages such as government favor . It brings disadvantages also such as lack of peace, false accusation, cruelty, meanness, insubordination, financial loss due to theft/fire and loss of male child.

(2) Compound Wall of the plot/house

Before starting the construction of the dwelling unit, it is essential to build a compound wall on all the four sides of the plot for the safety and security of material and man force working there. As per Vaastu guidelines the Compound wall should be symmetrical to both the axis of the same height. South and West walls should be higher than the North and East walls to receive more Solar energy. Resident will feel comfortable and peaceful.

(3) Water Bodies-Well/Tube well/Underground tank

Water Bodies i.e. boring and underground water tank will be ahead of Main gate in the North-East (Eshaan) direction touched with compound wall. The used water and rainwater should flow towards East. This will provide a good atmosphere to the resident. He will be healthy and happy.

(4) Swimming Pool

If open area of the plot/house allows construction of swimming pool, it can be constructed exactly in the North-East compound wall restricting some walking area around and at some distance from boring. It makes healthy and brings good luck, good name and fame, bank balances, credit in the society and so on for the residents. But in India most of the houses have no swimming pool.

(5) Overhead Tank

It can be fixed on the roof of the Toilets, which are near bedrooms in South-West direction. Here water flow will be normal. This situation will make the resident healthy, wealthy and happy.

(6) Septic tank

A Septic tank can be built in the outside center of the house in the South-East direction along with compound wall. It will protect from dirty air and unhealthy environment. Thus, house owner and his family member's health will be free from diseases and they will feel healthy, peaceful and happy.

(7) Cattle Shed

Cattle shed should be in an open area and toward West side. Water is essential for them, so boring or underground water tank is must nearby the cattle shed or cattle shed nearby boring or underground water tank. It will protect them from bad health and sanitation. Resident's health will also be protected.

(8) Garage

Garage should be near Main gate along with East side compound wall. Now-a-days there is a verandah along with Main gate. People keep their car in verandah or outside Main gate. It is an easy approach, but not a safe one.

(9)Trees, Plants, Garden and Small Playgrounds
Trees and plants are planted outside the South-West side wall of the house. Grassy area should be nearby cattle shed or Pooja room. Small playgrounds such as Volleyball, Basketball, Badminton, Table tennis grounds are to be developed here. For self and family members these games are necessary for good health and happiness.

<u>**Inner area planning of the Plot/House**</u>

(1) Basement
Now the plots are small or very small because of shortage of land. This is the reason that people are constructing basements in the houses. A Basement can only be built in the North-East or East or North direction as per house plan measurement. North-East/North/East direction basement is beneficial for only storage of domestic items, office work and recreational activities. The condition is that no bedroom should be built over it.

(2) Pooja room (Place of worship)
Pooja room is made on the upper side of South-East side wall of the house. Here worshipping and meditation will provide the resident peace and prosperity.

(3) Kitchen and Dining
It is built in the lower side of the South or South-East (Aagneya) direction. It will generate and enhance positive energy, suppressing and even eliminating negative energy in the house. The house owner and family will enjoy joyful and peaceful life and succeed in every field of life. Soon they will be wealthy and prosperous. Dining room should be built in the center of the house down to the kitchen. From the bedroom the Dining room should be in North-East side down to the drawing room or in the North-West from the main gate. Such situation brings happiness, peace and unity in the house. It also creates respects to elders.

(4) Drawing room
A Drawing room/Drawing room can be constructed in the North-East corner direction (Eshaan) or North-West corner direction (Vayavya). East or North side is also good for a Drawing room. It should be constructed in the middle of East and West wall far from main entry of the house. Such situation brings happiness and peace in the house. New baby entry is possible in the family room or in the North-West from the main gate. Such situation brings happiness, peace and unity in the house. It also creates respects to elders. Guest room is especially built in the lower portion of the North side wall or North-West wall. Guest will stay there for a short period and feel good. It favors the resident and family. They will feel comfortable.

(5) Study room

For encouraging children study room is essential. A table with chairs should be there. They can sit and study books independently. It should be built nearby West wall with bedroom. It will give them healthy atmosphere for studies and thoughts of bright future.

(6) Bedrooms-Master bedroom & other bedrooms

Master bedroom & other bedrooms are built nearby South-West and West direction because of the fact, if any problem comes with the children that may be solved immediately and easily. The children will be safe and secure. They will enjoy good time.

(7) Storeroom

This room should be in the South-East corner down to the kitchen in the South. It is essential to store food items such as grains, pulses, ghee, vegetables and other items to cater the family needs. It makes the house owner economically sound.

(8) Toilets

Toilets nowadays are attached to the bedrooms. Toilets and bath are at one place towards South side wall. This position saves time and area of the house. It is an easy access especially to parents and grandparents for using rest room and taking bath.

(9) Staircase

It will be better that Stairs may be built on West side wall along with the Main entrance of the plot/house to reach to the roof. It will be easy approach for Master bedroom and Drawing room. This position is good for safety purposes and healthy atmosphere.

(7) House Plan for South-West (Dakshin-Paschim) facing Plot

This is a **South-West direction (Dakshin-Paschim Disha) facing plot**. It is called Nairutya direction. The Main Road or front is in the South-West (Dakshin-Paschim) direction. So, the main entrance will be in the South-West (Nairutya) direction. It is the residence of **Putna,** the Demoness. It leads to mental and physical disabilities in family life. Planet **Rahu** rules this direction. Therefore, this is the most inauspicious and evil direction. Gates here many times bring misfortunes. This space should be filled with heavy stuff to pull down the negativity of this direction. **The Lord of the demons** is the lord of this direction. It bans all auspicious functions to this direction. See the following house plan Figure-60 along with the inner portions of the house i.e. the position of basement, pooja room, master bedroom, other bedrooms, toilet and bath, drawing and dinning, store/service room, kitchen, staircase etc. with certain area measurement of each portion.

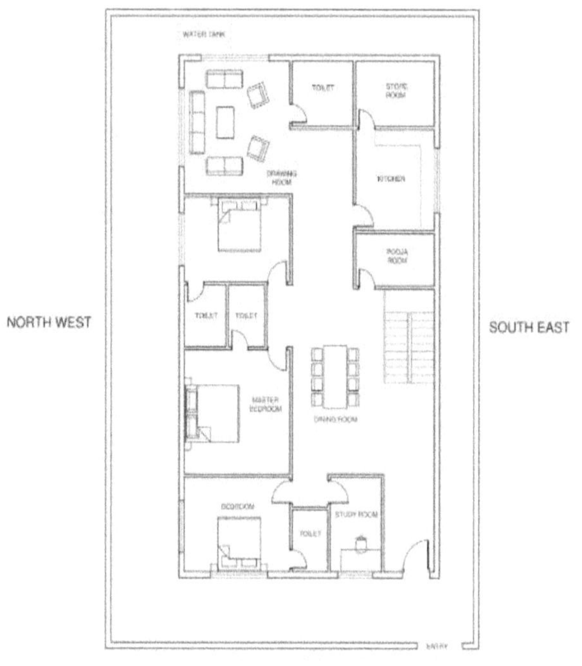

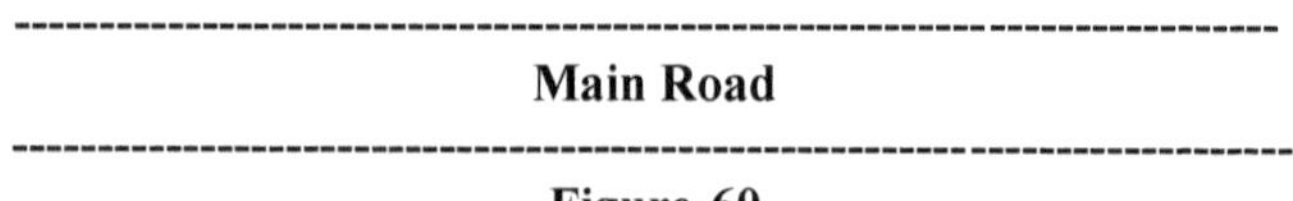

Main Road

Figure-60

<u>Open area planning of the Plot/House</u>

(1) Main Gate of the Plot/House

Its main gate entry is on the upper side of the South-West (Nairutya) direction as the main road is in the South-West (Nairutya) direction. According. to Vaastu guidelines this South-West (Nairutya) direction results some advantages such as Good position, Financial growth, Human growth, Mental peace. It brings some disadvantages too such as Financial loss, Unwanted expenses, Enmity, Ungratefulness and Trouble to son.

(2) Compound Wall of the plot/house

Before starting the construction of the dwelling unit, it is essential to build a compound wall on all the four sides of the plot for the safety and security of material and man force working there. As per Vaastu guidelines the Compound wall should be symmetrical to both the axis of the same height. South and West walls should be higher than the North and East walls to receive more Solar energy. Resident will feel comfortable and peaceful.

(3) Water Bodies-Well/Tube well/Underground tank

Water Bodies i.e. boring and underground water tank will be ahead of Main gate in the North-East (Eshaan) direction touched with compound wall. The used water and rainwater should flow towards East. This will provide a good environment to the resident. He will be healthy and happy.

(4) Swimming Pool

If open area of the plot/house allows construction of swimming pool, it can be constructed exactly in the North-East compound wall restricting some walking area around and at some distance from boring. It makes healthy and brings good luck, good name and fame, bank balances, credit in the society and so on for the residents. But in India most of the houses have no swimming pool.

(5) Overhead Tank

It can be fixed on the roof of the Toilets, which are near bedrooms in South-West direction. Here water flow will be normal. This situation will make the resident healthy, wealthy and happy.

(6) Septic tank

A Septic tank can be built in the outside center of the house in the South-East direction along with compound wall. It will protect from dirty air and unhealthy environment. Thus, house owner and his family member's health will be free from diseases and they will feel healthy, peaceful and happy.

(7) Cattle Shed

Cattle shed should be in an open area and toward West side. Water is essential for them, so boring or underground water tank is must nearby the cattle shed or cattle shed nearby boring or underground water tank. It will protect them from bad health and sanitation. Resident's health will also be protected.

(8) Garage

Garage should be near Main gate along with East side compound wall. Now-a-days there is a verandah along with Main gate. People keep their car in verandah or outside Main gate. It is an easy approach, but not a safe one.

(9)Trees, Plants, Garden and Small Playgrounds

Trees and plants are planted outside the South-West side wall of the house. Grassy area should be nearby cattle shed or Pooja room. Small playgrounds such as Volleyball, Basketball, Badminton, Table tennis grounds are to be developed here. For self and family members these games are necessary for good health and happiness.

<u>**Inner area planning of the Plot/House**</u>

(1) Basement
Now the plots are small or very small because of shortage of land. This is the reason that people are constructing basements in the houses. A Basement can only be built in the North-East or East or North direction as per house plan measurement. North-East/North/East direction basement is beneficial for only storage of domestic items, office work and recreational activities. The condition is that no bedroom should be built over it.

(2) Pooja room (Place of worship)
Pooja room is made on the upper side of South-East side wall of the house. Here worshipping and meditation will provide the resident peace and prosperity.

(3) Kitchen and Dining
It is built in the lower side of the South or South-East (Aagneya) direction. It will generate and enhance positive energy, suppressing and even eliminating negative energy in the house. The house owner and family will enjoy joyful and peaceful life and succeed in every field of life. Soon they will be wealthy and prosperous. Dining room should be built in the center of the house down to the kitchen. From the bedroom the Dining room should be in North-East side down to the drawing room or in the North-West from the main gate. Such situation brings happiness, peace and unity in the house. It also creates respects to elders.

(4) Drawing room
A Drawing room/Drawing room can be constructed in the North-East corner direction (Eshaan) or North-West corner direction (Vayavya). East or North side is also good for a Drawing room. It should be constructed in the middle of East and West wall far from main entry of the house. Such situation brings happiness and peace in the house. New baby entry is possible in the family. Guest room is especially built in the lower portion of the North side wall or North-West wall. Guest will stay there for a short period and feel good. It favors the resident and family. They will feel comfortable.

(5) Study room
For encouraging children study room is essential. A table with chairs should be there. They can sit and study books independently. It should be built nearby West wall with bedroom. It will give them healthy atmosphere for studies and thoughts of bright future.

(6) Bedrooms-Master bedroom & other bedrooms
Master bedroom & other bedrooms are built nearby South-West and West direction because of the fact, if any problem comes with the children that may be solved immediately and easily. The children will be safe and secure. They will enjoy good time.

(7) Storeroom

This room should be in the South-East corner down to the kitchen in the South. It is essential to store food items such as grains, pulses, ghee, vegetables and other items to cater the family needs. It makes the house owner economically sound.

(8) Toilets

Toilets nowadays are attached to the bedrooms. Toilets and bath are at one place towards South side wall. This position saves time and area of the house. It is an easy access especially to parents and grandparents for using rest room and taking bath.

(9) Staircase

It will be better that Stairs may be built on West side wall along with the Main entrance of the plot/house to reach to the roof. It will be easy approach for Master bedroom and Drawing room. This position is good for safety purposes and healthy atmosphere.

(8) House Plan for North-West (Uttar-Paschim)) facing Plot

This is a **North-West direction (Uttar-Paschim Disha) facing plot**. It is called Vayavya direction. The main road or front is in the North-West (Uttar-Paschim) direction. So, the main entrance will be in the North-West (Vayavya) direction. It governs interpersonal relationship. People of the family depend on each other. Moon rules this direction. For total happiness of the family no basement, underground water tank, kitchen, dining room and master bedroom should be in this direction. Any type of extension in the house/building should also be avoided in this direction. **Lord Hanuman** is also symbolic of this direction. This is the Direction of Movement. Thus, according to Vaastu Girls, who are not Getting married after reaching a marriageable age, generally get married Soon. **Vayu Devta**, the lord of Air is the lord of this direction. See the house plan in Figure-61 on next page along with the inner portions of the house i.e. the position of basement, pooja room, master bedroom, other bedrooms, toilet and bath, drawing and dinning, store/service room, kitchen, staircase etc. with certain area measurement of each portion.

Open area planning of the Plot/House

(1) Main Gate of the Plot/House

Main entrance of the house will be on the upper side of the North-West direction as the Main Road is in the North-West direction. According to Vaastu guidelines this North-West (Vayavya) direction results some advantages such as All types of gain, Financial growth, Human growth, Happiness for the resident. This also brings some disadvantages such as

Sickness, Enmity, Government harassment, Imprisonment, Financial loss, Accidental injury, Tragic death.

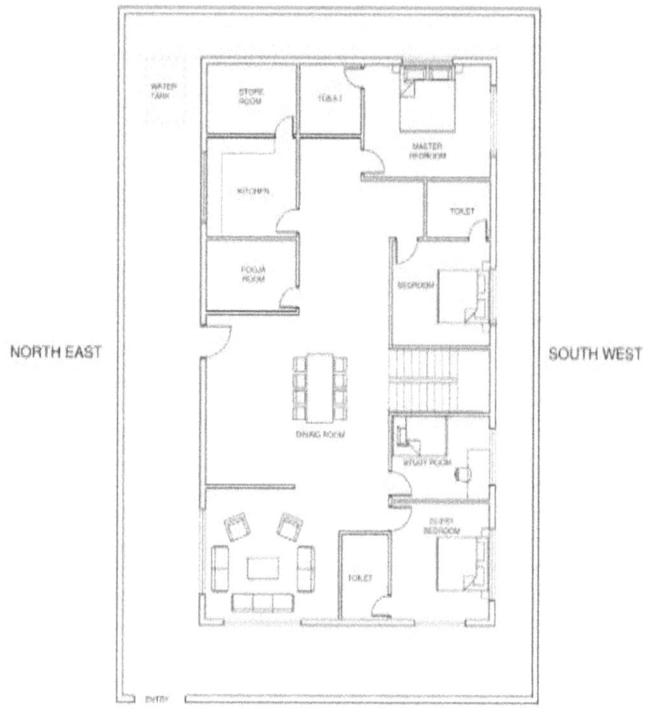

Main Road

Figure-61

(2) Compound Wall of the plot/house

Before starting the construction of the dwelling unit, it is essential to build a compound wall on all the four sides of the plot for the safety and security of material and man force working there. As per Vaastu guidelines the Compound wall should be symmetrical to both the axis of the same height.

South and West walls should be higher than the North and East walls to receive more Solar energy. Resident will feel comfortable and peaceful.

(3) Water Bodies-Well/Tube well/Underground tank

Water Bodies i.e. boring and underground water tank will be ahead of Main gate in the North-East (Eshaan) direction touched with compound wall. The used water and rainwater should flow towards East. This will provide a good environment to the resident. He will be healthy and happy.

(4) Swimming Pool

If open area of the plot/house allows construction of swimming pool, it can be constructed exactly in the North-East compound wall restricting some walking area around and at some distance from boring. It makes healthy and brings good luck, good name and fame, bank balances, credit in the society and so on for the residents. But in India most of the houses have no swimming pool.

(5) Overhead Tank

It can be fixed on the roof of the Toilets, which are near bedrooms in South-West direction. Here water flow will be normal. This situation will make the resident healthy, wealthy and happy.

(6) Septic tank

A Septic tank can be built in the outside center of the house in the South-East direction along with compound wall. It will protect from dirty air and unhealthy environment. Thus, house owner and his family member's health will be free from diseases and they will feel healthy, peaceful and happy.

(7) Cattle Shed

Cattle shed should be in an open area and toward West side. Water is essential for them, so boring or underground water tank is must nearby the cattle shed or cattle shed nearby boring or underground water tank. It will protect them from bad health and sanitation. Resident's health will also be protected.

(8) Garage

Garage should be near Main gate along with East side compound wall. Now-a-days there is a verandah along with Main gate. People keep their car in verandah or outside Main gate. It is an easy approach, but not a safe one.

(9) Trees, Plants, Garden and Small Playgrounds

Trees and plants are planted outside the South-West side wall of the house. Grassy area should be nearby cattle shed or Pooja room. Small playgrounds such as Volleyball, Basketball, Badminton, Table tennis are to be developed here. For self and family members these games are necessary for good health and happiness.

<u>**Inner area planning of the Plot/House**</u>

(1) Basement
Now the plots are small or very small because of shortage of land. This is the reason that people are constructing basements in the houses. A Basement can only be built in the North-East or East or North direction as per house plan measurement. North-East/North/East direction basement is beneficial for only storage of domestic items, office work and recreational activities. The condition is that no bedroom should be built over it.

(2) Pooja room (Place of worship)
Pooja room is made on the upper side of South-East side wall of the house. Here worshipping and meditation will provide the resident peace and prosperity.

(3) Kitchen and Dining
It is built in the lower side of the South or South-East (Aagneya) direction. It will generate and enhance positive energy, suppressing and even eliminating negative energy in the house. The house owner and family will enjoy joyful and peaceful life and succeed in every field of life. Soon they will be wealthy and prosperous. Dining room should be built in the center of the house down to the kitchen. From the bedroom the Dining room should be in North-East side down to the drawing room or in the North-West from the main gate. Such situation brings happiness, peace and unity in the house. It also creates respects to elders.

(4) Drawing room
A Drawing room/Drawing room can be constructed in the North-East corner direction (Eshaan) or North-West corner direction (Vayavya). East or North side is also good for a Drawing room. It should be constructed in the middle of East and West wall far from main entry of the house. Such situation brings happiness and peace in the house. New baby entry is possible in the family. Guest room is especially built in the lower portion of the North side wall or North-West wall. Guest will stay there for a short period and feel good. It favors the resident and family. They will feel comfortable.

(5) Study room
For encouraging children study room is essential. A table with chairs should be there. They can sit and study books independently. It should be built nearby West wall with bedroom. It will give them healthy atmosphere for studies and thoughts of bright future.

(6) Bedrooms-Master bedroom & other bedrooms
Master bedroom & other bedrooms are built nearby South-West and West direction because of the fact, if any problem comes with the children that may be solved immediately and easily. The children will be safe and secure. They will enjoy good time.

(7) Storeroom

This room should be in the South-East corner down to the kitchen in the South. It is essential to store food items such as grains, pulses, ghee, vegetables and other items to cater the family needs. It makes the house owner economically sound.

(8) Toilets

Toilets nowadays are attached to the bedrooms. Toilets and bath are at one place towards South side wall. This position saves time and area of the house. It is an easy access especially to parents and grandparents for using rest room and taking bath.

(9) Staircase

It will be better that Stairs may be built on West side wall along with the Main entrance of the plot/house to reach to the roof. It will be easy approach for Master bedroom and Drawing room. This position is good for safety purposes and healthy atmosphere.

Vaastu Assessment of A residential house

Before moving in the house one can assess the degree of one's residential house. According to the learned author Engineer Pawan Kumar Goel one can oneself get the Vaastu Assessment of one's house through its ten-point formula as per facing side. Suppose it is East facing. The table given below:

Ten Points formula table for Vaastu Assessment of A residential house

Sr. No.	Different locations, if best, better, good, average and below average	Total Marks	Marks obtained
1.	Shape-size-slope of the house	15	15
2.	Main Gate of the house	15	13
3.	Master bedroom	15	6
4.	Other bedrooms	15	11
5.	Guest room	15	11
6.	Storeroom	15	5
7.	Kitchen	15	8
8.	Well/Tube well/Underground water	15	12
9.	Toilets	15	
10.	Resident feelings	15	13
Total		150	100

Conclusion:

For each point 15 marks are fixed, and ten points total is 150 marks. For total assessment, if total is obtained 150, the house is **best** one, 120 to 149 is **better** one, 100 to 119 is **good** one, 76 to 99 is **average** one and up to 75 is **below average**. Below average house will neither be beneficial nor favorable for a resident. As per table the assessment of East facing house is good for resident.

Chapter
17
Farmhouse/Resort

Nowadays big cities like Delhi, Kolkata, Chennai, Mumbai have become polluted. Environment has been poisonous. Many people of such big cities now are in the practice of having farmhouses and resorts in the rural area quite away from polluted and poisonous environment. They have constructed their farmhouses and resorts according to Vaastu guidelines far from the big city and begin to reside there. There they feel happy and enjoy healthy, wealthy and prosperous life.

A Scene of a Farmhouse and Resort

Figure-62

Figure-63

While selecting a land/plot for a Farmhouse and Resort, hilly earthen area is good. It should be higher on South side and slope towards North or

North- East or East side. Following Vaastu guidelines may be considered.

<u>**Vaastu guidelines**</u>
1. Bedrooms
Bedrooms should be built in the West or South-West or South side of the plot for privacy, total relaxation and mental peace.
2. Study room
Study room should be in North-East side. It is the best source of Solar energy in the house. The children will sit here peacefully to concentrate on their studies.
3. Library room
It should be in West side. It will help to search the required matter independently through reading library books. Children may be good researchers.
4. Kitchen
It should be in South-East side, the Aagneya direction. It is the place where healthy and nutritious food is cooked. Resident and family will enjoy and prosper.
5. Pooja room
Pooja room should be in North-East side. It increases our positive energy. Meditation controls our worries and gives us happiness. We get peace of mind.
6. Swimming pool
Swimming pool should be in North-East side. Swimming is the best exercise to remain healthy.
7. Health club, Steam bath, Gymnasium, Yoga and Massage rooms
All these should also be in the East direction to get more energy. They provide good health to the resident and family.
8. Badminton, Tennis and other courts
These courts should be in North-West side far from the main gate to get good atmosphere and happiness.
9. Heating equipment and air conditioners
Heating equipment and air conditioners should be fixed in the South-East side the Aagneya direction for overall comforts.
10. Trees, plants and greenery
Trees, plants and greenery should be in South-West (Nairutya) direction for peaceful and happy atmosphere.
11. More open and spacious place
More open and spacious place should be in North and East side of the farmhouse to get more and more energy.

Chapter
18
Multistoried Flats

The system of multistoried flats on Vaastu based structures are seen in countries like UAE (United Arab Emirates) and big cities Dubai, Abu Dhabi, Sharjah, Muscat in Oman, in Singapore and in Malaysia Kuala Lumpur and in United States of America, in England city London, in Australia, Switzerland, Saudi Arabia, Kuwait, Norway and Sweden etc. The same craze of dwelling in multistoried flats has now begun in India because of decreasing land, increasing population, and non-availability of low-cost houses. In big cities like Capital city Delhi, Millennium city Gurugram in Haryana, New city Noida in Uttar Pradesh, other cities Mumbai, Bangalore, Chennai, Kolkata etc. multistoried flats are in full swing. Presently it is people's first choice due to provision of many facilities such as Steam bath, Gymnasium, Yoga, Massage room, Health club, Badminton, Tennis etc. courts all in a gated area along with full protection and Security benefits.

A Scene of Multistoried Flats

Figure-64

Construction of Multistoried Flats

It is rather difficult to construct multistoried residential flats as it is not so simple to fix proper zones for kitchen, bathroom, water closet, master bedroom, drawing-dinning etc. as per Vaastu guidelines. However, if multistoried flats are constructed keeping in view the following points under consideration or already constructed flats are to be rearranged accordingly, then favorable results may be obtained. Occupants may feel happy, healthy and prosperous. Some of the basic Vaastu guidelines for multistoried flats are to be kept in mind.

Vaastu Guidelines

1. Multistoried flats area
Multistoried flats must be constructed in a rectangular area or a square area so that each and every flat component must be a rectangular or a square unit i.e. each and every portion at 90° degree. This will make the occupants healthy and happy.

2. The main gate of the campus
It must be towards any of the sharp direction i.e. North, South, East or West, or towards North-East or North-West but in no case, it should be towards South-West or South-East. It will provide more energy. Residents will feel happy and healthy.

3. More open space
The placement of the building should be done in such a way that more open space should be left towards East and North than West and South. This will make the occupants active and energetic.

4. The main gate of the flat
It should open towards the interior of the room. It must not be of sliding nature. Sharp South-West corner should never be allotted to the gate of the flat. It will lead to loss of energy and resident will feel uncomfortable.

5. Center of the flat
It should be free and open. It should be kept empty and clean. No domestic loaded item should be placed there, because it is called Brahamsthan.

6. Pooja corner
Each flat must have bathroom in the North-East zone, leaving sharp corner for a small temple. Residents can pray to Almighty God and enjoy the habit of meditation there for peace of mind and prosperity.

7. Kitchen
It should be towards South-East sharp. It must never be towards North-East. Second preference of kitchen may be given towards North-West for better cooking of items for family meal. Residents and family will enjoy the quality food for good health.

8. Master bedroom
It should be towards South-West of the flat for better health and happiness. Other beds may be given toward North-West or North or East.

9. Bathrooms
Bathroom must be followed with a W/c towards East that is away from North-East corner. W/c may be given to South-West or North-East zone also.

10. Storeroom
It must be towards South-West zone, or it should be in the middle of the West to keep things better for use.

11. South portion

South portion should be made somewhat elevated for peace and prosperity. Its weight up to 500 kg should always be present in the sharp South-West corner.

12. Ventilators

The flat must have more ventilators towards East and North or towards North-East zone to get light and fresh air.

13. Well or tube well in the campus

The Well or tube well in the campus of the apartment building must be in North or East or North-East.

14. Water storage tank

Any kind of water storage tank area should be towards North-East leaving sharp corner for the common temple of the complex or towards East or North, but it should not be towards South-East area.

15. The overhead tank of the complex

It should be given in South-West zone. If possible, select South-West sharp corner for it.

16. Drainage System

It should be towards South-West or North-West. It could also be towards West or even towards South-East away from the sharp South-East corner.

17. Water Stream

The water streaming should be done from South to North or from West to East or towards both North and East.

18. Staircases

Staircases are to be given in South, West or South-West but they should not be given towards North-East.

19. The electric mains and electrical switches

These should be given in South-East corner of the rooms in the flats and towards South-East zone or in the sharp South-East corner of the complex. Second preference may be given to North-West.

20. Parking

Parking for light vehicles may be given towards North-East and parking for the heavy vehicles may be given towards West or Middle of North.

21. Plantation

It should be done in North and West and following plants should specially be planted in the campus in favorable directions i.e. Ashoka, Champa, Rose and Bamboo towards North, Jamun and Mango towards West and wild pepper Sambhalu in the East.

Remedies for Anti-constructed Flats

In a flat of a multistoried building, we cannot bring about any constructional change. Hence in such a case following simple remedies can be performed to overcome the defects.

1. No heavy load on Brahamsthan

If the 'Brahamsthan' (center) is under heavy load, shift the load towards South-West or West or even towards South.

2. **Alum crystals**

Always keep one kg. Alum crystals opened in the drawing room and the Master-bedroom to get fresh air.

3. Sufficient amount of common salt crystals

If the toilets are in unfavorable directions, keep sufficient amount of common salt crystals preserved in a plastic bucket in the toilet permanently. It will nullify the bad energy there.

4. Residents should pray the Almighty God every day regularly and enjoy the habit of meditation there for peace of mind and prosperity.

5. A small 'Havan' on every 'Amavasya'

A small 'Havan' should be performed. A cow dung cake is burnt and then over that burning dung cake a mixture of the following should be burnt as 'aahuti' Sandal powder, Black Sesame, Barley, Camphor, Raal, Powder of Ashwagandha and Desi ghee.

Note:

Doing so regularly would cure the bad effects of Vaastu defects and residents of the flat may feel healthy, wealthy, peaceful and prosperous.

A Table of Ideal Directions of Rooms in a Multistoried Flat

Room	Ideal Direction As Per Vaastu	Pointers
Gates	North and East	The waves that rise from the gates influence the mind of the person entering from the gate.
Master Bedroom	Southwest corner	If your flat has more than one floor, then make sure the master bedrooms on the top floor. The ceilings of the floor must always be in level.
Children's room	Northwest corner	No pointer
Bathroom	West or South	Bathroom drains must always flow in the north-east
Drawing room	Northwest	Furnishings must be placed in the south and west directions. Maximum open space must be kept in south and east directions.

Study Room	Northeast, Northwest, North, West, East corners	Make sure the study room and pooja rooms are adjacent to one other. This is considered very auspicious. The study table should be kept in Eastern or Northern wall
Pooja Room	Northeast	No pointer
Guest Room	North-West direction	The room in northwest is also considered to be very auspicious for unmarried girls.
Kitchen and Dining	South-East	The cook must always face east when cooking. The water taps in a kitchen must be in the Northeastern direction.
Storeroom	Southern part of the building	Grain and other supplies should be stocked inside the kitchen or in any other room. Things must never be stored inside the box beds, as it can cause sleeping disorders.
Wastes from the kitchen	South-West corner of the kitchen	The Waste Bins must always be kept covered.
General room	North-West	No pointer
Water-Tank	North-West	No pointer
Balconies	North, East Or North-East directions	Eastern balcony is very auspicious
Windows	Eastern and Northern sides of a building	No pointer

Chapter
19
Factories or Industries

Factories or Industries are the main source of our daily needs such as food items, clothes, transport facilities, medicines, electric and electronic items and so on. The Factories or Industries prepare such items in a lot to cater the demand of humans. Vaastu guidelines play a dominant role in selecting a square or rectangular site or premise for the factory or industry and further construction of different blocks inside, so that things are peaceful and fruitful. It is more important that where and what type of block should be constructed in a factory or industry. Main blocks are administrative block, office files block, staff quarters block, water system and its flow block, fixing of main machinery and plant block, putting of boiler, heater, electric generator etc. block, raw materials and finished goods stores, parking place, trees and greenery, a small temple, gate keeper's room on entrance and no profit no loss tea/coffee and food shop/canteen for employees. Now we take each block in the factory or industry for consideration as to where they have to be constructed.

A Scene of a Factory or Indus

Figure-65

<u>**Vaastu Guidelines**</u>

1. Main entrance
Main entrance should be in the East or North for best returns. West is also favorable. Other dishas (directions) or Vidishas (corner directions) are not good.

2. Compound wall
South and west compound wall should be made of heavy stones for safety of plant. North and East wall may be simple of light weight bricks.

3. Tube well/Water system
Water system tube well should be in the North or North-East or East side and flow of water towards North.

4. Gate keeper's room
If main entrance of the factory is in the East direction, then Gate keeper's room should be in the South-East. If main entrance of the factory is in the North direction, then Gate keeper's room should be in the North-West.

5. Reception counter
This should be in the North-East side well-furnished and attractive.

6. A small temple
A small temple of Sri Ganesha in the factory or industry should be in the North or North-East or East side nearby reception counter.

7. Administrative block
This may be in the East or South or West or North or South-West corner direction.

8. Office files block
In a factory or industry there are at least 15 types of office files. It is essential to keep them safe in a big cabin so that when it is needed, immediately can be put on the officer's or owner's table. **Putting of Files in a factory or industry**

i)   Personal files, Purchase files, Assets files, Raw material files, Income tax files, Store files and Cash purchase files in South-West of cabin.

ii)   Sales files, Share files, Finished goods files, Credit sales files, Staff and worker's files, Litigation files and Pending bill files in North-West.

iii)   Account files in South-East corner.

9. Fixing of main machinery and plant block
Fixing of main machinery and plant should be in the West or South-West or South direction of the factory or industry plot.

10. Fixing of boiler, heater, electric generator etc.
Fixing of boiler, heater, electric generator etc. should be either in the South-East or in the North-West side.

11. Raw material store

Raw material store should be built in the North or East or South-West or West direction.

12. Finished goods store

Finished goods store should be built in the North-West or North or East or South-East or West direction.

13. Tea/coffee and food canteen for employees

Tea/coffee and food canteen for employees should in the East or Northeast direction.

14. Trees and greenery

Trees and greenery should be nearby administrative office.

15. Parking place

Parking place for vehicles should be built either in the North-West or South-East direction.

16. Staff quarters

These should be constructed in the North-West or South-East direction of the factory or industry.

17. For Chemical factory

If it is a Chemical factory, water purifier system and disposal of waste should be made as per Vaastu for the safety and protection.

Chapter
20
Shops and Shopping Malls

A Shop or a Shopping Mall is a business that presents a selection of goods such as food items, kiryana, masale, vegetables, fruits, clothes, shoes, cosmetics, books, medicines, electrical and electronic items, vehicles and so on. For shops or shopping malls essential factors are offers to trade or sell them to customers for money or other goods. Shopping is an activity in which a customer browses the available goods or services presented by one or more shops/shopping malls with the intent to purchase a suitable selection of them. In modern days customer focus is more transferred towards online shopping. Now worldwide people order products from different regions and online shops, or shopping malls deliver their products to their homes, offices or wherever they want. The consumer does not need to consume his energy by going out to the shops or shopping malls and saves his time and cost of travelling. For a shop or a shopping mall following steps should be taken while constructing/buying a land/plot.

Vaastu Guidelines for Outer Plan for Shops and Shopping Malls

1. The plot should be square or rectangular.
2. If it is a little bit Shermukhi, it will be advantageous and beneficial to the owner.
3. The South and West walls of the shop/shopping mall should be made of heavy stones for safety purpose.
4. Verandah and balcony should be in the front side.
5. Heavy items should also be kept in the North-East direction.
6. Shopkeepers place in shop/shopping mall should be such that his face appears towards East or North direction.
7. Money box so called Tijuri should be in the North side.
8. Shops/shopping malls should be connected by walkways so that consumers can easily walk.
9. Malls can be built in an enclosed or open-air format.
10. Now Smaller shopping malls are replaced with large "Malls", of four-five stories often accessible by vehicle. Escalators are fixed to reach to the higher story.
11. From late 20th century, entertainment venues such as movie, theaters and restaurants began to be added. See below a scene of one big shopping mall.

It is a very good structure for those, who are desirous to get full return and benefits by constructing such shopping malls adopting Vaastu guidelines for internal planning.

A Scene of a shopping Mall/Complex

Figure-66

Vaastu Guidelines for Inner Plan for Shops and Shopping Malls

1. Main gate
It should be in the direction of major road of the plot. It should be free from all hindrances. There should be no obstacle in front of the main gate.
2. Worship place
A temple of Ganpati and Lakshmi should be in the North-East direction to get good benefits.
3. Water sources/Tanks
Water sources/Tanks should also be in the North-East direction.
4. Heavy items place
Heavy items should also be kept in the North-East direction.
5. Weighing machine
Weighing machine should be placed in the South-West side.
6. Power meters and switch boards
Power meters and switch boards etc. should be placed in South-East side.
7. Almirahs and show cases
Almirahs and show cases should be placed in the South-West side.

Chapter
21
Hotels and Restaurants

A Hotel is a commercial establishment that offers lodging to travelers. It is a part of the hospitality industry. Some may also offer lodging to permanent residents. Hotels may also have restaurants, conference rooms, stores, and other services that are available to the general public. It can also be defined as the place, where it provides lodging to the travelers, banquet halls for official parties, offers food to the guests make revenue on the owner's point of view.

A Restaurant is also a commercial project. It is also a part of the hospitality industry. It prepares and serves food and drink to customers. Meals are generally served and eaten on premises, but many restaurants also offer take-out and food delivery services. Restaurants vary greatly in appearance and offerings, including a wide variety of cuisines and service models.

A Hotel or Restaurant, if constructed on the basis of Vaastu guidelines, it will attract more and more visitors or guests. They will feel comfortable and relaxed while relishing their quality services and facilities. Vaastu Guidelines for Hotels and Restaurants are given below.

1. Shape and size of Hotel/Restaurant
A Hotel or Restaurant Should always be a square or rectangle Shaped. The North-East side of the Hotel or Restaurant should be kept clean and tidy to attract positive energy.

2. Main entrance of a Hotel or restaurant
The main entrance of a Hotel or restaurant should always be in East or North or North-East direction and first floor would be apt for the reception. The Conference Hall should also be on the first floor.

3. Landscaping and Fountains etc.
Landscaping and Fountains or Artificial Water Falls and a Fish Tank can be Constructed in the Northeast, North or East of a Hotel or Restaurant ensures all year-round Prosperity.

4. Reception counter
It should be in North-East (Eshaan) direction so that the receptionist may face to the North or East.

5. Kitchen in Hotel or Restaurant
Harmony and efficiency in the kitchen are the key to the success in any Hotel or Restaurant. So, the Kitchen of a Hotel or Restaurant should only be placed in the South-East Side with adequate provisions for light, ventilation and a large open space. The Cooks face should be in the East direction while cooking the food.

6. Storage room in a Hotel or Restaurant
The storage room for a Hotel or Restaurant to keep heavy goods should be built in the South-West (Nairutya) corner of the building.

7. Electrical equipment
Electrical equipment such as generator, transformer, AC plant should preferably be installed in the South-East corner.

8. Dining Hall or room
It should be in the West direction on an open area or the space. Low lighting is better here.

A Scene of a Dining hall in a Hotel or Restaurant

Figure-67

9. Waiters
They must be sober towards customers in serving food in a mannered way neatly and cleanly.

10. The Bed in the Hotel or Restaurant Rooms
The Bed in the Hotel or Restaurant Rooms should be placed such that the head of the guest is the South or West side only. Orange, yellow, cream and brown colors should be used in the interior.

11. Toilets in the bedrooms

The toilets in the bedrooms should be in the South-West (Nairutya) direction. These can be constructed in the North-West (Vayavya) direction but not in North-East (Eshaan) direction.

A Scene of a bedroom in a Hotel or Restaurant

Figure-68

12. Washbasins and Mirrors

Washbasin and mirrors can only be fixed in the North or North-East (Eshaan) direction.

13. Staircase

Stairs must be very near to the main entry of the Hotel or Restaurant

14. Parking place

It should be in the basement. Vehicles must face towards North or East.

Chapter
22
Banks

What is a bank?

A bank is a financial institution licensed to receive deposits and disperse loans. Banks may also provide financial services, such as wealth management, currency exchange, safe deposit boxes and lockers for depositors. In most of the countries, banks are regulated by the national government or by Central/Reserve bank.

Safety and security of the Banks

Safety and security are an important factor for the bank as well as other types of financial institutions. If banks buildings/rooms are constructed according to the Vaastu guidelines, then probably banks would never face problem of robbery or theft. The significant portion is the strong room for money deposits and confidential documents. The second is locker's room for depositors. Room for manager and employees is third factor. When designing a Structure and the rooms within it, the main consideration is to create a pleasant, comfortable environment to live/work in. If a Structure and the rooms are designed well, with a place and position for each item, it becomes a well-lit, airy, clutter free, efficient place to work in, which in turn makes us feel very happy and contented.

A structural Scene inside a Bank

Figure-69

Vaastu Guidelines for banks

1. North or East direction facing plot is an ideal plot for construction of a bank.
2. Main gate or entrance of the bank is recommended towards North or North-East or East.
3. Manager's room should be in the South-East corner of bank and his face towards North.
4. Employees of bank or staff must be seated in the West.
5. Wooden Cash counters must be placed in North with cashier facing East or North-East.
6. The Main Cash room must be in South or South-West and opening towards North.
7. Files, papers and other junk stuff must be kept at South-West, but Stationary in North-West.
8. Yellow color is prominent in making and stabilizing wealth matters, so use yellow color.
9. Keep stairs in West, South-West or South-East.
10. Water source, which is most auspicious, should always be in North-East.
11. Toilets or restrooms should be near water source in North-East.

Chapter
23
Hindu Temples

A **Hindu temple** or **mandir** is a structure designed to bring human beings and Gods together, using symbolism to express the ideas and beliefs of Hinduism. The symbolism and structure of a Hindu temple came from Vedic traditions. A temple incorporates all elements of Hindu cosmos symbolically presenting Dharma, Artha, Kama, Moksha and Karma The spiritual principles symbolically represented in Hindu temples are given in the ancient Sanskrit texts of India Vedas and Upanishads, while their structural rules are described in various ancient Sanskrit treatises Brihat Samhita and Vastu Shastras on architecture.

The layout, the motifs, the plan and the building process recite ancient rituals, geometric symbolisms, and reflect beliefs and values innate within various schools of Hinduism. A Hindu temple is a spiritual destination for many Hindus. Temples are the place of peace and harmony, where people generally seek God's grace to fulfill their wishes. Hindu temples come in many styles, are situated in diverse locations, deploy different construction methods and are adapted to different deities and regional beliefs. They are found in South Asia particularly in India and Nepal.

There are many temples especially in south India, which were constructed with Vaastu guidelines are still famous and prosperous in terms of peace, harmony and economically sound. The names of such temples are Vivekanand temple near Kanyakumari (Tamilnadu), Shiva Temple in Rameshwaram (Tamilnadu), Rangnath Swami temple in Trichi (Tamilnadu), Lord Venketeshwar temple on Tirumala hills (Andhra), Lord Jagannath Temple in Puri (Orissa) Chamudeshwari Devi temple in Mysore (Karnatka). In North India Vaishno Devi temple in Jammu and Kashmir, Sikh Gurudwara in Amritsar (Punjab) Sai temple in Shirdee (Mahrashtra) and The Shri Swaminarayan Akshardham Mandir in Delhi. The Vaastu facts are-

1. Entrance Facing in East direction

Every shrine must be constructed facing East direction with entrance in the same. East direction is sacred in Vaastu because sun rises from here which the sole energy giver and symbol of light. Therefore, according to Vaastu guidelines a shrine should always be constructed East facing and entrance while the idols of God facing the appropriate direction as well.

2. A regular shaped Site/Plot is the best

Ensure that the plot of temple is regular shaped and avoid irregular shapes while constructing a shrine because shapes like triangular, circle or oval are prohibited & considered inauspicious. Temple is best on the site, where there is hill, sea, mountain lies in East or North direction.

3. Shoes keeping point outside temple

Shoes keeping point in the temple should be best located in Southern side while drinking or water resource can be arranged in Eastern side.

4. Ideal Gates in East and North

A temple plot should have at least two sides facing East and North so that there may be two gates one in East and second in North. If there is only one gate to the temple then the best to have in East direction. Avoid entrance main gate in the South direction. Main gate must be huge and stronger than other gates of temple.

5. Provision for windows

Provision for window should be made on Eastern side only.

6. Place for God's idol

Place for God's idol must be higher than the ground and all the idols must be placed in such way facing East while only Lord Hanuman, Lord Dakhinamurti and Goddess Kali can Face South.

A Scene of a Famous Temple of Jagannath, Puri (Orissa)

Figure-70

7. No residential/commercial places in front of temple

Avoid building other residential or commercial places near or in front of temple. The shadow of temple should not fall on the places around the temple.

8. Water storage

Water storage must be located in North-east corner if underground and over-head tank must be situated in South-west.

9. Kitchen in temple

Kitchen in temple must be situated in South-east corner as this is the place for element Fire.

10. Charity box

Charity box must be kept in East or North direction.

11. Parikrama area

Parikrama area should be wider so that there is no clash between Darshanarthis.

Chapter
24
Orphanages and Shelters

An **orphanage** is a residential institution devoted to the care of orphans i.e. children whose biological parents are deceased or otherwise unable or unwilling to take care of them. Biological parents, and sometimes biological grandparents, are legally responsible for supporting children, but in the absence of these, no named godparent, or other relatives willing to care for the children, they become a ward of the state and orphanages are one way of providing for their care, housing and education.

It is frequently used to describe institutions abroad, where it is a more accurate term, since the word orphan has a different definition in international adoption. Most children who live in orphanages are not orphans, four out of five children in orphanages having at least one living parent and most having some extended family. Few large international charities continue to fund orphanages. However, they are still commonly founded by smaller charities and religious groups. Especially in developing countries, orphanages may prey on vulnerable families at risk of breakdown. There are 153 million orphans in the world, according to UNICEF. Many of them live in institutional orphanages with deplorable conditions, where their most basic needs are not met. The children are often hungry, scared, confused and lonely.

Most institutional orphanages are overcrowded and dilapidated, some rife with corruption, neglect and abuse. Even when managed by people with good intentions, orphanages often lack the necessary funds, resources and knowledge to properly provide for the children in their care. The fact is, most of the children in these institutions don't stand much of a chance of breaking out of the cycle of poverty and thriving as independent adults.

A **shelter** is a small building or covered place which is made to protect people from bad weather or danger. A shelter is a building where homeless people can sleep and get food. **A shelter** is a free place to sleep if you have nowhere else to go. Shelters are also sometimes called 'hostels'. If you are homeless, feel unsafe in your own home, or are in an emergency situation where you need a place to stay, you should think about going to a shelter. You can stay at some shelters for a short time, and others will let you stay longer.

Shelters also have basic services like bathrooms, showers, laundry, clothes and meals. Some shelters also have healthcare services, counseling, legal help, and job search training. Each shelter has its own rules about who is allowed to stay, for how long, and what services it provides. Shelter services are free. Shelters have highly trained and knowledgeable staff. Even though they try their best to keep shelters as safe as possible, some shelters might be safer places for you than others. Some females may feel safer in a women's shelter.

Vaastu Guidelines

1. Orphanages and Shelters should be compact with a boundary wall.
2. Number of Rooms should be according to the number of orphans and shelter seekers.
3. One room area should not be more than six beds with one toilet and bath.
4. There should be fixed partition or wall between male and female area.
5. If it is only for children, then boys' and girls' area should be separate.
6. Rooms and outer area should be neat and clean.
7. There should be a manager to look after activities and a guard to control the building.

Chapter
25
Hospitals

What is a hospital?

A **hospital** is a health care institution providing patient treatment with specialized medical and nursing staff and medical equipment. The best-known type of hospital is the general hospital or civil hospital, which typically has an emergency department to treat urgent health problems ranging from fire and accident victims to a heart attack patient. A district hospital typically is the major health care facility in its region, with large numbers of beds for intensive care and additional beds for patients who need long-term care. Specialized hospitals include trauma centers, rehabilitation hospitals, children's hospitals, seniors (geriatric) hospitals, and hospitals for dealing with specific medical needs such as psychiatric treatment (see psychiatric hospital) and certain disease categories. Specialized hospitals can help reduce health care costs compared to general hospitals.

A Scene of a ward in Civil Hospital

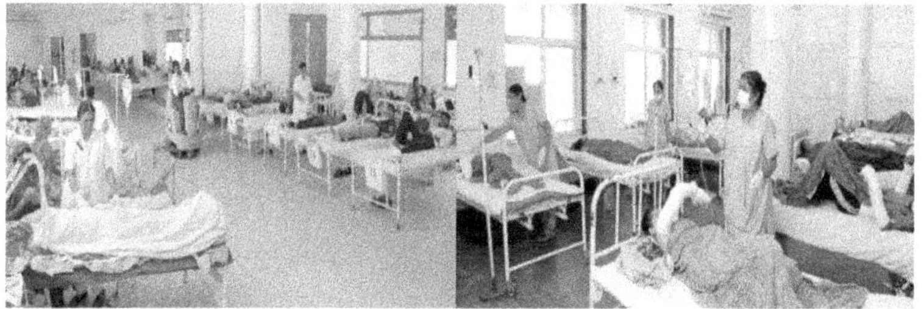

Figure-71

Vaastu Guidelines for Hospitals

1. Hospital should face the East possibly and the entry should be in the East or North-East.
2. The middle portion of the hospital should be open to the sky.
3. The slope of the flooring should be towards North, East or North-East sides.
4. In case of any roof the ventilated roof should be 2 ft. to 3 ft. higher than the top floor roof.

5. The racks for medical books and medicines should be in the South or West.
6. Cash counter should be in the South or West and should open towards the North or East.
7. Parking should be done on the Northwest / West sides.
8. Drinking water should be kept in the North-East.
9. Cleaning, changing rooms, toilets should be on the South or West sides.
10. Bathrooms should be on the East or Northwest sides.
11. X-Ray room, Electrical equipment etc. should be in the South-East room.
12. Operation-theatre should be in the West, patient's head on stretcher, should be towards the South.
13. Patient should be kept in North-West.
14. An emergency case, or serious case should never be kept in the South-West corner room.
15. The doctor should operate facing East or North or West side, but never to South side.
16. While examining patients in the North room, the doctor's face should be in the East or North.
17. Patient should lie down with head in the South or East and never in the North.
18. The patient's rooms should be in the South or North-West.
19. Inquiry counter should be in the South-East and waiting room on the South side.
20. The Staircase should be in the West, South-West, South-East or North-West.
21. Nurse's quarters should be in the South-East or North-West place to the Hospital.

Chapter
26
Mortuaries and Crematoriums

What is a mortuary?

A **mortuary** is a building or a room in a hospital, where dead bodies are kept before they are buried or cremated, or before they are identified or examined. When a person dies in a hospital, his body is usually moved to a mortuary before an autopsy takes place. Another word for a mortuary is a morgue, which is more commonly used in the United States of America. In the year1500 and onward mortuary was used as an adjective meaning "pertaining to death," from the Latin root word mortuus, or "dead." So, mortuary is a room for dead persons in the hospital. After autopsy it is handed over to the concerned family, relatives and friends to have a look (darshan) before funeral.

What is a crematory?

A **crematory** also known as a **crematorium** or **retort** is a place where people's bodies or remains are burned down to the bones, eliminating all soft tissue. Crematories are usually found in funeral homes far from the residential houses or area. **Cremation** is the combustion, vaporization and oxidation of cadavers to basic chemical compounds such as gases, ashes and mineral fragments retaining the appearance of dry bone. Cremation may serve as a funeral or post-funeral rite as an alternative to the internment of an intact dead body in a coffin, casket or shroud. They may be retained by relatives and dispersed in various ways. Cremation is an alternative in place of burial or other forms of disposal in funeral practices. In many countries, cremation is usually done in a crematorium. Some countries, such as India and Nepal, prefer different methods, such as open-air cremation also.

Vaastu Guidelines-For a mortuary

1. It is a part of the hospital. It is a small room to keep the dead body safe.
2. The room should be neat and clean.
3. A dead body is kept there for a short time or a day after surgery.
4. When the family members or relatives come, the dead body is handed over to them.
5. Some take it away to the house first for rituals and then crematory for funeral. Some take it direct to crematory for funeral.

6. Ambulance on demand should be present there.
7. There should be place of parking in front of mortuary room or nearby.

Vaastu Guidelines-For a crematory

It is called funeral place for dead bodies. It covers a big Area covered with tin sheds.
1. There is one crematory in a small village or town.
2. In big cities crematories are more than one. These may be two or three in number as per people's strength.
3. Cremation is usually done in a crematorium covered with sheds.
4. In India and Nepal, people prefer open-air cremation.
5. Crematory should be far from residential area with open area for parking.
6. Water bodies are also a part and parcel of the crematory.
7. There is a hall/verandah for the people's sitting.
8. There is a store for woods for funeral.

Chapter
27
Educational Institutions

An **educational institution** is a place where people of different ages gain education. It includes preschools, childcare schools, primary-elementary schools, secondary-high schools, colleges and universities. They provide a variety of learning environments and learning spaces. A school, college or any other educational institute plays a major role in building the future of the Nation. It is very essential to construct such buildings as per Vaastu guidelines to get the maximum benefit of the five elements of nature. Educational institutes should be designed in such a way that students reading there can concentrate on their studies and career prospects properly.

Institute can vary from educational to vocational organization to impart academic training and every such institute requires proper analysis so as to secure goodwill and results. Vaastu Shastra of an educational institution is also necessary to make the ambience peaceful, progress of students and to achieve higher standards in terms of vocationalism and goodwill. Vaastu Shastra lays down some basic guidelines regarding institutes.

Basic Guidelines

1. The Main Gate for the Entrance of the building should face East or North direction.

An Educational Institution Building

Figure-72

2. Leave more space towards the East and North-east while other parts like South, West and South-west must be used for construction.
3. The Prayer Hall should be constructed in the North-East.
4. There should be a statue or picture of Vidhya Devi Ma Saraswati in the prayer hall.
5. The Administration block should be preferably in the North or East direction.
6. Principal's office must be constructed in South-west or South direction only so that she/he can sit facing North.
7. The Staff room must be made in North-west side.
8. Reception and cashier room must be located in Eastern or Northern side.
9. The classrooms should be made with entrance in East and blackboard in West.
10. The classrooms should have larger windows on the Northern and Eastern walls.
11. The students should face North or East while studying.

12. Platform of teacher's desk must be made some feet high from the ground.
13. The electrical equipment like generators, inverters are to be kept in the South-East.
14. Library in the institute can be made in Western portion.
15. The toilet cum bath blocks should be in the North-West corner of the entire building.
16. The Playground for the students should be in the North, East or North-East side.
17. The Canteen should be preferably in the South-East.
18. Light colors should be used in the building. White color may also be used.

Chapter
28
Government Offices

A building in which the business of a department of government administration is carried out is called an office. Especially the office is an area where administrative or management related specific duties are performed. The term "office" may refer to business related area for operational tasks. Our homes and the office both should be in harmony to enjoy maximum peace, joy, prosperity, happiness, health and bliss. Workplaces should be matched as much as possible because many people spend the prime hours of the day at work. Though the workplace or office does not belong to them, they spend precious time within the office. Rushing through work and not respecting the environment can be a cause of tension and hostility for them.

According to Vaastu guidelines, the place of business or the office should be in tune with the five elements of air, fire, water, earth and ether, so that the management and employees work in harmony to achieve success. These guidelines are made keeping in mind various energy fields emanating from different directions. These diverse energy fields affect the various dimensions of our life. If we make an office against Vaastu guidelines, we will find ourselves standing against the natural forces. One of the basic aims of Vaastu is to extract the maximum out of natural forces so that we can get maximum energy for each and every field of life. If we stand in opposition to nature, some of the energy fields obstruct our work and we will find ourselves lagging behind in several spheres of life. Vaastu guidelines to follow are given below.

Vaastu Guidelines

No obstacles: Business and work has to be about free and unending opportunities. In order to promote the number of opportunities make sure that at the entry point there are no obstacles in your office between you and your entrance. The office should be well lit.

1. **Keep the center empty:** The center of your office room or workplace should be kept empty. Don't use any object within that circle.
2. **Location of the reception:** Make sure that the reception to your business is located in the North-East side of the office. When the

receptionist faces the clients/customers, his/her face should be in the North or the East direction.

3. **Using the water bodies:** Flowing water can be really beneficial for such areas, so make sure that the water bodies should be placed in the North/East corner of the office.
4. **An aquarium for Fishes:** You can have an aquarium with 1 blackfish and 9 goldfish. This will enhance your business.
5. **Executives' location:** The highest level of operators and workers in the company should be located in the West/South/South-West side of the office.
6. **The middle level management:** The middle level management offices should be in the North/East direction while field staff offices in the North-West corner to promote maximum cooperation.
7. **Accounts department:** The accounts department should be constructed in the South-East corner of the office for prosperity to attract more returns.
8. **Marketing department:** The marketing department should be located in the North-West side to promote harmony easily.
9. **Decision makers not under beam:** Beams have been used in construction for a long time now, but people did start covering these beams with false ceiling a long time back. Office Vastu Shastra would state that it is very bad for people, especially working people, to be seated under a beam, so make sure that the office's ceiling does not expose any of the beams. It would be all the more desirable if executives or decision makers avoid sitting, working right under the beams even if the beams are concealed by false ceiling.
10. **Right type of desk:** Vastu is so good that it can also promote the kind of desks one would work best on. For example, people who are involved with distribution or are the owners should have a rectangular table, while others can have creatively distributed tables depending on what assignment they have taken up.
11. **Lunchrooms:** Lunchrooms, pantry cart, etc. are to be located on the northwestern part of the office or the north-eastern part. This helps unity of the workers, for it provides them with one single facility that one cannot ignore.
12. **Toilets:** The locations of the toilets are also determined by the guidelines of Vastu Shastra for office. The toilets should certainly be located in either the southwest or the north- eastern.
13. **Keep important documents together:** it is better for one to have all important papers in one single place. Such a practice brings in some amount of tidiness. It would also help people to find what they want quickly, thereby averting any form of delay or trouble. Keep all the documents in one secure place. The papers should be kept in cupboards that face the southwest.

A Scene inside a Government Office

Figure-73

14. **Employees' placement:** The employee should sit facing the West side to imbibe some amount of intelligence. If people are made to sit facing a Vaastu compliant direction, they will feel adequately energized to bring about their stellar performance.
15. **Pictures of God:** In Vastu Shastra, it is considered quite appropriate for people to display their points of view. Hence, having some pictures and gods would help in promoting the general good spirit and also the spirit of good luck and prosperity.
16. **Staircase:** Staircases in the building are quite reminiscent of the times gone by. They also represent the tiresome and strenuous climb to the top in our lives. The staircase construction should be towards to south of the building. This is the best and most important place to make complete use of Vastu Shastra in full measure in the office.
17. **Using the right colors:** In the office, Vastu Shastra would recommend that you use colors like white, grey and blue so as to put across the right meaning ambience and Certain colors can help a person feel better and it can certainly help them cheer up as well. Hence, using these colors for office Vastu Shastra would certainly be a good idea.

Chapter
29
Military Camps

A military base or military camp is a facility directly owned and operated by or for the military or one of its branches that shelters military equipment and personnel, and facilitates training and operations. In general, a military base/camp provides accommodations for one or more units, but it may also be used as a center, a training ground, or a competence providing ground. In most cases, a military base relies on some outside help in order to operate. However, certain complex bases are able to manage and endure by themselves for long periods because they are able to provide food, water and other life support necessities for their residents while under siege.

Recruit training, more commonly known as **basic training** and colloquially called **boot camp**, is the initial instruction given to new military personnel, enlisted and officer. After completion of basic training, new recruits undergo Advanced Individual Training (AIT), where they learn the skills needed for their military jobs. Officer trainees undergo more detailed programs that may either precede or follow the common recruit training in an officer training academy which may also offer a civilian degree program simultaneously or in special classes at a civilian university. During recruit training, drill instructors do everything possible to push a recruit to his or her physical and mental limits to mold him or her to best efficiency levels.

Vaastu guidelines:

1. Military Camp area should be 10 to 15 hectares so that all types of military based trainings may be provided to the trainers.
2. Main gate of the boundary wall should be wide so that military trucks may easily enter and exit.
3. There should be an open bigger training hall for giving instructions to the trainers.
4. An open vast parade ground of at least two-three hectares for the Parade of trainers should be leveled. If possible, the length and breadth should be equal to form a square shape.
5. Plantation of trees and Greenery is also required in the area for bringing about a good atmosphere.

A Scene of a Military Camp/Recruiting Site

Figure-74

Figure-75

6. Tent area for the stay of trainers/campers should be neat and clean.
7. Officer's area and mess for officers and campers should not be near but at a reasonable distance from the training area.

Chapter
30
Community Clubs/Community Centers

Community clubs or **community centers** are public locations, where members of a community tend to gather for group activities, social support, public information, and other purposes. They may sometimes be open for the whole community or for a specialized group within the greater community. Examples of community centers for specific groups include Hindu Sabha centers, Christian community centers, Islamic community centers, Jewish community centers, youth clubs, lion's club etc.

Community Clubs are common spaces for people of all shades to come together, build friendships and promote social bonding. Community Clubs also connect residents with the Government for providing relevant information and gathering feedback on national concerns and policies. Each Community Club serves about 15,000 households or an average of 50,000 people. A central location with sufficient car parking is best, close to shops and other well-used facilities and to public transport. A site that is equally accessible to established and new areas of development can instill a sense of ownership across the community.

Health clubs and recreation centers are the part of a growing industry. Gym facility and steam bath for all age persons is a good idea. Sports club is a home to numerous sports and other activities open to the community. Exercise classes, badminton, wrestling, karate, yoga and weekly Teen Night. Scouts and many other recreational activities are available, and each provider charges a nominal fee for participation. Thus, several other clubs and centers are serving the community in their own ways for the happiness, peace and prosperity of the whole country.

A Scene of club inside Activities

A Scene of club inside Activities

Figure-76

Vaastu Guidelines

1. Community clubs or community centers should be near the locality of members.
2. Environment of the area should be attractive and praiseworthy and place neat and clean.
3. There should be a compound wall of the land and club/center face towards North-East or South-East.
4. Open space should be provided for community clubs or community centers for different activities inside the compound wall.
5. There should be a Meeting Hall with seating facilities for at least 200 persons the hall's entrance gate should face North- East.
6. A very good Water system is primary necessity of the community club or center.
7. Safe Parking facilities of vehicles are also required outside or inside the main gate.

Chapter
31
Remedial measures through Vaastu & Feng Shui

Regarding Vaastu Shastra Saar and Feng Shui Art in **Atharva Veda** there is a Sanskrit Shloka which explains "Let the everlasting air and light make comfortable the house that is built up with skill and knowledge and measured and erected by learned architects." Indian Vaastu and Chinese Feng Shui both are the household names. They have many similarities and only one end to make life happier, healthier and more prosperous for those, who follow the guidelines of architecture.

(a)Remedial measures through Vaastu

First, we take Indian Vaastu. It is strongly believed that Vaastu, which is Science of Structure, is a promise to heaven and prosperity. But when most of us live urban life, where buildings/flats are constructed mostly without Vasstu concepts due to scarcity of land, then mostly perfect Vaastu compliance is almost impossible! However Indian Astrology provides many a scientific and comprehensive solutions for proper alignment of Vaastu elements and to rectify Vaastu Doshas without any change in building/flat. Following are some suggestions/religious measures for getting peace and prosperity in life.

i) Chanting of Mantra for releasing the mind from hindrances and impediments:
Planetary mantras, which are the parts and parcel of our traditions of Vedic astrology and create sounds, are based on simple physics. By chanting mantras, we remind our universe to fill the vacuum or missing areas. If we want to enhance the energy of a planet to make it more positive and favorable to us, we will have to repeat relevant planetary mantra daily to the extent of numbers given in the table. We are not to spend money on it. Chanting of Mantra or Mantra Japa associated with a specific planet adds its vibrations to attain cosmic balance in human body and mind. It releases the human mind from hindrances and impediments. Evil effects of the deficient direction of Vaastu are compensated. So, if the resident has any problem of Vaastu in his/her building/flat because of certain planet, it can be removed by Mantra Japa. Planetary Sanskrit Mantras in English language table is given below:

Planetary Tantrik Sanskrit Mantras in English Language
Numbers, Timings and Charity Items

Sr. No.	Planets	Tantrik Mantras Beej Mantras	Numbers &Timing	Charity Items
1.	Sun	Om Hram Hreem Hraum SA Suryay Namah	7000 at Sunrise	Wheat, molasses, saffron, red cloth, copper piece, ruby.
2.	Moon	Om Shram Shreem Shraum SA Chandramase Namah	11000 at Sunset	Rice, sugar candy, camphor, white cloth, silver piece, pearl.
3.	Mars	Om Kram Kreem Kraum SA Bhaumay Namah	10000 at Sunrise	Wheat, molasses, lentil pulse, red cloth, red flower, copper, coral.
4.	Mercury	Om Bram Breem Braum SA Budhay Namah	9000 before Sunset	Sugar candy, ghee, kidney beans, green cloth, gold piece, emareld.
5.	Jupiter	Om Gram Greem Graum SA Guruve Namah	19000 at Sunset	Grams, gram flour, salt, turmeric, yellow cloth, gold piece, topaz.
6.	Venus	Om Dram Dreem Draum SA Shukraya Namah	16000 at Sunrise	Rice, ghee, sugar, milk, curd, white cloth, silver piece, diamond.
7.	Saturn	Om Pram Preem Praum SA Shanye Namah	23000 at Noon	Musturd Oil, black sesame seeds, black cloth, coins, steel pots.
8.	Rahu	Om Bhram Bhreem Bhraum Sa Rahve Namah	18000 at Midnight	Coconut, sesame seeds, blanket, lead, iron piece, zircon.
9.	Ketu.	Om Sram Sreem Sraum SA Ketve Namah	17000 Before Sunrise	Coconut, sugar, blanket, sesame seeds, iron weapon, cats' eye.

ii) Application of Yantras for helping in rectification of aura problems:

Planetary Yantras and other Yantras basically are for symbols. They are a source for energy, mental peace and happiness. They change our minds and enable formation of good thoughts. If we are worried and scary, they make us strong, courageous, fearless and happy. Application of these Yantras creates a rhythmic molecular memory on a metal piece through a ritual. By using sounds of Beej Mantras, divine fire, smoke vapors of divine plants and harmonized water the rituals create a quantum memory on metal pieces. Thus, they rectify a portion of an aura in the house/flat. Planetary yantras and some other yantras table is given below.

Planetary Yantras and other Yantras Table

MERCURY YANTRA

7	12	5
6	8	10
11	4	9

VENUS YANTRA

9	14	7
8	10	12
13	6	11

MOON YANTRA

5	10	3
4	6	8
9	2	7

JUPITER YANTRA

8	13	6
7	9	11
12	5	10

SUN YANTRA

4	9	2
3	5	7
8	1	6

MARS YANTRA

6	11	4
5	7	9
10	3	8

KETU YANTRA

12	17	10
11	13	15
16	9	14

SATURN YANTRA

10	15	8
9	11	13
14	7	12

RAHU YANTRA

11	16	9
10	12	14
15	8	13

Roghar Yantra

70	77	2	7
6	3	74	73
76	71	8	1
4	5	72	75

Dushthdrishti SafeYantra

148	13	138	6
2	146	13	139
63	7	140	1
20	134	9	147

Manokamna Yantra

1	14	11	8
12	7	2	13
6	9	16	3
15	4	5	10

Vyapar Vridhi Yantra

52	59	2	7
6	3	56	55
58	53	8	1
4	5	54	57

Ajivika Prapti Yantra

242	257	254	249
253	248	243	256
247	250	259	244
255	245	246	251

Dhan Prapti Yantra

7	12	1	14
2	13	8	11
16	3	10	5
9	6	15	4

Lost Return Yantra

73	78	2	7
6	3	76	75
77	74	1	8
4	5	81	70

Suit Winning Yantra

592	599	2	7
6	3	596	595
598	593	8	1
4	5	594	597

Exam Success Yantra

2	9	2	7
6	3	6	5
8	3	8	1
4	5	4	7

iii) Precious Stones/Gems for polarizing energy and mental peace.

Precious Stones such as Ruby, Pearl, Coral, Emerald, Yellow Sapphire, Diamond, Blue Sapphire, Hessonite and Cat's Eye have wide effects on human aura. They have their own polarized energy spectrum representing specific planets. They give maximum benefit to the resident. Thus, the traditional practice of using gems can prove to be a comprehensive remedial measure at all levels. Planetary Gems table is given below:

A table of Planetary Gems

Sr. No.	Planets	Gems	Signs of Zodiac
1	Sun	Ruby	Leo
2	Moon	Pearl	Cancer
3	Mars	Coral	Aries & Scorpio
4	Mercury	Emerald	Gemini & Virgo
5	Jupiter	Yellow Sapphire	Sagittarius & Pisces
6	Venus	Diamond	Taurus & Libra
7	Saturn	Blue Sapphire	Capricorn & Aquarius
8	Rahu	Hessonite	--
9	Ketu	Cat's Eye	--

iv) Color Schemes for peace and prosperity

Light is one of the basic elements that improves and creates holistic environment outside. Same way vibrations of Colors used in clothing and surroundings can effectively improve response of outside environment towards human body. Directional deficiencies can be rectified by the use of such definite colors. For selecting colors for the use in case of a building/flat as per Vaastu guidelines the zodiac sign preferred colors of the resident should be kept in mind and priority should be given to them. Directional colors are also used. So, there is an option for use of colors. Use of bright colors in building/flat is better than the dark colors. In practice people may use first Color Scheme as per their Zodiac Sign in their horoscopes. If there is no horoscope of the resident, then second Color Scheme will be better for happy and peaceful dwelling. A friendly color accentuates the virtues of the great element, while an enemy color diminishes the effects of element. Zodiac sign-wise elements are shown in the table. See both the Color Scheme tables below:

Color Scheme based on Resident's Zodiac Sign

Sr. No.	Resident's Zodiac Sign	Lord Planet	Preferred Color	Element	Sole Mate	Friend	Foe
1	Aries	Mars	Red	Fire	Air	Earth	Water
2	Taurus	Venus	White	Earth	Water	Fire	Air
3	Gemini	Mercury	Green	Air	Fire	Water	Earth
4	Cancer	Moon	Pink	Water	Earth	Air	Fire
5	Leo	Sun	Off-White	Fire	Air	Earth	Water
6	Virgo	Mercury	Whitish Green	Earth	Water	Fire	Air
7	Libra	Venus	White Cement	Air	Fire	Water	Earth
8	Scorpio	Mars	Red, Pink	Water	Earth	Air	Fire
9	Sagittarius	Jupiter	Golden Yellow	Fire	Air	Earth	Water
10	Capricorn	Saturn	Brick Red	Earth	Water	Fire	Air
11	Aquarius	Saturn	Blue, Pink	Air	Fire	Water	Earth
12	Pisces	Jupiter	Yellow, Bright White	Water	Earth	Air	Fire

Table of Color Schemes and its Characteristics

Sr. No.	Colors	Color Characteristics
1.	Saffron	It relates to Sun. Represents sacred fire. Stands for knowledge and truth.
2.	White	It relates to Moon and Venus. Stands for Purity, peace, knowledge and nobility.
3.	Red	It relates to Mars. Stand for spiritual power, faraway the evil, endows power, bravery, protection. Encourage sense of charity.
4.	Green	It relates to Mercury. Stands for harmony and peace. Source of soothing and treating disease.
5.	Yellow	It relates to Jupiter. Excites the mind. Leads to awareness and self-confidence.
6.	Blue	It relates to Saturn. Represents stability, serenity, infinity, defuses emotions, improves judgment, removes heat, brings clarity and gives knowledge.

Color Scheme based on Plot Directions and Planets

Sr. No.	Directions	Planets	Color
1	East	Sun	Saffron/Bright White
2	Northeast	Jupiter	Golden Yellow
3	North	Mercury	Green
4	Northwest	Moon	White
5	West	Saturn	Blue
6	Southwest	Rahu	Green
7	South	Mars	Red, Pink
8	Southeast	Venus	Silver White

Figure-77

v) Herbal Bath for cleanliness, health and happiness

Herbal Bath for cleanliness and happiness of a human body is of immense importance and almost a ritual in the Eastern part of the country. Various types of oils, salts and herbs are used as a cleaning agent while bathing. These agents not only clean the human's body but also relieve the human bodily aura or planetary deficiencies in the house/flat and give comforts to the body. Resident feels peaceful and happy. Wearing of a Talisman given by a saint or maulvi also helps in nullifying the evil influence of any Vaastu Dosha on the person residing in a house/flat. Planet-wise herbal table is given below:

Planet-wise Herbs for Bath or Talisman Name to wear table

Sr. No.	Planet	Herbs for bath	Utensil for Ritual Bath	Talisman's name
1	Sun	Manjistha	Copper	Bale-Mool
2	Moon	Koshtha	Conch	Shirni-Mool
3	Mars	Chikanmul	Silver	Naag-Jivha
4	Mercury	Gehula	Earthen	Vardara
5	Jupiter	Nagarmotha	Gold	Bharang-Mool
6	Venus	Safed Shirus	Silver	Vaghoti-Mool
7	Saturn	Halad	Iron	Vattul
8	Rahu	Sharponkha	Bull Horn	Malay-Chandan
9	Ketu	Lodha	Sword Guardrail	Ashvagandha

vi) Ganesh Puja, Navgrah puja and Hawan/Yagya for happiness, peace and prosperity

Ther is another way of making the body sensitive for receiving planetary energies. At a Shubh Muhurta, which matches with specific planetary influence the resident can manage Shri Ganesh Puja, Navgrah Shantipath/Shanti Puja and Hawan or Agnihotra yagya with the help of a capable Pandit. Reciting Puja and Hawan related Mantras will help in getting happiness, peace and prosperity.

(b) Remedial measures through Feng-Shui

Now we will take Chinese Feng-Shui measures, which are suggested to diffuse negative energy and to activate positive energy in a house/flat. They lastly give happiness, health, wealth and prosperity the residents. There are nine main measuring items of Chinese Feng Shui, the people are using these days. The names are:

i) Wind Chime and Buddha Statue for diffusing negativity and having Prosperity.
ii) Lion for confidence and power, Camel for growth of career.
iii) Pyramid and Pakua Mirror for maximum source of energy
iv) Doves, Dolphins and Tortoise for happiness, harmony and stability.

(1) Wind Chime

Wind chime is one of many people's favorite item used for Feng Shui cures as well as home decor. The Feng Shui wind chime is very nice to look at. It is decorative and musical. It makes a very good mellifluous soothing sound each time, when wind moves them. It is widely used to diffuse negative energy and activate positive energy that can be causing problems for a house resident. It is also good tool for attracting money and friends as well as to promote harmony and health within the family.

Type and size of Wind Chime

It may be of Silver or copper, bamboo or wooden, ceramic or glass. If one wants wind chime to work for the best, it should be hung correctly. It cures against possible negative influences of environmental forces. For the best effect, choose the wind chimes with suitable size to your space. If you want to attract good luck in your lives, use six or eight rods wind chime. See below the symbols of two types of wind chime having eight rods.

Designs of Wind Chime

Figure-78

(2) Prosperity Statue

There are certain specific statues used in Feng Shui for prosperity and success. Laughing Buddha is one of them. It is regarded as one of the Gods of wealth (Kuber). It brings prosperity, success and financial gains in the house. The location of placing the laughing Buddha is very important. The energy that enters the house from the main gate is greeted by laughing Buddha and the energy is activated and turns highly prosperous. It is to be placed on a side or a corner table which is diagonally opposite to front gate and facing the main gate. One important thing to remember is that laughing Buddha should be in sitting position because we want stability in wealth and prosperity. See Laughing Buddha's sitting statue as below.

Seated Laughing Buddha Statue

Figure-79

Types of laughing Buddha:

1) Laughing Buddha with a bowl-The bowl depicts a monk's life. It is associated with renunciation of material possessions and attaining enlightenment.

2) Laughing Buddha with a fan-This one symbolizes happiness and joy. It is said that waving of fan by Buddha sculpture depicts deportation of troubles.

3) Laughing Buddha with a sack-The Buddha carrying sack symbolizes a traveler. One version is that the sack means that he collects people's sadness and woes and puts them in his sack. While another version is that the sack symbolizes wealth and good fortune.

4) Laughing Buddha with beads-The one with beads is considered to be a monk representing meditation practice. The beads also symbolize 'pearls of wisdom.'

5) Laughing Buddha playing with children-It symbolizes good fortune coming from heavens. It also brings good luck and positive energies.

Placement of laughing Budha

(1) One should place a Buddha statue in the East side or in a direction, where it   be seen by all the family members, when they are seated in the Drawing room or the main hall.

(2) Buddha's birthday falls on 8th May. It is considered auspicious. If a candle is lightened on his birthday, it is said that it fulfils all desires of the resident.

(3) If the Buddha statue is placed facing Feng Shui Kua Formula, then it is said to bring wealth, helpful in self-development, well-being and victory. It helps in achieving one's goals.

(4) If Laughing Buddha statue is displayed in the South-East direction of the main hall, dining room or bedroom in the house, it brings windfall luck and increased income in the family.

(5) Placing Buddha statue in the office gives clear mind, reduces tensions and eliminates enemies' effect.

(6) Keeping Buddha statue on one's desk enhances luck and fulfils aspirations.

(3) Lion for confidence

The lion is most powerful big cat. He always looks like the most confident animal. His features are majestic and royal. He is a symbol of king's throne in the palaces. He has his specific desires. He eats, when he wants. He sleeps as much as he wants. He paces, where he wants. He roars as loudly as he wants. As per Feng Shui one can get several benefits by placing a brass lion in the North-East (Eshaan) direction of the house. It will change one's personality. One will feel confident, courageous and powerful getting much more energy. One's personality strengthens. Lion ensures wealth and prosperity in the house/office. Lion produces glory and grandeur to the resident. See a scene of a lion with kids as under.

A Scene of Lion with Kids for Confidence

Figure-80

The lions are traditionally carved from decorative stone, such as marble and granite or cast in bronze or iron. Because of the high cost of these materials and the labor required to produce them, the private use of guardian lions was traditionally reserved for wealthy or elite families. Indeed, a traditional symbol of a family's wealth or social status was the placement of guardian lions in front of the family home. However, in modern times less expensive lions, mass-produced in concrete and resin, have become available for use. Now it is no longer restricted to the elite.

Use of Lion Symbols
The lions are always presented in pairs, a manifestation of Chinese Yin and Yang, the female representing yin and the male yang. The male lion has its right front paw on a type of cloth ball simply called an "embroidered ball" which is sometimes carved with a geometric pattern coincidentally, resembling the figure called "Flower of Life" in the New Age movement. The female is essentially identical but has a cub under the left paw to the male, representing the cycle of life. Symbolically, the female lion protects those dwelling inside, while the male guards the structure. Sometimes the female has her mouth closed, and the male open. This symbolizes the enunciation of the sacred word "Om". However, Japanese adaptations state that the male is inhaling, represents life, while the female exhales, represents death. Other styles have both lions with a single large **pearl** in each of their partially opened mouths. The pearl is

carved so that it can roll about in the lion's mouth but sized just large enough so that it can never be removed.

Feng Shui Lions for Confidence

Figure-81

Correct Placement

According to Feng Shui, correct placement of the Lions is important to ensure their beneficial effect. When looking out of a building through the entrance to be guarded, looking in the same direction as the lions, the male is placed on the left and the female on the right. So, when looking at the entrance from outside the building, facing the lions, the male lion with the ball is on the right, and the female with the cub is on the left. Chinese lions are intended to reflect the emotion of the animal as opposed to the reality of the lion. This is in distinct opposition to the traditional English lion which is a lifelike depiction of the animal. The claws, teeth and eyes of the Chinese lion represent power.

(4) Camel for Career
Camel gives growth in one's career. Camel is known to be a protector of the people, guiding them through exhausting endeavors and difficult journeys. The golden camel depicted here is standing confidently on a big coin and Its body is inscribed with many small coins of prosperity.

Camels can be your savior in a time of turmoil in your work life or great difficulty in daily life. They are excellent symbols for serving as remedies for overcoming hardship and coming out unscathed or even reaping some benefits from what was first perceived as a difficult situation. This is because of their natural persistence and resilience, above and beyond all other animals, to endure in extreme or desolate environments.

Consider the camel is trekking through the desert without food or water and able to endure great strife to deliver the owner along with their belongings safely to a far-off destination. Camel is called 'ship of the desert'. Camels can toil through freezing cold and blistering hot conditions. They survive challenges that humans cannot even imagine because of how their humps and stomachs store large amounts of energy and then slowly draw off them. Camels can drink up to 30 gallons of water in one sitting after they have been without for some time. These magnanimous creatures inspire great strength and the ability in the beholder of their icon, because of their known abilities in enduring the unimaginable ordeals. They help the beholder to surmount massive hurdles. Thus, camels are hardy and loyal creatures more than willing to carry you through difficult or even extreme conditions.

A scene of a desert Camel of Career

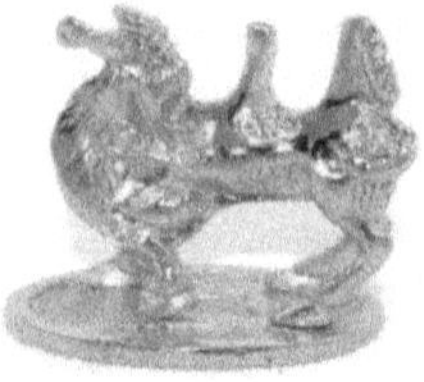

Figure-82

By sharing their desirable energy stores and their qualities of drive, dedication, endurance, honorability and long lasting-energy a camel can symbolically lead you safely through difficult times. If you are facing great challenge or see something unpleasant in the road ahead, inviting the presence of the camel is a desirable choice. And for those whose career is safely on-track camels are good on the desk or in a public workplace or office to safeguard the road ahead and help you endure on your road to success. The determination and patience of the camel are its other desirable traits. Camels have double rows of eyelashes protecting them from harsh storms and their feet tread lightly on all types of ground.

(5) Pyramids

A **pyramid** is a structure or monument, usually with a quadrilateral base, which rises to a triangular point. In the popular imagination, **pyramids** are the three lonely structures on the **Giza** plateau at the edge of the Sahara Desert but there are over seventy pyramids in **Egypt** stretching down the **Nile** River Valley and, in their time, they were the centers of great **temple** complexes. Although largely associated exclusively with Egypt, the pyramid shape was first used in ancient **Mesopotamia** in the mud-brick structures known as ziggurats, and continued to be used by the Greeks and Romans. Pyramids are also found south of Egypt in the Nubian kingdom of **Meroe**, in the **cities** of the **Maya** throughout Central and South America, and, in a variation on the form, in **China**.

A Scene of a Pyramid

Figure-83

Note:

A pyramid is a 3-dimensional geometric shape formed by connecting all the corners of a polygon to a central apex. This lesson will define what a pyramid is and discuss the different types of pyramids and formulas surrounding them. It is useful for getting more positive energy in the house that gives peace and happiness to the resident.

(6) Pakua Mirror

This type of mirror protects a house or place of business from the negative energy known as shar chi or poison arrows. A standard Pakua mirror is octagonal in shape with a wooden back. Eight trigrams surround the round mirror in the center, one trigram on each of the octagonal sections. Outside of the trigrams, toward the outer edge of the Pakua mirror, is a Luoshu diagram with one symbol on each of the octagonal areas. There is generally a hook placed on the back to ensure hanging the mirror properly. Always hang a Pakua mirror with the Chine trigram, the one with the three solid lines, at the top and the Kun trigram on the bottom. This placement allows the Pakua to repel negative energy. See the symbol of Pakua Mirror

A Symbol of a Pakua Mirror

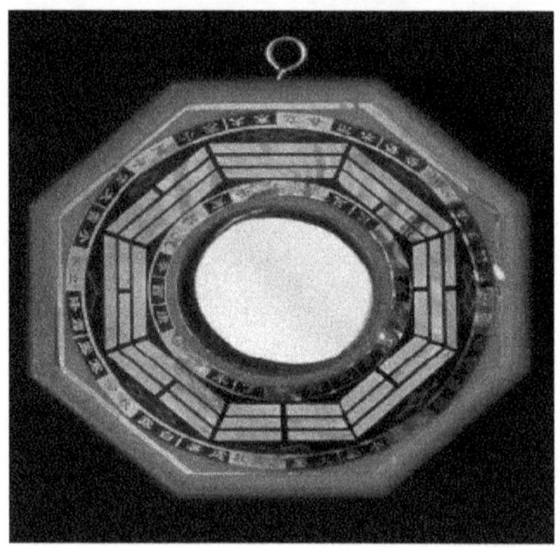

Figure-84

Types of Pakua Mirror
There are three types or designs of the Pakua mirrors. The shapes are-
(1) Concave
(2) Convex and
(3) Flat

Concave mirrors absorb the bad chi (Vibrations) as their curve is inward towards the edge. Convex mirrors have an outward curve towards their edge reflecting away the negative and harmful chi (Vibrations). Using convex type of mirror requires special care as improper placement may harm neighbors. A flat mirror is considered neutral.
The first style mirror has an octagon shaped wood back and measures between four and six inches in diameter. In the center is a two-inch round mirror. The second style mirror has an octagon shape and is on a six-inch wood frame. The mirror has a plate glass covering in the shape of an octagon. The cover has the **yin yang** and bagua symbols painted on the

inside of the glass. The second style bagua mirror is installed on front door as per practice is acceptable in Feng Shui. The third style mirror adds a symbol of a gate guard under the mirror. The symbol is usually a god riding a tiger. The god holds a staff in one hand, keeping away evil and a plaque in the other hand telling the people of the house of their good fortune.

(7) The Mandarin Doves

The Mandarin doves are the most popular, well known and widely used traditional Feng Shui cure for love matters. Note the word traditional, or classical Feng Shui, which means that a cure is based on culturally specific images, symbols, and overall historical use. If you are looking to attract a love partner, "Choose the Mandarin doves as a Feng Shui cure to attract love and to feel the energy of love and devotion when you look at them. "Because in symbolic Feng Shui level one works with images and symbols to represent the desired energy, the Mandarin ducks have become the perfect Feng Shui cure for love.

A Pair of Mandarin doves

Figure-85

That is, in Chinese culture. Does that mean you have to use it? If you like it, certainly go for it; if you do not feel the love attraction when you look at the Mandarin doves, rest assured there are hundreds of images out there that can speak to you of love and devotion. The traditional placement of the Mandarin doves is in the Love & Marriage area i.e. in the Southwest area on the upper right corner of your Master bedrooms. Always display your

Mandarin doves as a couple. Have them face the same direction and be sure the energy around them is clean, well lit, attractive and fresh.

(8) Dolphins

We all know that a Dolphin is an intelligent and versatile aquatic animal. It can be trained to perform interesting feats. In Feng Shui Dolphin is considered auspicious and hence respected. By keeping it at house, we can get prosperity and happiness among family members. It drives away scarcity of money. A dolphin showpiece or its photograph (as below) should be placed in the North of the house. If Dolphin is made of crystal, then it should be placed in the West direction. Crystal Dolphin, on one hand boosts happiness, on the other hand it absorbs negative energy.

A Scene of Dolphins

Figure-86

In Feng Shui, Dolphin is a powerful symbol of protection and perfection. So, for better performance in business Feng Shui Dolphin can be placed in the Western direction in the office. When kept at North and West directions, it produces better results. The Dolphin is particularly beneficial for youths as it helps them in making new friends. Dolphin develops intelligence among them. They feel happy and fresh.

(9) Tortoise

A tortoise is gifted with long life. Therefore, in Indian Vaastu and in Feng Shui its symbol is used for Long Life. As per Puranas, the religious books in Sanskrit, Lord Vishnu second time took the form (Avatar) of a tortoise to uphold the earth during the Sagar Manthan. Lord Vishnu's this form (Avatar) is called as Kurma Avatar. These days you can find tortoise in all houses because of the belief that this symbol gives a happy long life as per Indian Vaastu and Chinese Feng Shui. These symbols are made up of Resins, Metal, Glass, Mud, Crystals or else of Wood.

A Scene of Moving Tortoise

Figure-87

There are few Vaastu guidelines, which you should know and follow them, while placing a tortoise at your house or in your office. These guidelines will give you more benefits in your life. As per Vaastu Shastra a tortoise brings serenity, harmony, peace, long life, and wealth in your house. Now the question arises, where it is to be placed in the house/office to get all above things or   benefits in life. Read following guidelines.

1. **Earthen material Tortoise-** If it is made up of earthen material such as resin or mud, they should be placed in the North-East or in the Center or in the South-West.
2. **Metal made Tortoise-** It is to be placed only in North and North-West.
3. **Crystals made Tortoise-** It should be either placed in South -West or North-West.
4. **Tortoise figurines made of wood-** It is to be placed either in East or in South-East.
5. **Always face towards East Direction-**You must always remember that wherever you place your tortoise figurine, it should always face towards East Direction.
6. **For family harmony in Drawing room -** If you are wishing to place a tortoise family in your Drawing room; then it is the best option as it will help you to increase your family harmony.
7. **Tortoise figurine keeps in water-** It always must be kept in water. Tortoise figure can be kept in similar material depth in a dish. Add some water and colored stones. This will make the figurine a nice décor and attractive.

Conclusion

Always take care to check that the tortoise figurine is well placed in above mentioned direction and the water level is maintained. Water must be enough in dish to soak the feet of tortoise figurine. This conclusion ends with the following Shloka:

सर्वे भवन्तु सुखिनः, सर्वे सन्तु निरामयाः।
सर्वे भद्राणि पश्यन्तु, मा कश्चित् दुःख भाग्भवेत्।।
Om Sarve Bhavantu Sukhinah, Sarve Santu Niramaya |
Sarve Bhadrani Pasyantu, Ma Kaschit Dukh Bhag Bhavet | |

इति भारतीय वास्तुशास्त्र सम्पूर्णम।
Iti Vaastu Shastra Saar Sampurnam | |

www.ingramcontent.com/pod-product-compliance
Lightning Source LLC
Chambersburg PA
CBHW041314120726

48005CB00014B/2004